PICKUP AT UNION STATION

A NOVEL

GARY REILLY

Running Meter Press

DENVER

Published by
Running Meter Press
2509 Xanthia St.
Denver, CO 80238
Publisher@RunningMeterPress.com
720 328 5488

Cover art by John Sherffius
Composition by D.K. Luraas

ISBN 978-0-9908666-1-9
Library of Congress Control Number: 2015933268

First Edition 2015

Printed in the United States of America

Other Titles in The Asphalt Warrior Series

The Asphalt Warrior
Ticket to Hollywood
The Heart of Darkness Club
Home for the Holidays
Doctor Lovebeads
Dark Night of the Soul

CHAPTER 1

I was sitting inside my taxi outside the Oxford Hotel when a call came over the radio for a pickup at Union Station. I had just dropped off a fare at the hotel, which is half a block away from the train depot. It was six-thirty Wednesday evening, it was April, and it was raining buckets. Don't ask me how the word "it" can be so all-inclusive, but it is. I guess that's the magic of language, but I didn't have time to parse the baffling splendor of the King's English because I had thirty minutes to drive my cab back to the Rocky Mountain Taxicab Company (RMTC) before my shift ended. I also had two seconds to deliberate taking the call. If I waited three seconds, another cabbie might jump the bell. The weather was so inclement that cabbies all over Denver were reaping the whirlwind. By this I mean that people were calling for taxis, so it was a seller's market and I was one of the rip-off artists on duty that night.

I caved in fast. Union Station was thirty seconds away and I have an uncontrollable craving for money. Money is like all of my uncontrollable cravings—it makes me do things I sometimes regret, although the regret usually takes place after the craving has been slaked and I'm sitting around idly thinking about nothing. Ironically I sometimes find myself regretting not having slaked a craving. If you go on dates, you probably know what I mean.

"One-twenty-three!" I said, grabbing the microphone off the dashboard.

"Union Station, party named Zelner," the dispatcher said.

"Check." I hung up the mike and made an illegal U-turn on 16th Street. To my knowledge "illegal" is the only kind of U-turns they have in downtown Denver.

I drove across Wynkoop Street and into the driveway that fronts Union Station. Coincidentally the driveway is shaped like a U. I figured the customer for someone who had just gotten off the Zephyr coming from either Chicago or Oakland. I once rode the Zephyr to Oakland. So did Jack Kerouac but not at the same time. I pulled up at the cabstand and peered through the pouring rain toward the front door of the station, hoping the fare would be standing by the entrance waiting anxiously for his ride. Not that I like it when people are anxious, but it hurries things along.

I had my fingers crossed that the fare would ask me to take him to one of the big hotels in midtown—the Fairmont or the Hilton. I might pick up a fast five bucks and still have time to make it back to the cab company before my shift ran out. The trip would come to only two bucks or so, but people tip like madmen when it rains, especially when their taxis show up fast.

I had shown up fast. Maybe too fast. I sat staring through the wet windshield toward the front door of the terminal. The wipers were going back and forth but the rain was coming down so hard that they were virtually useless, like everything else in my life not counting TV.

I didn't see anybody.

This made me anxious. It meant I might have to get out of my cab and go into Union Station and look around for my customer. On the upside I would get to yell "Rocky Cab!" at the top of my lungs, which I have done before in the terminal. I enjoy that. My voice echoes off the high ceiling and makes me feel like a railroad conductor. I wanted to become a conductor the first time I hollered "Rocky Cab!" in the terminal but by the time I got back into my cab the ambition had faded, like most of my ambitions. If you've ever seen Grand Central Station in New York

City, Union Station is sort of like that, in the way that Denver is sort of like a city.

But I had one problem that night. If I walked into Union Station I would get wet. As I said, it was "raining buckets." Normally I don't employ clichés but I have learned over the years that people respond more readily to clichés than to James Joyce, who once took an entire page to make it clear to his readers that it was snowing all the hell over everything in Ireland. Okay Jimbo, we get the point, but where's the plot?

Aaah, don't get me started on James Joyce.

My anxiety increased. I could feel my left hand reaching for the door handle. But I kept staring at the brightly lit doorway of the terminal trying to "will" my customer to appear with a suitcase. Cab drivers do this frequently. The only thing besides the rain that stopped me from getting out and rushing toward the terminal was the fact that I had gotten there so quickly that I knew the customer might still be standing at the phone booth gathering his things together and sighing with resignation, believing that his cab might never show up. Customers do that frequently, especially when the weather is bad, or when cabs are tied up because there's an NBA championship game being played by the Denver Nuggets. That never happens frequently, believe me.

I glanced at my wristwatch and noted that barely a minute and a half had passed since I had taken the call. This was what ultimately kept me inside my taxi. Nobody in their right mind would expect a cab to show up that fast. The fare might even be at the snack counter buying cigarettes or a cup of coffee before going to the door and peering out to see if his cab had arrived.

That was what I was thinking.

I was fabricating scenarios. I was making excuses for my fare who had yet to appear in the doorway, which was really starting to annoy me. I dislike being annoyed at fares because they give me money, and I like people who give me money. It's the instant gratification in me. It makes me impatient with people who don't give my inner brat what it wants right now!

Then a thought occurred to me that made my heart sink. What if another cabbie—say a Yellow Cab driver—just happened to be at Union Station when my call came over the radio and he had stolen my fare? I know how that works. I've done it plenty of times at the mall. I hate it when other people treat me the same way I treat them—it makes me feel like such a commoner.

I began to audibly curse the Yellow Cab company when suddenly my back door opened and a man climbed in wearing a snap-brim hat and a trench coat. He scared the hell out of me.

I reached to the breast pocket of my T-shirt where I keep a nasal-spray bottle filled with ammonia, but let's not delve too deeply into that.

"Did you call a cab?" I said.

"Yes," he said in a voice so husky that I thought he had a cold.

"Is your name …?" I started to say, but I abruptly stopped. "What's your name?" I said, feeling clever.

"Zelner."

"Where to, Mr. Zelner?" I said, dropping my flag and turning on the meter.

He reached inside his trench coat and began digging around for something. Not a gat I hoped. Maybe a nasal-spray bottle. I reminded myself not to loan him my own bottle. I had learned that the hard way.

He pulled out a small square of paper and held his arm across the front seat. "I need to go here," he said. I glanced at his face as he spoke. He had a ruddy face. He looked older than me, for what that's worth. I'm forty-five. His hat was dripping water. It occurred to me that he might have been standing in the rain all this time waiting for me. This made me wonder why he hadn't come dashing to my taxi as soon as I pulled up at the stand.

I switched on the overhead light to read the paper. This threw his face into shadow. The address was right across the Valley Highway in North Denver, at a place called Diamond Hill, a small business park.

"Is this very far?" he said.

"No, sir," I said, putting the cab into gear. "Maybe five minutes away."

He sighed with what I took to be satisfaction, pocketed the paper, and sat back. I turned on my headlights and pulled out of Union Station. Already I was thinking what a sweet deal this was. I would probably earn five dollars from this ride, and after I dropped him off I could swing down to the Valley Highway and head north to Interstate 70 and over to the cab company—or the "motor" as we drivers call it—and sign out with at least ten minutes to spare. This was the kind of ideal situation that cabbies are always hoping for. It rarely happens, but when it does happen you have to milk it for all the joy you can get. When you drive a taxi for a living, you rarely get the opportunity to feel ecstatic.

"Is it permissible to smoke inside your taxicab?" Mr. Zelner said, as we pulled away.

I glanced in the rearview mirror and nodded a preamble to saying yes. I was using the power of positive body language to indicate to him that I was amenable to anything that would increase the size of my tip. "Yes sir," I said. "There's an ashtray in the armrest on the door."

"Thank you," he said. He spoke very slowly and distinctly with a foreign accent. By foreign I mean European, although I do realize that Europe itself is not a country in spite of attempts by tyrants throughout history to alter that construct.

I heard the rustling of fabric, the faint scrape of fingers dealing with cellophane, then the man leaned forward and said, "I am sorry but I do not seem to have any matches. Is it possible that you have matches or a lighter that I might make use of?"

"Yes, sir," I said. I reached for my toolbox and popped the lid open. I keep all sorts of things in my box, like matches, small change, toothpicks, pocket Kleenex, anything that might feasibly increase the size of my tips. I had to refrain from saying, "Want me to smoke it for you, pal?" That's an army joke guaranteed not to increase the size of your tips. I've often wondered whether "army joke" is an oxymoron, but let's move on.

I handed him a book of matches and told him to keep it. I pick up free matches at 7-11 stores, even though I don't smoke cigarettes, although I used to. I pass the matchbooks along to people who are trying to give up smoking. Name anybody who smokes—I guarantee you that he's trying to give it up. The only reason I succeeded at giving up the habit is because I have always been good at giving up.

"Interesting odor," I said, complimenting his smoke. "What brand is that?"

"Gauloise," he replied hoarsely.

I nodded as if I knew what a golwoss was, then headed down to Speer Boulevard and took the 14th Street viaduct across the valley. We were halfway across when I saw a flash of red lights in my rain-spattered rear window. They had come on suddenly, as opposed to appearing in the far distance the way emergency vehicles often do, such as fire trucks and ambulances. I groaned inwardly, then glanced at my speedometer. I was doing the speed limit. Obeying the law is a habit I got into the same day I received my taxi license fourteen years ago. It's one of my better habits. Given the fact that most habits are performed unconsciously, I figured that obeying the law would be a good habit to nurture assiduously. But I still groan when red lights flash on. Habit.

"What is that?" Mr. Zelner said, turning around and peering out the rear window.

"I believe it's a police car, sir," I said, as I took my foot off the accelerator.

"Why is a police car following us?" he said in a voice that communicated suppressed panic. I am familiar with that voice. I practically invented it. If you ever want to hear it, just call my answering machine.

"I don't know," I said. "I must have violated a traffic law."

I had no intention of pulling over and stopping in the middle of a viaduct under wet-weather conditions, so I gave my brakes a couple of taps and turned on my right blinker to signal to the policeman that I was aware of his presence. I intended to pull into a gas station at the west end of the viaduct.

"Can you elude him?" Mr. Zelner said.

"What?" I said.

"I am late for an appointment."

I glanced at the rearview mirror. Mr. Zelner was turned almost completely around, peering at the red lights of the cop car that was perhaps thirty feet behind my taxi.

"I have to stop, sir," I said. "I can't try to elude a policeman. I would lose my license."

He turned around and looked at me. Then he began touching the pockets of his coat. For one second I thought he was going for a gat. By now we were at the far end of the viaduct and I had to take care of the business of pulling into the station and parking beneath a roof that protected the gas pumps and possibly diving out of my taxi. I could hear Mr. Zelner making rustling noises in the backseat. As I wheeled into the parking lot I glanced at the mirror and saw him tamping out his cigarette. He closed the ashtray and twisted around to look at the cop car, which had parked directly behind me.

"This is a local policeman, yes?" Mr. Zelner said, turning and facing front.

I craned my head around and looked into the backseat. His arms were folded and one hand was touching his chin. I forget which hand. The only thing I remember is what his body language communicated: he was prepared to bolt. I had seen this before in other passengers, which we cabbies refer to as "runners." These are people who hop out of a backseat at intersections and run away without paying. I don't know who the genius was who invented the word "runner," beyond the fact that he must have been a taxi driver. I suppose that many a hired coachman in Auld Angland must have chased "runners" down the foggy streets of London town.

"Yes," I said. "It's a Denver Police Department car."

He nodded, closed his eyes, and bowed his head as if to hide his face. His body language was freaking me out, especially the syntax of his skull.

I faced forward, rolled down my window, and prepared myself mentally for the excruciating experience of signing a traffic ticket. You know what I'm talking about. Don't even try to kid me.

"Good evening, officer," I said.

"Good evening, sir," he said. "The reason I pulled you over is to let you know that your left-rear taillight is out."

I started to say, "It is?" but I had been trying for years to wean myself from the habit of making cops repeat themselves. "I wasn't aware of that," I said.

He nodded. "I'm not going to give you a ticket. I just wanted to let you know about it." He ducked his head and glanced into the backseat. "Running a fare?"

"Yes, officer."

"All right. You might be able to buy a replacement bulb in this station. If not, you better get that taken care of as soon as possible."

"I'll do that. Thank you, officer."

He tapped the bill of his cap and said goodnight, then walked back to his car.

As he pulled away and drove up Speer Boulevard, I started thinking about the break he had given me. If I had been a civilian he probably would have ticketed me, but cops always seem willing to give cab drivers a break. Cops and cabbies have a lot in common. We drive automobiles on the job, we work the mean streets, and we frequently deal with weird strangers. The list is almost endless but it's not. At the bottom of the list is the fact that cab drivers don't carry .38 caliber revolvers. At least I don't. Bottled ammonia is as far as the Founding Fathers were willing to let me go.

"I'll take you up to Diamond Hill first, sir," I said glancing at the mirror. "Then I'll come back here and replace the light bulb."

He didn't say anything. I put the transmission into gear, pulled out onto the street, and made my way up to the business park in silence. I thought about turning on my Rocky Cab radio and listening to the dispatcher, but I decided against it. My fare would be getting out in a couple of minutes, and after I replaced the bulb I would be heading back to the cab company to sign out for the night, so I wasn't interested in listening to the perpetual drone of addresses on the receiver. I would opt for AM radio as soon as I was alone, which is what I usually am when I rock to the Stones.

Another option would have been to fill the silence by starting a conversation with Mr. Zelner so that we could drift idly down The Pointless River to The Sea of Forgotten Chatter. But I hate talking to people as it is, and I saw no reason to jump-start a conversation with a man who would be getting out of my backseat in less than two minutes. When you've driven a taxi as long as I have, you get good at estimating how long it will take before a fare climbs out of a backseat. I'm usually right to within a range of ten to fifteen seconds. I'm not bragging, just stating a scientific fact.

But I was wrong.

Mister Zelner would not be climbing out of my backseat within two minutes. He would never be climbing out of my backseat. I guided my cab into an asphalt parking lot and stopped in front of a building. I looked at the meter, switched on the overhead light, and turned around in the seat.

"Three-twenty," I said, meaning three dollars and twenty cents. Mr. Zelner appeared to have fallen asleep. I won't insult your intelligence by pretending that I did not know he was dead. I knew it as soon as I looked at him. I will admit it was odd that I knew he was dead, because the only other dead body I knew of that I had encountered "on the job" was in a mortuary. I was delivering flowers for a living at the time. But since it was a mortuary I had no problem figuring out that the horizontal body on the clinical table was a corpse. However on that rainy night in April I felt psychic as I looked at the fare in my backseat. I felt every hair on my body stand erect. I don't want to get grotesque here but I mean every hair, and I sport a ponytail.

There was something about the way he was sitting that told me he was a goner. He wasn't just slouched against the backseat with his chin resting on his chest with a bit of drool hanging from his lower lip, while his partly curled palms lay slack on his lap. He looked "crumpled." I guess that's where the phrase "crumpled corpse" comes from.

I got out of the driver's seat fast.

I leaned down and looked through the window and said loudly, "Mister Zelner, we're here!" But I did not say it loud enough to wake the dead.

CHAPTER 2

B rother, you haven't lived until you've stood for ten minutes in a rainstorm trying to ignore a corpse.

I remained outside the cab waiting for the evening supervisor to arrive along with an ambulance. As soon as I had ascertained with certainty that another awful thing had occurred in my life, I had reached in and radioed the dispatcher. There is a code word that RMTC cab drivers use to let the company know that a fare has died in his cab. I won't tell you the code, but they taught it to us during our one day of training back when I first started driving. Everybody laughed when the instructor told us the code. Nobody expected to use it. Who dies in taxis? Mister Zelner did, and that's why I was soaked when the evening supervisor, Mr. Bailey, showed up in an unmarked cab. Supervisors drive gray cabs, which are former police interceptors. Mr. Bailey cruises the mean streets of Denver observing the driving habits of RMTC cabbies and reporting violations like curb jumping, rolling stops, etc. He has never nailed me for violating the rules. I'm a good driver. By that I mean I'm a paranoid driver. I get along well with Bailey, as I get along well with everyone who never catches me.

"What's the story, Murph?" he said, after he pulled up next to my cab and got out. He didn't put on a raincoat. I liked that.

"My fare is dead," I said. "He must have had a heart attack or something."

Bailey nodded and went over to the right-rear door of my cab, pulled a pair of rubber gloves out of his back pocket and yanked them on. He opened the door and leaned in to examine the corpse. I couldn't watch. Call me a sissy—as if I give a damn.

Bailey came back around the cab and told me that an ambulance and a police car were on the way. He pointed a thumb at his vehicle. "Hop in."

I climbed into the shotgun seat and began telling him about picking up Mr. Zelner at Union Station and driving him across the viaduct. The ambulance showed up while I was talking. Red lights but no siren. I assumed that the medics had their own code for the dead. A police car showed up a few minutes later. That made me nervous for reasons that have nothing to do with reality. Cops always make me nervous. That's their job.

By then the rain had stopped. I got out and stood by the vehicles feeling lousy while the medics did what they were paid to do. That's one job nobody could pay me to do. It's part of a rather long list of jobs aside from taxi driving. Name any job—it's on my list.

But I don't want to dwell on the scene. Instead I will dwell on how I felt after the policeman finished interviewing me, and the ambulance went away with no siren or red lights. By then it was a quarter after seven, but Bailey told me I wouldn't be charged a late fee when I got back to the motor. The code word for this situation is "compassion." He asked me if I was okay. I lied and said yes. But I wasn't okay. I didn't want to get back into 123 and drive to the motor. I don't believe in ghosts, but there are a lot of things I don't believe in that often affect my behavior. Bailey said he would meet me at the motor. I would have to write up an "incident" report.

I reluctantly got back into 123, and only then did I realize I had not shut off my meter. As a result, the meter read nine dollars and sixty cents. The waiting-time clock had been running all along. I shut it off fast. Strangely, this made me feel better, as though I had exorcised Zelner's ghost from my backseat. It got me to thinking about body language, symbolism, and moronic gestures in general. As I drove up the Valley

Highway I contemplated the odd little rituals, moves, and hand signals that people learn as children, which are often accompanied by face making. This took me up to the teen years where body language drifts toward "acting cool." This includes diddybopping, slouching, eye rolling, and the unfortunate obscene gestures that we all learn in the gutters and soda shops of America. I realized that during the teen years, face making is replaced by a kind of stoic somnambulism that is supposed to hide true emotions and express disdain for such things as classical music and gym coaches. I was raking the army over the coals and thinking about the peculiarity of the salute when I arrived at the entrance to the Rocky Cab parking lot. I had to put my sack of hypotheses back into the mental steamer trunk where I keep most of my pointless observations, and prepare myself mentally for writing down on an official form the things that I described above—not counting the theory and practice of acting cool from grades 9 through 12.

During the ride from Diamond Hill to the motor I never once looked into my rearview mirror. If I have to explain why to you, then you don't know me very well, which is probably a good thing.

I wrote the incident report upstairs in Mr. Hogan's private office. Hogan is the managing supervisor at RMTC, but he was gone for the day. I get along well with Hogan. Don't ask me why. It seems like every time I find myself in his office the police are there too, usually investigating a crime for which I am a "person of interest," which is cop lingo for "suspect." Murder, kidnapping, bank robbery—you name it, I've been found not-guilty of it. Maybe that's why Hogan and I get along so well. I don't look forward to the day when I make him ashamed of me. When I was a younger man, my supervisors were that frequently.

After I finished writing the report I carried it downstairs and handed it to Bailey, who was standing by the cage talking to Stew, the night cashier. The Word was out: an RMTC fare had "exited en route." You can't keep a euphemism like that a secret in the small world of cab driving. But it wasn't the sort of gossip that would be joked about in the on-call room the next day—even cab drivers have a sense of propriety, in spite of the way we dress.

I told Stew that the left-rear taillight needed to be replaced on 123. He made a note of it on my trip-sheet.

"I'll be back on Friday," I said to Mr. Bailey for no apparent reason. But I felt the need to say it. I felt the need to tell somebody besides myself that I wasn't going to let a bad day stop me from coming back to work. If I ever let that happen I would never get out of bed, and that's not an exaggeration. I possess documented proof—I call it "Cincinnati."

I walked outside, crossed the parking lot, and got into my '64 Chevy. I drove in the direction of home. Home is an apartment on Capitol Hill. I call the apartment my "crow's nest," and that's exactly where I wanted to be right then, at the top of the mainmast of a schooner sailing across an ocean with the ruins of civilization at my back. Denver is as close as I've ever gotten to the ruins of civilization.

I made a quick stop at a Burger King on east Colfax. I wasn't in the mood to cook that night. Death does that to me. The difference between stopping at a fast-food joint and cooking a burger on my stove is five minutes but I needed that five minutes. I needed it bad. Real bad. I intended to use it to sit in my easy chair and stare at the wall above my TV. I had learned long ago that the best way to overcome traumatic events is to sit and do nothing.

I refer to doing nothing as "the great equalizer." When you do nothing to avoid anything, the thing bothering you melds with everything that you don't do—ergo, you develop the proper perspective. Which is to say, it's all equally meaningless. The absence of meaning is the key to peace of mind. If I ever thought that anything I did meant something, I would develop a psychological tic and become prudent, and that's one cross I refuse to bear. I've lost count of all the crosses I've borne in my lifetime. But that's no surprise—I'm lousy at math.

It warmed my heart when I pulled into the parking lot behind my building and looked up at my apartment on the third floor where the kitchen light was on. It also pissed me off. I had forgotten to turn the light off when I went to work that morning. I hate leaving a light on when I go to work. There's no rational basis for this because my utilities are covered by the rent. But it's a psychological tic. If a light is burning all day I feel like a rain forest is going to disappear, and I don't want the blame.

I parked my Chevy in the choice V-spot where two wooden fences meet at a 90-degree angle. I climbed out with my sack of burgers and fries. The sack felt like a warm puppy. This made me think of Rod McKuen's smash bestselling record album, *Listen to the Warm*. If you're too young to know who Rod McKuen was, I'll gladly trade places with you.

When I got inside I set my cab accoutrement on the kitchen table, then went into the living room and quickly placed my taxi profits into my copy of *Lolita*, which I keep on a bookshelf. I have perhaps the only bookshelf in the world made of books. Okay. I'll admit it. The books are unpublished manuscripts. They were unpublished by me. I'm an un-published novelist, but its been a long time since I haven't published anything. I keep promising myself that I'll sit down and start another unpublished novel one of these days, but if you know anything about unpublished writers then you probably know that the worst thing that can happen to one is to run headlong into a wall of free time. That's when his bluff is called. That's when he knows he has to get creative—and he does. You've never seen a writer get more creative than when he starts thinking up alibis for not writing. I'm as prolific as James Michener when it comes to excuses.

But I didn't have that problem when I got home on Wednesday night. I had the greatest excuse in the world not to write: death. If I had been a cab driver when I was ten years old I could have stayed home from school an entire week with an excuse that good. My Maw was always a sucker for good excuses. When I was in the sixth grade our sheltie dog— Shelteen—died. I got a two-day break from homework out of that bitch. Shelteen I mean.

I went into the kitchen and grabbed a beer from the fridge, then carried my sack of warm food into the living room and sat down in my easy chair. I picked up my TV remote and began searching for *Gilligan's Island*. Standard Operating Procedure for a work night. Unfortunately Gilligan's was over. The death of Mr. Zelner had seen to that. I had missed the end of the show by ten minutes. Out of curiosity I picked up my *TV Guide* to see what I had missed. Big mistake. It was an episode where Mary Ann wore a bikini. I closed the guide and vowed that I would never again read a blurb for a Gilligan episode. I had enough torment in my life even when my cab fares didn't die.

I toyed with the idea of watching an episode of *The Secret Life of Henry Phyfe*, which is broadcast out of Chicago on Wednesday nights. Red Buttons kills me, although he's no Bob Denver. But the death of my taxi fare had drained me of the will to laugh. There are some things in life that a man cannot avoid, and death is one of them. Try it sometime, and let me know how it works out.

That got me to thinking about what might have happened if the castaways had started kicking the bucket before the show was canceled. I assumed that Mister Howell would be the first to go. Later on, Mrs. Howell. There would probably be a knee-slapping episode where the rest of the survivors haggled over the Howell estate. The professor would probably don the robe of a judge and make a division of the booty, with Ginger and Mary Ann fighting over Mrs. Howell's jewelry. The skipper would get the jaunty yachting cap that Mr. Howell always wore. And of course it goes without saying that—due to a legal technicality—Gilligan would end up with Mrs. Howell's dresses.

As I sat there in the easy chair thinking about this, I got so wrapped up in the endless possibilities that it was like I was watching an episode of *Gilligan's Island* that had never been broadcast. I got to laughing so hard that I choked on a French fry and had to run into the kitchen to drink a quick glass of water. I was terrified of getting the hiccups.

I stood for a few minutes holding the glass of water and listening to my esophagus to make sure I wasn't going to hiccup—or "hiccough" as the tight-asses say. Listening to my body made me think of Rod McKuen. I was having a terrible night—hysterical laughter followed by commercial poetry. By the time I got back to the living room I was so full of water that I couldn't drink any more beer. But rather than let my half-can of booze go to waste, I carried it into the kitchen and stored it in the fridge. I do not believe in wasting beer. Beer is like a rain forest. This got me to thinking about Rod McKuen again, so I decided to call it a night.

I often turn in early after close encounters with death, manual labor, or old friends, so hitting the sack early wasn't unusual for me. I had learned to do it in the army. In basic training they never let us sleep at all—except between the hours of nine p.m. and five a.m. Admittedly that's eight hours, but what's that got to do with my life? Prior to getting drafted I was a twelve-hour man. "Twelve-up and twelve-down," that was my motto. On the first day of basic training I tried to explain my sleeping requirements to my drill sergeant.

I really don't want to talk about that any further.

I turned off the lights in the kitchen and living room, then I went into the bedroom. I kicked off my Keds, turned off the table lamp, and collapsed into bed. I got undressed too, but I'll leave that to your imagination. As I lay in the darkness staring at the ceiling, I started thinking about poor ol' Mr. Zelner. Died in a taxi. I wondered who he was, how old he was, where he had been going, and what he had been planning to do when he got there. What was on Diamond Hill? All of the office buildings appeared closed for the night. Was he planning to meet someone there? Or did he live nearby? I wondered if he had died without ever seeing a single one of his dreams realized. I often wonder that about dead people. I wonder it about myself too—in the future tense I mean. But I am consoled by the fact that I once caught a glimpse of Mickey Rooney in person, so my life isn't a total waste.

CHAPTER 3

I woke up at ten o'clock on Thursday morning feeling blue. I went into the kitchen and made breakfast, which consisted of three boiled eggs chopped up on a plate of saltines. As I was crumbling the crackers and sprinkling them onto a paper plate I felt bad about feeling blue, since I am never blue when I don't have to work. I will go on record and state that not working has always been my primary goal in life. I blame homework of course. When I entered first grade I was astonished when I found out that the nuns expected us to "take school home" with us and continue our studies unsupervised. It not only sent me into a state of shock, it sent me into gales of laughter.

Unsupervised study. Give me a break.

I pulled a soda from the fridge and sat down at the kitchen table to eat. I felt too blue to watch TV, which shows how depressed I was. But it felt just plain "wrong" to watch TV when I was down in the dumps, especially when I was so happy about not working. I've never handled conflicting emotions very well, but I have found that not watching TV helps me to pretend to deal with the situation. It almost makes me feel "mature." Anybody who has never watched TV knows what I mean.

Then the phone rang.

A knot immediately appeared in my stomach. Rings always do that to me. I held a spoonful of egg-and-crackers poised in front of my lips as I waited out the chimes. Time was temporarily suspended. I counted the bells, five, and then the answering machine kicked in.

My recorded voice told the caller to please leave a message after the beep. I wondered how Alexander Graham Bell would have felt if he had known that he would one day be responsible for the proliferation of the word "beep."

I never answer the phone before twelve noon—or after twelve noon. You do the math. But I knew who it would be. It would be a telephone solicitor trying to talk me into giving him money. This would have sent me into gales of laughter if the joke wasn't so old. I have nothing against businessmen trying to get their hands on other people's money—that's their job. But there's something cute, if not pathetic, about trying to get money out of me.

For some reason that I don't understand, I squinted as I listened to the silence coming from the telephone. After all, you can't see silence, you can only not hear it. Suddenly the image of Rod McKuen welled up in front of my eyes, which killed my appetite.

I set the spoon back on the plate and frowned while simultaneously listening to the silence in the living room. I heard a few clicks coming from the answering machine. Then I experienced the blessed relief of the dial tone, perhaps the most beautiful sound on earth next to the melodious fluting of Zamfir.

I sighed.

Anybody who calls my machine and doesn't identify himself right away is living in a fool's paradise. When people say, "Hi Murph, it's me," they might as well say, "Hi Murph, don't pick up the phone." I do occasionally get calls from Hogan—as well as the police. The police are especially conscientious about identifying themselves. This sometimes has to do with my car that gets stolen every now and then by street punks or junkies. I'm on a first-name basis with the operator down at DPD. Her name is Gladys. She giggles whenever she tells me that my Chevy has been found within a mile radius of my apartment. The thieves always abandon my car after a test drive.

The answering machine shut itself down.

The silence coming from the living room was now organic rather than electronic, but by then I was no longer paying attention. I was thinking about Mr. Zelner, the man who had suffered either a heart attack or a stroke in my taxi and died between Union Station and Diamond Hill. I was the last person on earth to whom he had spoken. That would make anybody blue.

I stared at the crackers spread across my plate like scattered hopes and dreams. I decided to go ahead and finish breakfast even though it felt "wrong." But my stomach felt "hungry." Don't get me started on the digestive track, which is closely related to the concept of work. I don't know how many movies I've seen where a bossman says to an underling, "If you don't work, you don't eat." Facile intellectualism kills my appetite. Underlings know what I'm talking about.

After I finished eating I "did" the dish, which consisted of throwing it into the wastebasket. I had started using paper plates a few months previously after I decided to streamline my life. That didn't take long since I own nothing and practically never do anything. I go to the laundromat once a month, and I walk on the same places on my floor when I go from room to room in order to reduce the amount of wood that I have to mop, so I had a tough time trying to figure out how to do less than I already did. I scouted the apartment looking for any kind of clutter that I could eliminate from my life and I happened to open the silverware drawer in the kitchen and saw my fork. I own a fork, a knife, and a spoon, as well as a plastic plate. That's when it dawned on me that by using paper plates I could eliminate the twenty seconds it took to wash my dish after eating dinner. I bought a stack of paper plates and never looked back.

The plastic plate is getting kind of dusty though. I suppose I will be forced to wash it a couple times a year. Back in the old days when my friends used to drop by, they sometimes inspected my kitchen, opening the silverware drawer and the refrigerator and so forth just to see how I lived. This got to be both annoying and embarrassing. Again—the conflicting emotions deal. I wasn't able to solve the problem by not watching TV, so I simply told my friends to stop coming over. It worked! Maybe I could sell that technique to a self-help video guru.

After I tossed the "dish," I went into the living room to listen to the silence on my answering machine. Okay. I'll admit it. I wanted to double-check whether the lottery people had left a message. I sometimes turn the answering machine sound all the way down in order to stream-line my life even further, but I get worried that someone might phone to give me money, so I turn the sound back up. I know what you're think-ing, so let's move on.

I squinted as I listened to the silence. All I heard were the clicks, which I interpreted to be the sounds of a phone being set back on its cradle at the other end of the line. I pictured an embarrassed person try-ing to hang up secretly. Then I undertook the most soul-satisfying act a human being can perform. I erased the message.

I no longer felt blue.

Thursday had begun in earnest.

I had cleansed my answering machine of what I like to think of as a "virus." It almost made me feel like doing my laundry. But I save that for "spring break" as I call it, the nine days that I take off work from Rocky Cab once a month. I always do laundry on the ninth day, when my mind, body, and spirit are completely revitalized. Unlike people who order things from self-help infomercials, I had developed this technique through trial-and-error, which I guess means I own the copyright, or the patent, or whatever delusion that makes businessmen think they're pro-tected from rip-off artists.

By now it was almost eleven a.m. and I had absolutely nothing to do, which gave me the same giddy feeling that it gives me 64 percent of every year, since I work only 11 days per month, or 132 days per annum. But that's just an approximation, partly because I am sometimes forced to work on weekends, but mostly because I am lousy at math. Let's just round it down to a whole number or whatever it's called and say that 60 percent of every year I am giddy, and the rest of the year I work. To translate this from arithmetic into English: I didn't know what to do with myself for the rest of the day.

The two most viable options were to start writing a new novel or else watch TV. In theory I could have gone to a zoo or else looked for a job that paid better than cab driving, but those options involved leaving the apartment, and I got enough of that nonsense three times a week.

I was stumped.

Then the goddamn phone rang again.

I was ambivalent about this. I can't tell you the number of times my inability to make a decision has been interrupted by a telephone call, sometimes to my advantage. For instance, one time I almost absconded with one hundred thousand dollars in stolen money, until my phone rang and blew the whole deal. It's a long story and I probably wouldn't have gotten away with it anyway.

I counted the number of rings. Five of course—it never fails.

I rolled my eyes with impatience and waited to see who was calling—assuming that I can say "see who was calling" without violating the sacred rules of English grammar. Again, I obviously couldn't "see" the sound of a voice. This made me wonder if Rod McKuen might be on the line. A call like that would make a nice addendum to my "Mickey Rooney Moment."

The machine spoke:

"Hello Mr. Murphy. My name is Arthur Heigger. I am the family lawyer for Mr. Zelner, the man who passed away in your taxicab last night. I have something important to discuss with you. If you are there, could you please pick up the phone?"

I froze.

I avoid the word "important" whenever I can—but it was my dead fare's lawyer on the line.

I picked up the receiver. "This is Mr. Murphy."

"Ah, Mr. Murphy, I am so happy to get hold of you. As I said, I am the lawyer for the Zelner family, and according to the police report you were the taxi driver who was present when Mr. Zelner died last night. This is correct, yes?"

"Yes, sir."

"I wonder if it would be possible for you to come to my office? It is located on Tenth Avenue near Grant Street. The family requested that I speak with you. If you could come by my office today I would be willing to pay you for your time."

I started to explain that he wouldn't have to pay me, but I quickly checked myself. I prefer that people believe that the slightest favor on my part is tantamount to one of the twelve labors of Hercules. It discourages follow-ups.

"I guess I could do that, sir," I said. "May I ask how you got my phone number?"

"From the phone book," he said.

I felt stupid. He may have thought I was "accusing" him of something. I kept forgetting that I didn't have an unlisted number, since nobody I knew ever called me. But even if I did have an unlisted number, they still wouldn't call me. I began to develop a psychological tic. I finessed that by saying, "I could come over right now, sir."

"That would be very helpful," Mr. Heigger said.

He gave me the address. I told him I would be over in fifteen minutes.

I hung up and went through the onerous process of trying to make myself presentable to the public on my day off. Three minutes later I was driving along on 13th Avenue in the direction of Lincoln Street.

I turned left onto Grant Street. A number of Denver streets were named after American Presidents, but it didn't seem to have worked. I drove as far as 10th Avenue. The building came in sight. I slowed as I approached the address. It was a three-story mansion made of red sandstone, a striking example of nineteenth-century Gothic architecture. I had driven past it many times and had assumed it was merely an apartment building that I could never afford to live in. I had no idea it contained offices. The exterior walls had been sandblasted so it glowed against the backdrop of nearby mansions that possessed the gritty charm of weather-stained gray sandstone. The roof was made of slate, and the sidewalk was made of flagstone. I began to have a new respect for the genius who named the Rocky Mountains.

I parked in front of the building. The streets were narrow in that part of town. They had been laid out before the advent of horseless carriages. It was a residential neighborhood that had doubtless been rezoned for businesses, but not to the point that it had parking meters. A well-manicured lawn fronted the place. There were steps leading up to a wide veranda. I tried to imagine what it must have been like to live in such a fancy mansion during the cowboy days. Unfortunately that made me think of *Gone With the Wind*, so I stopped imagining. I'll admit it. When I was in college I read *Gone With the Wind*. The thing I liked most about it was the fact the Margaret Mitchell had been a newspaper reporter before she became a best-selling author. She worked the police beat, smoked cigarettes, drank corn liquor, and was a scandal to her family. I may be her biggest fan for all the wrong reasons.

I stepped up onto the veranda and pushed open the front door. The interior of the building had been refurbished so that it looked more modern than the exterior, meaning it lacked character. It could have been a building in the Denver Tech Center. A broad staircase led to the second floor, but the office I was seeking was on the first floor toward the rear. The place was silent. Office buildings are always silent. Factories are always noisy. I've worked in both environments. I still do in a sense. A taxicab is like a rolling office where you can crank up the windows to shut out the factory racket of life. I was thinking about this as I walked down the hallway. I found a door with a sign that read "Heigger & Associates." The sign consisted of white letters against a black background bordered by a silver frame. It was elegant yet subdued, like so few things in my life.

I knocked and waited.

CHAPTER 4

The door opened and a man about my age stood smiling at me. He was wearing wire-rim glasses and had curly hair that looked a bit "longish" for a man his age. I myself sport a ponytail so I don't know where I get off by that remark, except he was wearing a well-tailored suit and possessed what I would describe as a "dignified bearing." Need I say more?

"Brendan Murphy," he stated.

"Yes, sir."

The man smiled broadly and held out his hand. "How do you do?" I was immediately struck by his accent. There was something slightly Germanic about it. I've seen a lot of sub-titled movies.

"How do you do, sir," I replied, shaking his hand. He had a firm handshake.

"Step into my office," he said. "Thank you so much for coming here on your day off."

"No problem," I said, then wished I hadn't said it. When you say a thing like that it spreads like a virus.

"Please have a seat," he said, as he walked around his desk. The office was nicely appointed. That's as far as I'm willing to go in terms of descriptive prose. You've seen offices. Believe me, they're all the same.

He sat down behind the desk and got a serious look on his face. I knew what he was doing. He was "cutting to the chase." He held his torso very erect. This too struck me as Germanic. Let me say here that I have no bias against Germans. I love Billy Wilder movies even though he was Austrian. But I suddenly became leery.

Let me explain:

When I'm in my taxi I have a tendency to start talking like the people I meet, and in this situation I was afraid that given enough time and rope I might start talking like Colonel Klink. This has to do with ingratiating myself with my fares in order to increase the size of my tips, talking the way they talk, agreeing with their views on politics, economics, or any other subject that can be crammed into a ten-minute ride. This is just an "act" of course. In reality I don't talk like anybody I know, and I don't agree with anybody on anything, so I'm pretty flexible.

But I knew I had to do my best to act mature during this sad encounter with Mr. Zelner's lawyer, which was not beyond the realm of possibility. I've had quite a bit of experience acting mature, mostly in the presence of detectives.

"Again, zank you for coming in on your day off," he said.

His accent wasn't actually that thick, but I did hear the faintest whiff of a "Z" in his voice. Rod McKuen couldn't have said it with more contrived subtlety.

"You're welcome, sir," I said.

Mr. Heigger then frowned a businesslike frown. "Could you describe for me the circumstances of the taxi ride during which Mr. Zelner passed away?"

"Certainly," I said. "I picked him up at Union Station and drove him across the Fourteenth Street viaduct. He wanted to go to a location called Diamond Hill, which is just across the Valley Highway. When I got to the address though, I found out that …" I stopped. I felt foolish stating that Mr. Zelner was dead. It always bothers me when people state the obvious in my presence as if I was some kind of a dolt—but Mr. Heigger was a lawyer so he was probably used to it. "… that Mr. Zelner was dead," I concluded.

"I see," Mr. Heigger said. He nodded and looked down at some papers on his desk, then looked up at me. "I have a few questions that I would like to ask of you, Mr. Murphy."

I nodded.

"What was the disposition of Mr. Zelner's luggage?"

"Mr. Zelner didn't have any luggage." Heigger's eyebrows arched.

"He did not?"

"No, sir."

"Do you mean to say that when he came out of the railway station he was not carrying a suitcase?"

"No, sir."

"Perhaps he might have been carrying a small valise?"

"No, sir. When he climbed into my backseat he didn't have any luggage at all."

As I was replying I was thinking that this may have been the first time in my life that anyone had actually said the word "valise" to me. Fares usually said "carryall" or "travel case."

An expression flitted across Heigger's face that I would describe as "perplexed." But it quickly went away.

"May I ask if Mr. Zelner might have been carrying anything at all in his hands when he came out of the railway station?" he said.

I wanted to reply "Yes, you may ask" but somehow I managed to say, "I didn't see him come out of the station."

"What do you mean?" Heigger said. "Were you not parked at the taxi stand in front of the station?"

I cleared my throat with the same preparatory misgivings that I often incorporate when being interrogated by the police. I described my initial encounter with Mr. Zelner: the call from half a block away, the fast drive to the station, the slap of the windshield wipers that couldn't keep up with the driving rain, the darkness, the sudden opening of my rear door, the trench coat, the hat, the note handed to me, the face thrown into shadow. I was starting to overdo it in the drama department but Heigger interrupted my narrative by asking me to describe the note.

"It was just a small piece of paper that had an address for Diamond Hill written on it," I said.

"What was the address?" he said.

I swallowed hard. I suddenly felt like I was being interrogated by a cop—or a nun. The cop's name would have been "Duncan," whereas the nun's name would have been "Xavier," as in "Sister Mary."

"I don't know," I said.

"You do not know the address that you were going to?" he said with a disapproving lilt in his voice.

I started to get rattled because Heigger now sounded like my Maw. This in turn kick-started the general wariness and disdain that I have for all forms of authority except Leonard Maltin. When I was in the army, a lieutenant colonel once asked me to recite the chain-of-command from the President on down to my battalion commander. I nearly fainted.

"I knew the address last night but I didn't memorize it," I said.

"Why not?" he said.

An electric bolt of umbrage welled up inside me, thank God. Umbrage has always helped me to pretend to be mature. "Mr. Zelner handed me a piece of paper with the address written on it, so I used that as my guide."

"Could you possibly recall the address?"

The answer was no, but I pretended to think it over. I always know what I don't know, and I knew I didn't know the address. I had glanced at the slip of paper only long enough to read the number, which was like hearing a fare articulate an address that remained inside my brain long enough to haul the customer to the destination. My brain is like the print-spooler on my word processor, which holds a failed novel long enough to print it out before it is deleted from the RAM and replaced by a rejection slip.

"All I can recall is that it was an address on Diamond Hill," I said. "After I found out that Mr. Zelner was dead I sort of forgot everything else."

"If I were to accompany you to Diamond Hill could you point out the building to me?" Heigger said.

I stared at Heigger in silence for a few moments. I began to experience a number of emotions that, while not conflicting, certainly were different from each other. One of the emotions was amusement. Heigger had made the classic blunder of offering me a chance to say no. But he was also suggesting that I take time out of my three-score-and-ten to go somewhere on my day off. I might as well admit here that asking me to do anything at all is a risky proposition, which may explain why I have so few friends. On top of all this, his attitude communicated to me an assumption that I would do this favor for him because he was a lawyer and I was a lowly cab driver, which, while not necessarily untrue, didn't sway me. He seemed awfully determined to find out where Mr. Zelner had been going the previous evening, and since I was starting to be irked by his officious attitude, I decided to yank his chain.

"Why would you want me to do that?" I said.

"It may be that Mr. Zelner had his luggage sent on ahead, perhaps by another taxi. If so, his family would like me to retrieve his personal belongings."

"I don't think any of the office buildings were open for business last night," I said.

"He may have sent his luggage along earlier in the day," Heigger replied.

So far every answer he had given made perfect sense. I was out of my element.

"I vill pay you of course," Heigger said.

The V-sound in the word "will" wasn't really there, yet I heard it. I also heard the word "pay."

"Would twenty dollars compensate you for your time and trouble?" Heigger said.

I made a quick calculation. As bad as I am at math, I am a whiz when it comes to mileage/money calculations. If I had been taught cab driving in grade school I might not have failed arithmetic. I calculated that the mileage from 10th Street to Diamond Hill would be twelve dollars, which meant I could scam Heigger out of eight dollars. Not really, of course. This was a legitimate offer that he was making, but it did have the delightful odor of a rip-job.

"You got a deal," I said.

CHAPTER 5

Mr. Heigger immediately stood up to leave for Diamond Hill. It took all my willpower not to imitate his move. I don't know about you, but when people abruptly stand up in my presence I look around for danger. Three times in my life I have entered a room unexpectedly only to cause a woman to scream. Fortunately there were other people present who could identify me.

As the lawyer stood there looking down at me, he picked up a briefcase from the desk and tucked it under one arm. I casually got up and followed him out of the office.

After we stepped outside, Mr. Heigger asked if I would mind driving my car to Diamond Hill. He said he would follow me in his car. He then sweetened the deal by offering to give me an extra five dollars to cover the cost of my gas as well as making use of my private automobile to complete his business.

I kept a straight face and nodded, but inside I was doing back flips. I wasn't even on duty and I was scoring a half-day's pay. This almost made me want to quit cab driving and become a lackey for lawyers. I'll admit it. I've never completely abandoned that idea.

I climbed into my Chevy and watched in the rearview mirror as Mr. Heigger climbed into a Cadillac parked farther down the block. My shoulders drooped. I realized I should have gone to law school instead of English degree school.

I sighed and pulled out onto the street and headed for Speer Boulevard. As I drove I watched Heigger in my mirror. He stayed right on my tail. I sped up a little to see what would happen. He remained on my tail. He was good. He was like a man who had a lot of experience chasing ambulances. We crossed the 14th Street bridge and drove to the top of Diamond Hill. I parked in the asphalt lot where I had parked 123 the previous night, but not in the same slot. I wanted to leave it vacant so Heigger could get a clear picture of the scene even though there wasn't a chalk outline of my cab on the asphalt.

After Heigger climbed out of his gas hog and walked up to my pollution factory, I pointed at the empty slot. "I parked here last night," I said. "Then I looked into the backseat and saw Mr. Zelner sort of slumped down." I paused a moment before I went ahead and said something that I felt foolish saying. "I sensed right away that he was dead."

Heigger nodded. "That is understandable."

"It is?" I said.

"I have been told by clients on previous occasions that the presence of a dead body in a room can be sensed even when the observer has not yet discovered the corpse."

"Really?"

"Yes. But I believe there is a scientific explanation. The deterioration of a human body commences immediately upon expiration. The air surrounding the body is tainted with a molecular residue that can be unconsciously smelled by the observer."

I nodded and started breathing through my mouth. The idea of Mr. Zelner's molecules bouncing around inside my nostrils made me uneasy. But mostly I was disappointed to learn that I was not mystical. My psychic ability to sense death had been disproved by scientific rationalism, like most of my abilities.

"Can you point out which building Mr. Zelner wished to go to?" he said.

I turned and pointed at a glass-walled building. "I don't recall the specific address from last night, but this is the place," I said.

Then I saw the address printed on a tastefully designed rectangle of wooden signage planted on the grass near the front door. Heigger pulled out a pen and jotted down the number.

He snapped the top of the pen with his thumb and slipped the pen into his shirt pocket. He raised his chin and gazed at me. "I have another question I wish to ask you."

"All right."

"During your trip to this location, did you engage in a conversation with Mr. Zelner?"

I shook my head no, then stopped abruptly. This was a bad habit that I had gotten into when I was a kid. I call it "denial." Whenever an adult asked me a question concerning a dicey situation—such as stolen donuts—I would automatically shake my head no while simultaneously trying to recall if I actually did know something. I usually did, but that's neither here nor there.

I began to nod. "When Mr. Zelner handed me the piece of paper at Union Station he asked me if it was very far away. I told him it would take five minutes to get here. He seemed pleased by that."

"Did you engage in any further talk?" Heigger said. "I know that taxi drivers sometimes strike up conversations during a ride. Small-talk, as it were. They become inquisitive about their fares. I wonder if perhaps you might have asked him where he had come from, and where he was going."

"No," I said. "We didn't have a conversation about anything. I knew that the trip wouldn't take very long so I didn't make any small-talk."

"He told you nothing about himself?"

"No. He seemed to want to sit back and, you know, enjoy the ride. Oh wait … he did ask me for a light. He smoked a cigarette on the way over the bridge."

Heigger's eyes were darting around my face as I spoke, as if he was trying to detect something hidden behind my words. Believe me I know the look. I was practically raised by nuns.

"He seemed sort of tired," I continued. "But I figured he was probably just worn out from his train trip."

"Did he tell you that he had arrived on a train?"

"No, but I deduced that from the fact that he came out of the train station. You notice little things like that when you drive a taxi for a living."

"But you told me that you did not actually see him come out of the station."

Shoot.

"That's true," I said. "I guess I just assumed that he came out of the station." I hated using words like "guess" and "assume" in the presence of a scientific rationalist, but guesses and assumptions are the cornerstones of my life.

Heigger pursed his lips and raised his chin and looked beyond the place where I was standing. I turned around. I could see the roof of the main building of Union Station far in the distance. It had been constructed during the nineteenth century. It was originally end-of-track for a spur line that came down from Cheyenne, Wyoming. Tracks were eventually laid to Colorado Springs—and on down to Mexico City for all I know, however my knowledge of railroad history pretty much ends at Pike's Peak.

"Vell, zank you for accompanying me to zees blace," he sort of said. He reached into his coat and pulled out a wallet and handed me two crisp new sawbucks and a fiver.

"Thank you, sir," I said. I felt funny saying "sir" to a man my own age, but the fresh injection of long green ameliorated my emotional conflict.

I tucked the money into my T-shirt pocket as if I was on cab duty, then I said, "Do you need me for anything else?"

"Your help has been quite satisfactory," he said. He glanced at the building, then looked back at me. "You have done all that you can do. Thank you very much. I am now going into this building to make a few inquiries."

He abruptly jammed his hand toward me. I reached out and shook it. I wanted to ask him who Mr. Zelner was, where he had come from, and where he had been going. I wanted to know if Mr. Zelner had died without ever seeing a single one of his dreams realized. But mostly I wanted to know where Mr. Heigger had learned to speak English. His syntax was weirding me out. I was willing to bet he hadn't gone to a Catholic school where they really hammer on syntax—unless it was a German-Catholic school. I once met a guy who was German-Catholic. He drives a taxi in Wichita.

I climbed into my Chevy and headed out of the parking lot. I looked into the rearview mirror as I drove away. I saw Heigger standing there watching me. His briefcase was tucked under one arm. I slowed as I guided my heap down the hill. I kept glancing at Heigger expecting him to turn away and goosestep toward the building, but he just stood there watching me until I rolled out of sight.

I drove on down the hill and pulled up at a stop sign. It was at this precise moment in time that something occurred to me: I had forgotten to fill out my trip-sheet. By this I mean that after I had gotten back to the motor on Wednesday night I had not filled in the box at the bottom of my trip-sheet for Mr. Zelner's ride to Diamond Hill. His death had caused me to forget the paperwork. Which is to say, all the tees had not been crossed and all the eyes had not been dotted. I groaned and leaned my forehead against the steering wheel.

Let me explain.

Without going into too much detail, I had been involved in situations in the past where I had failed to properly fill out my trip-sheets and I subsequently found myself in what might be termed "hot water" with RMTC. The situations sometimes involved homicides, kidnappings, bank robbery—it all becomes a blur and isn't really important—but I knew that if I didn't go to RMTC and complete the paperwork I might get into trouble, though not so much with my supervisor, Mr. Hogan, as with the top brass, and the insurance company, and all the other faceless entities who yank the puppet strings of my life. Every once in a while they tug the "You're-suspended-from-cab-driving" string and I find myself unemployed. It's always temporary but it's a pain in the neck because it sometimes causes me to look for another job.

End of explanation.

I cut down to Interstate 25 and headed north. I retraced the route to the motor that I had driven from Diamond Hill after Mr. Zelner died—up I-25 and across I-70. As I drove along I started wondering how the federal government went about the process of naming highways. I wondered if I-70 really was the 70th federal highway built in America. I knew that I-80 ran through Cheyenne, Wyoming, but were there really 80 highways in America? These are the kinds of questions that could easily be answered if I used libraries to do educational research rather than borrowing bestsellers that I'm too cheap to buy.

CHAPTER 6

I arrived at the motor and parked in the lot, climbed out of my Chevy, and walked toward the door of the on-call room. Since this was my day off I felt like a kid walking toward a school that I did not actually attend. It made me feel like I could step inside and walk past the principal and snap my fingers in his face and strut on down the hall with a smug smirk. Being in places where I don't belong has always made me feel this way, not counting the army—although one time I saluted an officer with my left hand and got away with it. But he was only a second lieutenant so it wasn't that big a deal. I'll admit it. I never tried to pull a fast one on a general. You don't get to be a general by taking guff off draftees.

I entered the on-call room and walked up to the cage. Rollo was on duty. The man in the cage is sort of like a palace guard, in that visitors have to get past him if they want to speak to the managing supervisor or anybody else in authority at RMTC.

Rollo glanced at me. I knew what he was thinking: "Why isn't Murph at home asleep?"

I smiled at him and said, "I need to talk to Mr. Hogan. Is he here?"

"Go on up," Rollo said. He was eating a donut and reading a newspaper.

I'm going to tell you something that I will probably get canned for revealing, but getting canned is nothing new to me. There is a shotgun mounted on the wall inside the cage. It is clearly visible to anybody who stands directly in front of the cage. It is within easy reach of the cashier.

The cage has a thick Plexiglas window that in all probability could not withstand a blast at close-range from a 12-gauge shotgun, like almost anything else you could name.

Perhaps this is the reason why Rollo and I never let our mutual disagreements drift beyond a battle of the intellects. You be the judge.

I stepped into the hallway, climbed the stairs to Hogan's office, and knocked on the door.

"Yeah," Hogan muttered.

I pushed the door open and stepped inside. Hogan was seated at his desk fiddling with paperwork. He glanced up and smiled. "Thanks for coming in on your day off."

I frowned with puzzlement.

He lifted a trip-sheet and held it out to me. I stared at it—then looked at him.

"What's this?" I said.

"Your trip-sheet from last night."

Was I in the Twilight Zone again? I stepped closer to his desk and looked at the sheet. When I didn't take it from his hand, he shook it the way you would shake a cracker at a parakeet.

"Excuse me, boss, but can I ask you a question?" I said.

"Sure."

"Why … why … why …" I stopped. I didn't even know how to phrase the question. I wanted to know how he knew that I was here to fill out my trip-sheet from Wednesday night.

"Problem, Murph?"

"I came to fill out that trip-sheet," I said. "I forgot to fill it out last night."

"I know."

"How could you possibly know that?"

"I noticed it when I was looking over the paperwork this morning."

"No ... what I mean is ... how could you know that I came here just now to fill it out?"

He lowered the sheet and gazed at me. I began to wonder if my managing supervisor had psychic abilities.

"You got my call, right?" he said.

"What call?"

"I left a message on your answering machine half an hour ago asking you to come down and fill out the sheet."

Suddenly everything made sense. I didn't like that. In spite of my puzzlement I had been enjoying being in a situation that defied rational explanation. Ergo, Mr. Hogan's explanation ruined everything. It was like finding out how a magician really pulls a rabbit out of a hat. I've often wondered about the psychological makeup of people who become professional stage magicians. Do they have some deeply rooted need to "trick" people? Magicians must live tormented lives.

"Oh," I said.

I raised an index finger and started to explain my confusion to him but I somehow managed to stop myself in time. I had long ago learned the futility of trying to explain myself to people who have absolutely no interest in the driftwood that bobs on the surface of my brain.

Instead I said, "By the way, I just wanted to let you know that I accompanied Mr. Heigger over to Diamond Hill this morning."

"Who is Mr. Heigger?"

"He's Mr. Zelner's family lawyer," I said. "I thought you might have been told that by the insurance people."

"Not yet," he said. "Why did you go to Diamond Hill?"

"I showed him the building where Mr. Zelner was headed for last night. He wanted to check on whether Mr. Zelner had shipped some luggage ahead. But there's something I wanted to ask you, boss."

"What's that?"

"Did you get any kind of medical report on Mr. Zelner? I mean, do you know what he died of?"

"No. The insurance people will let me know all that as soon as they get things sorted out. Why do you ask?"

"I just wondered." I paused a moment, then said, "I feel sort of bad, ya know? I feel like maybe I could have done something to help him."

"Don't start thinking like that, Murph," Hogan said. "It could have been a stroke, a heart attack, who knows? Things like this have happened to other drivers before. You did everything you could have done. You followed procedure. That was all that was required of you."

I nodded. I already knew that but I needed to hear it from somebody else. People rarely tell me that I did everything I could have done—probably because I never do anything.

"All right, thanks," I said.

Hogan nodded. He was already losing interest in this conversation. I could see it in his eyes. I recognized it. I often saw it in the eyes of women at beer blasts.

"You can give the trip-sheet to Rollo after you fill it out," he said.

"All right."

"Thanks again for coming in on your day off, Murph."

I started to say, "No problem," but I dodged that bullet. I was getting pretty good at making people think they had intruded on my valuable time. This might come in handy if I ever got any valuable time.

I would have preferred to fill out the sheet right there but I could see that Hogan was busy and wanted to be left alone. I have never understood busy people, but I am familiar with the concept. I took the sheet down to the on-call room and sat at a table where idle cabbies are not allowed to play poker by Colorado state law. I proceeded to fill out the last series of boxes on the sheet, which included the time, destination, and cost of the ride.

This was not as easy to do as it might appear on the surface because I had to regroup and try to remember the details of the trip with Mr. Zelner, and I make a habit of forgetting everything that happens to me as quickly as I can. I have found this to be a valuable tool on a witness stand.

Unfortunately the events involving Mr. Zelner had taken place less than twenty-four hours earlier so I had not been able to fully expunge them from my "memory bank" as I like to call the place where I keep my *TV Guide*.

I began regrouping:

It was six-thirty when the call came over the radio. I arrived at Union Station at approximately six-thirty-and-a-half. I rounded it up to six-thirty-one on the trip-sheet, but keep that under your hat.

I wrote down the Diamond Hill address and the time we arrived. The ride had taken five minutes. Then I came to the last box on the sheet where the meter fare was supposed to have been filled in, and suddenly an electric bolt of adrenaline went up my spine. I remembered that I had forgotten to shut off the meter when I parked on Diamond Hill. While I had been dealing with the death of Mr. Zelner, the meter had kept on ticking. The amount on the meter reached $9.60 before I shut it off. But that wasn't the only cause of the bolt. The bolt was also caused by something that Mr. Zelner had said to me halfway across the viaduct. "Can you elude him? I am late for an appointment." This was in reference to the policeman who had stopped me. Ergo, I realized that I had virtually lied to Mr. Heigger when he had asked me if Mr. Zelner had said anything else during the trip.

Fer the luvva Christ.

I raised my head and slowly looked around the on-call room as if I was "casually" looking around, which I was, but it had the quality of a furtive move. I often do this after I lie. Rollo was chewing on a donut and leafing through a stack of trip-sheets. There was nobody else in the room at the moment. Cabbies enter the on-call room at different times of the day, depending on the type of lease they work, but The Big Rush doesn't take place until five o'clock. Even though nobody could see me, I slid my left arm slowly in front of me on the tabletop so I could peek at my wristwatch to see what time it was.

12:45.

I don't know why I did that.

Time held no relevance to the situation at hand, which was the fact that I had told Mr. Heigger that Mr. Zelner had not spoken to me the previous night, when he not only had spoken but had said something so strange that I had no problem dismissing it from my memory bank. I'm pretty good at remembering numbers if they have a dollar sign on the left side, but odd statements by customers have about as much longevity in my brain as requests for favors.

You wouldn't believe some of the odd things fares have said to me during the past fourteen years. I would give you examples but I can't remember them beyond the fact that they existed long enough to make my tympanic membranes flutter. I do remember a woman who climbed into my cab and said, "The cure for cancer is in the earth!" but she later explained that she was talking about herbal cures. Her statement came to within a hair's breadth of being forgotten by me forever. But verbal explanations make things stick in my mind, although they don't occur often enough for me to view them as anything more than freaks of na-ture—sort of like the platypus but not as fun.

I suddenly felt trapped in a moral quandary. Should I get in touch with Mr. Heigger and tell him that I had forgotten Mr. Zelner's state-ments? Or should I do what any rational human being would do and forget it forever? After all, Mr. Zelner was dead and gone. If he had sent his luggage to Diamond Hill earlier in the day, his lawyer would probably track it down. As far as I was concerned, my involvement in this situa-tion had ended the moment I said goodbye to Heigger. I had made the mistake many times in my life of getting involved in the personal lives of my fares only to regret it. Most often I got involved in their lives in an attempt to help them solve a problem. But this was the first time that I had considered getting involved in the personal life of a dead man.

I stared at the empty box on the trip-sheet, then slowly and deliberately printed the numerals 9.60 in the box. I didn't have to draw the dollar sign. Dollar signs are preprinted on the forms. I think of this as a "gentle reminder" to cabbies who are not very good at distinguishing rectangles from one another.

The cost of the fare had been three-twenty but I wrote nine-sixty because it had been recorded on the meter, and if the IRS or Hogan had to go over my records with a fine-tooth comb, they or he might have conceivably discovered that I had short-changed the amount by $6.40, which would have forced me to explain the difference. Hogan wouldn't have had any problem understanding that I had forgotten to shut off the meter after my fare died. He had long ago gotten used to my inability to do certain things under certain circumstances. But that didn't matter because the only money RMTC cares about is the seventy bucks I lay on Rollo every morning. I could have written "one million dollars" on my trip-sheet and it wouldn't have meant anything to anybody, except perhaps an inquisitive IRS agent.

After the sheet was filled out, my only legal obligation was to carry it to the cage and hand it to Rollo. At that point the entire affair would have ended and I would have been free to walk out the door and forget it forever.

But instead I sat there wondering if I should go back up to Hogan's office and explain my "gaffe" and ask him to get in touch with Mr. Heigger. Perhaps I could phone in my gaffe. I've done that on a number of occasions, mostly involving apologies to women. In spite of my hatred of telephones, I have found that phones are the least dangerous means by which to end a relationship.

I glanced at Rollo. He now appeared to be eating a ham sandwich with lettuce and reading a newspaper. But I knew what he was really doing. He was playing "mind games" with me. You might wonder how I had come to this conclusion, but the answer is simple: the sonofabitch was always playing mind games with me. His very existence was a deliberate ploy. He was waiting for me to approach the cage so that he could "say" something. What—I did not know. But Rollo had been a taxi driver before he began working the cage, and when you drive a taxi for a living you learn to read people's eyes. Most taxi customers are unaware of the fact that a rearview mirror is a window to the soul. If I walked up to the cage and held my trip-sheet out to Rollo, one glance at my eyes would tell him that I was hiding a terrible secret. Instead of taking the sheet he would lay down his ham-and-lettuce and set into motion an inquisition of such piercing subtlety that I would probably crack on the spot.

I quickly reviewed the past forty-five years of my life and decided the best thing to do would be to forget it. Not my past life but the Zelner conversation. Just hand in my trip-sheet, get out of there, and never look back. I could not count the number of times that I had dug myself into a deep hole by trying to "fix" something only to regret it later, although the number 107 welled up in my mind. But I think that had something to do with an I.Q. test.

I tucked my pencil into my shirt pocket, stood up, and carried the trip-sheet to the cage.

"Here ya go," I said casually.

Rollo looked up from his newspaper, glanced at the sheet, then took it from my hand.

I turned to flee but Rollo said, "Hey Murph."

I froze.

"Look at this," he said.

He held up the newspaper. There was a half-page photograph of a single house standing amid the ruins of a forest fire that had recently ravaged the hills above Los Angeles.

"Fifty houses were burned down in this fire," he said, "but it by-passed this one house completely. How about that?"

I stared at the photograph.

The other houses had been flattened and charred, yet that one house remained unscathed. Was Rollo hinting at something? I had been to Los Angles a couple of times in my life but I sure as hell didn't have anything to do with that fire.

"Amazing," I said.

I hate the word "amazing." Nothing amazes me. But I have found that people respond positively to that word after they have said something boring to me.

"See ya tomorrow," I said.

Rollo nodded, set the newspaper down, and turned the page to the sports section. Just before I walked away I noticed that he tossed my trip-sheet onto his stack of trip-sheets. I experienced a fleeting moment of glee. Oblivious to the turmoil taking place in the on-call room that day, Rollo had inadvertently put a cap on the Zelner affair with his dismissive gesture.

As I walked away from the cage I secretly snapped the fingers of my right hand dangling near my thigh and thus hidden from Rollo's view. He may not have even heard the soft click of flesh-on-flesh.

But I did.

Just before the door closed at my back, I heard Rollo burp. I was home free.

CHAPTER 7

I drove back to my apartment experiencing the giddy feeling that I was actually "going somewhere" when in fact I was going where I would have been anyway if this had been a normal Thursday. But I always feel giddy when things are getting back to normal, which happens about six times a year. The a priori abnormalcy usually consists of having gotten involved in the personal life of a fare, and when it's over I vow that I will never do it again. But since I get involved in the personal lives of my fares on a fairly steady basis, I guess abnormalcy is normal for me. Even though I know the risks of helping people, I often respond like a skag addict and dive right into the alluring cesspool of altruism.

I have been told that helping people is a disease that cannot be controlled by daily injections of insulin, and while I believe that, I have never gone out of my way to cure myself of being nice. I am sometimes perplexed by the fact that I frequently turn my back on my natural inclination to do nothing, although a friend of mine named Big Al insists it's because I'm a raging egotist. You be the judge.

I thought about this as I drove toward my crow's nest. I knew that if I had found Mr. Zelner dying rather than already dead in my backseat I would have tried to help him. I would have radioed the dispatcher and then attempted CPR. We cabbies are taught a basic method of CPR, as well as other forms of first-aid. When I was in the army we were given in-depth first-aid classes. I became proficient at screaming "Medic!" and diving into a foxhole.

I also know how to deliver babies. They didn't teach us that in taxi class though—I learned it in the school of hard knocks. I don't have a very clear memory of my first delivery, although during the birthing process I do recall wishing that the cab company had taught us how to deliver babies. I don't know if that qualified as a form of circular logic or shell shock.

I arrived at my apartment building a little after one o'clock in the afternoon. I remember this because I was slightly chagrined by the fact that *The Afternoon Movie* had already begun. This is a daily local broadcast by a Denver affiliate. Since it's on a broadcast station I have to endure commercials if they are showing a movie that I want to watch. They often show "old" movies, black-and-white films made in the forties and fifties. I like to think it's because the program director has good taste but it's probably because the local affiliate can't compete with The Big Boys when it comes to sponsoring contemporary crap.

I got out of my Chevy and climbed the rear fire escape to the door on my third-floor apartment. The door opens to the kitchen, which is like a big box that was added on to the apartment at some point after 1885, which was when the building was constructed. My landlord told me this. The building was originally a private home belonging to a rich man. Capitol Hill is dotted with mansions that had been built during the silver boom of the nineteenth century before the federal government went off the silver standard causing the silver mines in the mountains to go bust. The mansions were turned into apartment buildings at some point during the twentieth century. I assume the changes occurred either during the Great Depression or else during the sixties when the influx of hippies lowered the property values. Either way, all the rich folks moved south. Thank God for economic bad times. I can't imagine the rat hole I would be living in if America was still on the silver standard.

I entered my apartment and walked into the living room, grabbed my copy of *Lolita* from the bookshelf, and placed my twenty-five dollar windfall between the pages along with the profits from Wednesday—and guess what? I realized that Mr. Zelner had never paid me.

I had completely forgotten the fact that I hadn't earned any money off my final ride Wednesday evening when I had been hoping to score at least five bucks by jumping a bell a half-block away. I'm usually leery of taking a call off the radio after six-thirty at night because my shift always ends at seven and I like to have that last half-hour for a leisurely cruise back to the motor without playing Beat the Clock. But the half-block to Union Station had broken my will that night, so I had jumped the bell. Every man has his price, and apparently mine is five dollars.

But the reason I had forgotten about getting paid was that Mr. Zelner had died, and the money he owed me was relegated to the insignificance that money has always had in my life. Unless we're talking about a million dollars, I'm not really interested. Hell, anybody can earn less than a million dollars, but I want The Big Score.

The Big Score has to do with writing a best-selling novel, but let's not get into that.

Of course for all I knew on Wednesday night Mr. Zelner might have been going to the Tech Center south of the city, which would have meant showing up after seven p.m. at the motor and paying a late fee, which would have caused me one minute of embarrassment. If I had driven to the Tech Center though, I would have earned more than enough cash to ameliorate my embarrassment. The Embarrassment/Profit Ratio (E/PR) of cab driving is almost as complicated as it is meaningless, but it's the kind of thing you think about toward the end of your shift. When you drive a taxi for a living you don't get many opportunities to feel like a financial wizard.

But it struck me as odd that I had completely forgotten about the fact that I hadn't gotten paid for the trip. Not that I'm complaining. I had already earned my standard fifty bucks profit for the day. By jumping the bell at Union Station I was sort of like a gambler in Reno who drops a silver dollar into a slot machine as he is walking toward the exit of a casino—drop the buck, yank the handle, watch the two cherries and lemon pop up, then trudge back to my motel and call my brother in California to wire me enough dough for bus fare back to Denver.

I erased Hogan's message from my answering machine, then went into the kitchen, opened the refrigerator and grabbed a beer. As I was popping the top I glanced at the light switch on the wall. I hate overlooking stuff like turning off lights, or a stove, or a shower—which is to say, I hate leaving trails of evidence demonstrating my inability to do things well. I never turn the lights on in my apartment during the daytime. Who needs light bulbs when the sun is free? This made me think of Rod McKuen. I took a long swig of beer and went into the living room to turn on the TV. That's one light bulb that never gets turned off. Okay. I'll admit it. I leave my TV off when I'm at work. But who doesn't? Security guards maybe. I'm talking civilians of course. When I was in the army they never let us watch TV while guarding the ammo dump.

I switched on the set and turned the channel over to *The Afternoon Movie*. I sometimes cynically wonder who the geniuses are who name things in this world, but I have never felt antipathy toward the program director who named *The Afternoon Movie*—as good a name as any, and better than most. A commercial was in progress, so I almost consulted the *TV Guide* to see what I was missing, but then I stopped myself. I realized I had an opportunity to get excited. Maybe it would be a black-and-white classic that I hadn't seen in years. Perhaps a Humphrey Bogart or a W. C. Fields. I decided to torture myself with exquisite anticipation, since it involved no effort.

As I waited for the movie to come on, the tension in my apartment began to mount. I sat through a commercial for toothpaste, which made me wonder if toothpaste was just a scam. After all, it's the bristles of the brush that get rid of the stuff on your teeth—and floss takes care of the detail work. What the hell is toothpaste made of anyway? It isn't soap, for crying out loud. I started to get angry. I imagined a cabal of greedy chemists in the nineteenth century cooking up a scheme to convince the

American public that tooth powder was vital to maintaining a healthy mouth. I've even heard about people who brush their teeth with ordinary salt. What in the hell is wrong with the human race?

But this gave me an idea for an invention—candy-flavored toothbrushes. They wouldn't actually contain sugar, but they would taste like cherry suckers. You wouldn't be able to pry the damn things out of your kids' mouths. American children would spend all their time brushing. They would have the cleanest teeth in the world. The dental industry might teeter on the brink of collapse. But the FDA would probably step in and declare my invention an illegal food product and outlaw it in order to protect the profits of The Big Boys. A cabal of dentists would probably blackball me, and I would have to travel to Canada to get my decay X-rayed.

Aaah, why complain? It's all a racket. I didn't know how I would have made my toothbrushes taste like cherry suckers anyway.

I was just starting to mull over the possibilities of blending molten plastic with artificial sweetener when *The Afternoon Movie* came on, thank God. I really should stop watching TV commercials.

The movie was *Georgy Girl*. I nearly broke my thumb switching channels.

I started to get depressed. Feel-good movies do that to me. I turned off the TV and thought about writing a novel. Nothing cheers me up like the possibility of earning a million dollars. But I was immediately faced with a critical decision: what should I write about?

It seemed like every time I decided to get started on a novel I was faced with the same onerous decision. I had read a lot of how-to books in my time but I noticed that nobody ever published "what-to" books. It seemed to me that the authors of how-to books could really cash in if they wrote books telling unpublished writers what to write. I even thought up a title: "Become An Old Pro Overnight." Maybe I could write a letter to an author of a how-to book and convince him to try a new angle. If the book sold well, we could split the profits fifty-fifty, since the book was my idea—after all, without me he would still be eking out a living.

It was at this point that I realized I had drunk one too many beers. I'd had only one, but any time I start thinking about sharing money, it's time to stop thinking.

I grabbed a soda and spent the rest of Thursday concentrating on cable TV. By the time I went to bed I had expunged most of the thoughts from my mind. I turned off all the lights, kicked off my Keds, and collapsed into bed.

I lay there in the darkness trying to go to sleep, but there was one thought that I couldn't get rid of. Unlike most of my thoughts, this one was real because it was grounded in guilt. Guilt is worse than caffeine when you're trying to sleep. I kept thinking about the fact that I had lied to Mr. Heigger, even though I had not actually lied, I had simply said something to him that wasn't true. I was too exhausted from watching cable to parse the difference—assuming that there is a difference between lying and not telling the truth.

This got me thinking about the death of Mr. Zelner, which in turn depressed me. That's exactly what I wanted. I have found that depression works much better than a sleeping pill—I start to feel so blue that I sink into a psychological quagmire, and the next thing I know I'm off to dreamland.

I started having one of those semi-nightmares where I was late for a Latin test in high school and couldn't find my classroom. I didn't know whether my anxiety was due to the fact that I was late or the fact that I had not studied for the test. When I was sixteen I never cared whether I was late, or if I failed, or both—so why would it bother me now? I finally concluded that my anxiety was caused by the fact that I was back in high school.

Okay. I'll come clean. Rejection slips make me feel like I've failed a Latin test. The only difference is that nowadays I have no idea when—or if—I'm going to graduate. I really ought to stop writing novels and try to fail at something more realistic, like cliff diving.

CHAPTER 8

I arrived at the motor at five minutes to seven on Friday morning determined to get things back to normal. I did this by recalling the things I do every Friday morning and then mimicking them as closely as possible. I frequently achieve difficult goals through mimicry. Large tips come to mind.

Whenever customers climb into my cab I become whatever they want me to be by acting either baffled, hip, funny, or profound. I know what you're thinking—how can you "act" profound. After all, you're either profound or you're not, in the same way that you cannot "act" as big as Hulk Hogan. But let me offer you a little insider's tip: Acting profound in a taxi consists of nothing more than agreeing with everything your customer says. I personally recommend the nod—"Safety through silence," that's my motto. In this way I increase the size of my tip and simultaneously make my fare happy. "Win-win" as they howl on infomercials.

As soon as I got inside I immediately regretted smiling. The place was as crowded as it always is on Friday morning, but the cabbies who glanced my way had the somber looks of people who were uncertain how to comport themselves around a man who had found a corpse in his backseat.

I had told myself that today I would act like "The Man of a Thousand Faces." He was played by James Cagney in the movie. Pretending to be him made me smile as I sauntered into the room—that Jimmy Cagney was a genuine two-fisted cocky little hoofer.

As I said, even cab drivers have a sense of propriety, so my smile was as inappropriate as a smile can get. But it was too late. I had to keep smiling otherwise they would "know" that I knew I was violating a precept of civilized behavior. If I dropped the broad grin on my face, they would see right through me and know that I was just pretending not to smile.

Fer the luvva Christ.

I wanted to whip a louie and go back home, but that would be so obvious that I would probably end up having to quit Rocky Cab and apply for a job with Yellow Cab, assuming word of my gauche behavior didn't precede my arrival at their employment office. Without going into detail, the odds of my getting a job at Yellow were zero. This had to do with a bet in which a number of Yellow drivers had lost a lot of money and blamed it on me. I say "a number of Yellow drivers" because I don't know the actual number, but the adjective "all" comes close.

I passed through the room glancing left and right at the gloomy faces of the cabbies. I started to feel sorry for them. They doubtless expected me to be depressed over the death of my customer on Wednesday evening, but there I was grinning like a hyena as I got in line at the cage. I could feel my facial muscles starting to seize up. I'll be honest. I don't smile very much. I have found that smiling occurs primarily when I'm around friends, and since I have no friends—well—you do the math.

When I got up to the window Rollo looked at me the way he looks when detectives are waiting to talk to me. "Trepidation" is as good a word as any, although in this case it didn't have anything to do with John Law. His eyes were sort of "rounded and inquisitive" as if he was waiting for an emotional outburst from me. It was obvious that he was prepared to call a brief truce in our perpetual battle of the intellects, although I doubted he would have taken it as far as pity. I'm not certain the bastard even knows the definition of the word.

I pulled seventy dollars out of my T-shirt pocket and slipped it under the Plexiglas window. My teeth were clenched. My lips were frozen open. I looked like I was having a rollicking good time.

Rollo quickly handed me a trip-sheet and the key to Rocky Mountain Taxicab #123.

"Engz," I said through clenched teeth. I sounded like the Frankenstein monster accepting a bowl of soup.

By the time I found my cab parked in the lot, the rictus had completely disappeared from my face. But the muscles of my cheeks were still sore so I exercised them by whispering "Wow wow wow wow." By the time I started the engine and radioed the dispatcher to let him know I was on the road, it was just another typical taxi Friday.

"Have a good day, Murph," the dispatcher said somberly.

My shoulders drooped. Even the dispatcher was showing compassion. He usually insults me when I sign on in the morning. This is a little game we play. It always ends with him threatening to send me to Hogan's office for a chewing out.

I decided to surrender.

"Thanks, Harv," I said. The morning dispatcher's name is Harvey. I'll try not to mention it again.

I headed to a 7-11 store to gas up. I was approximately halfway there when I suddenly realized what a mistake I had made. My God, people were actually feeling sorry for me! I hadn't scored a deal that sweet since Shelteen died. If I had played my cards right back in the on-call room I might have gotten a week's worth of solace out of every cab driver at RMTC. I had no idea what the benefits might have been, but as I said, my Maw let me stay home from school for two days after Shelteen kicked the doggy dish.

By the time I got to the 7-11 I was in a blue funk. I had let myself down. I had spent my entire life keeping my eyes and ears attuned for ways to milk sympathy from people, and now I had choked in the clutch. I felt like a rank amateur. Was I losing my touch? There was only one thing to do: earn my fifty bucks, go home, and watch TV. Normalcy was my only hope.

I filled a paper cup with coffee and grabbed a Twinkie. I was standing at the counter scowling to myself and examining the scratch tickets under the glass case when an old pro named Jacobson pulled up at the gas pumps. He climbed out of his taxi and walked into the store. He glanced at me, then stepped up to the counter and said, "This coffee is on me, pal." He slapped a buck down on the counter. The clerk took it. "I heard about that business on Wednesday night," Jacobson said.

I nodded sadly.

"See you on the asphalt, Murph," Jacobson said, then he wandered over to the candy aisle. He prefers Snickers to Twinkies, but each to his own I always say.

I paid for my gas and Twinkie, then trudged out of the store trying to keep from laughing. Free joe!

I sped away from the pump before Jacobson got outside and picked up where he had left off trying to make me feel good. This made me feel bad because if I had played my cards right at RMTC, I might have gotten a month's worth of free joe from the sonsabitches before they saw through me.

I sighed and headed for the Brown Palace Hotel where I normally start out my day. I parked in line behind three cabs and pulled a paperback book out of my plastic briefcase. I calculated that I had a minimum of forty-five minutes to sip my joe, eat my Twinkie, and read my book before it would be my turn to pray for a fifty-dollar trip to DIA.

When I was a newbie driver fourteen years ago I would start praying as soon as I parked my cab at a stand even if I was fifth in line. Pre-praying is the mark of a newbie. An experienced professional taxi driver waits until he is first in line before he plunges into the morass of futile hopes. The odds of getting a trip to the airport are fifty-fifty on an average day, although they rise to seventy-thirty on Friday. People fly on Fridays. If I get a morning trip to DIA out of the Brown I earn one-third of my gross, which is my only excuse for praying. So it's true what they say— there are no atheists at a cabstand.

Forty-five minutes later a customer came out of the Brown followed by a porter pushing a rack full of luggage. An obvious DIA trip, but I was second in line. The driver in front of me was in a Yellow Cab. I tried not to envy his good fortune. After he drove away I pulled forward one space, shut off my engine, sat back, and stared at the front door of the hotel.

William was on duty that day. He's a black man who became a palace guard at the Brown before I started driving. William and I get along well. I get along well with all the doormen at the big hotels in Denver. Doormen and cab drivers are like engineers and astronauts. I won't take that analogy much further except to say that cab drivers take off regularly, and doormen stay on the launching pad, and we both get funded by the same taxpayers: hotel guests. Tips are the ties that bind us. I do doormen favors every now and then, which mostly consist of not whining when a guest wants to go four blocks. Cab drivers are touchy about short trips—the rank amateurs anyway. They can't see The Big Picture. They can't see the doorman who surreptitiously "fixes" rides so that a cabbie whom he likes gets a trip to Aspen rather than a short trip to Larimer Square. Sometimes my favors involve allowing six people to ride in my taxi when only five people are legally allowed by Public Utilities Commission regulations. Keep that under your hat. If the PUC ever found out I was nice they would yank my license.

But the reason I bring this up is because a little old lady came out of the Brown and spoke briefly to William, who smiled and nodded at her, then turned and looked at the cabstand with one of the deepest frowns I had ever seen on the face of any human being. It wasn't the deepest though—that record belongs to a black security guard at the dog track whom I once made the mistake of annoying. It's a long story.

When William spotted me in the front seat of the first cab in line, the frown went away. He strolled up to my cab, leaned down to my window and said, "Listen, my man, I have a guest who wants to make a round-trip to The Bookbag."

My heart sank even as my lips formed a fake smile. The Bookbag was a bookstore four blocks away.

"She wants to run in and buy a novel and come right back to the hotel," William said.

"No problem," I lied, as I opened my door and climbed out to open the rear door.

William returned to the entrance of the hotel and escorted the woman toward my cab. She appeared to be about seventy years old. I don't want to sound sexist, but she also looked rich. Before she climbed into my backseat, she dipped her frail hand into her purse and pulled out a piece of paper currency and gave it to William, who quickly pocketed it. It may have been a fiver but William was too fast for me. He's an old pro.

After she climbed into my backseat I closed the door and beamed at William, who beamed back, then I got in, hit the meter, and pulled away from the curb.

"The Bookbag?" I said in a fake lively voice.

"That's correct," the woman replied. "I realize that this will be a short trip for you, but I will make it worth your while."

I don't want to sound sexist again, but why don't blonde starlets ever say that to me? I made a circuitous route around the spectacular one-way street system of downtown Denver before I pulled up in a no parking zone in front of the bookstore. I estimated that I drove ten blocks just to go four blocks. It reminded me of answers I used to write on my arithmetic tests, although "answers" is not an accurate description of the peculiar sums I jotted down.

I hopped out and opened the door for the woman. "I will be only a minute," she said.

I didn't escort her to the front door since the store had doors that automatically opened, one of the few marvels of superfluous technology that I admire. That, and the escalator. I see both of them as an extension of the automobile, devices that were conceived of by men who understood human nature better than the genius who invented the gymnasium.

Sure enough, one minute later she came out the door clutching a paper sack. I hadn't really believed her when she had said she would be only a minute. For reasons that I don't want to go into, little old ladies give me a psychological tic—this doesn't have anything to do with my Maw. I think.

"Thank you for waiting," she said—as if I had a choice. But she was just being courteous. The rich and the elderly wield courtesy like scimitars. There is literally no defense.

"You're welcome," I said.

I closed the door for her, then climbed into the driver's seat. Due to the nature of the one-way street system, the trip back to the Brown took only a minute. Maybe the street system was designed by a schizophrenic engineer who didn't understand that efficiency is a two-way street.

As we were making our way toward the Brown I heard the crackle of paper. The woman held up the book and said, "My nephew wrote this novel. It was published just this week."

I glanced at it, then looked straight ahead, pretending that I was adhering to the rules of safe driving when in truth I was hyperventilating. The fact that I was in the presence of a little old lady whose nephew had just published a novel reminded me that I was a taxi driver, and I try not to think about that as often as possible.

"What's the book about?" I croaked.

"I shall find out tonight," she said.

I glanced at her. She was smiling at the book. Then she looked at me. "My nephew lives in San Luis Obispo."

That almost did me in. I couldn't imagine anybody in San Luis Obispo writing a successful novel.

"After I finish it I am going to mail it to him and ask him to autograph it for me," she said.

I heard the crackle of paper. I glanced at her in the rearview mirror. She was putting the book away. She set the package aside, smiled out the side window, and gazed upon the wonders of 15th Street.

After I parked in front of the Brown, I twisted around in the seat and smiled at her. "I hope your nephew agrees to autograph his book," I said in a jocular tone of voice.

"I wouldn't worry too much about that," she said, as she gathered up her package. "He's in my will."

I climbed out and opened the door for her.

She got out and planted a twenty-dollar bill in the palm of my hand, then cupped my fingers closed around the money as if she was afraid the wind might blow it away. "My nephew once drove a taxi in Fresno," she said.

The twinkle in her eyes told me that I had no secrets hidden from her.

"Good luck, young man," she said, then she turned to William, who gently took her elbow and escorted her back into the hotel.

CHAPTER 9

After I climbed back into my cab I had a choice: circle the block and park again at the Brown, or start taking calls off the radio. Rather than follow my natural inclination, I chose to take calls off the radio. The emotional turmoil of being in the presence of a recently published novel made it impossible for me to touch my paperback.

Since it was a Friday there was a surfeit of calls. Fridays are like Christmas in many ways. The radio hops all day with the dispatcher dealing fares like a card-jockey in Reno. I try not to think about Christmas or Reno because they both remind me of my brother Gavin. Reno is on the route to California. I used to visit Gavin there once a year but I stopped going when I realized it was costing me too much money in Reno. With all the money I've dropped at Blackjack over the years I could have bought ten word-processors. Gavin bought me a PC last Christmas and one was plenty. So far I haven't successfully written any failed novels on it, although I have written a number of unfinished novels. I don't consider a novel to be failed until it has been rejected by at least one agent. You may not believe this but I once had a novel rejected by an actual publishing company. The novel was titled "Draculina." I was so excited about getting rejected by a New York publisher that I called my old college buddies to celebrate. I woke up in Reno. It's probably a long story. Let's move on.

I worked Capitol Hill until noon. Capitol Hill is always jumping with short trips on Friday. You can earn as much money in a single hour on The Hill as you can earn from a rich lady with a published nephew if you know what you're doing. This is one of the reasons why I rarely work The Hill—there's no challenge. You work twelve hours, pocket your one-hundred-and-twenty-dollar profit for the day, and go home feeling cheated. The real challenge of cab driving is to work as little as possible and still bring home fifty bucks.

It takes years of experience to fine-tune your skills to the point where you don't get ambitious and work five days a week instead of three. If I earned one hundred and twenty dollars a day five days a week, I would become an emotional wreck because it would make me want to earn even more money, but to do that I would have to get a real job. And let's be honest, where am I going to find a job that pays 30K a year? I'll tell you where: vocational training school. As soon as you graduate they help you find a job—that's what the infomercials say anyway. The next thing you know you're connecting pipes in a basement or laying tile in a kitchen and going home with sore knees and a fat paycheck. My knees haven't been sore since the last time I did squat-thrusts. Believe me, if I had been paid thirty grand a year in the army I would be a corporal by now.

I ran fares back and forth across The Hill, down to Cherry Creek, to dentist and doctor offices, to grocery stores and restaurants and bars. I don't pick up many people at bars in the daytime but I do seem to take a lot of people to bars around noon. On "Radio Days" as I call the rare days when I take calls off the radio, I know it's time to go to a delicatessen after my third bar-drop. I have noticed over the years that people who go to bars don't talk as much as people who come out of bars. But I understand. Whenever I take a cab to Sweeney's I sit quietly in the backseat and contemplate all the hilarious things I am going to say to the barflies when I arrive. I feel like a Denver Bronco psyching himself up for The Big Game—mostly playoffs.

I drove to a supermarket on Capitol Hill and bought a ham-and-lettuce sandwich. I had been thinking about ham-and-lettuce ever since Rollo had shown me that picture of carnage in Los Angeles. It made my mouth water.

I also bought a small cup of macaroni salad, which I rarely do. I usually go with potato chips because it's much easier to brush crumbs off my lap than mayonnaise.

"One twenty-three," the dispatcher said, as I was dabbing at my right kneecap with a napkin.

I grabbed the mike off the dashboard. "One twenty-three."

"You've got a personal, Murph."

A "personal" is a trip that you set up ahead of time with a fare. It might be a daily where you take the same person to work every morning. But I steer clear of personals because it entails an obligation, which is a sub-set of "doing things," and I don't ever want to be anywhere at all at any time doing anything.

"Check," I said.

I frowned with bafflement because I had not set up a personal with anyone lately.

Then the dispatcher gave me the address of Mr. Heigger's office. He said that Mr. Heigger had a client who needs to go to Broomfield, which is a town way north of Denver.

"Check," I said again. I love the word "check" because it has so many subtle interpretations, including the affirmative "Yes," or simple clarification, as in "I understand," or best of all, "We can stop talking now."

Heigger's office was less than ten minutes away. After I hung up the mike I looked at my knee. Here I was on my way to a hotshot lawyer's office and I had a mayonnaise stain to be embarrassed about. One of the nice things about being a cab driver is that fares rarely see your pants. If you took calls off the radio all day rather than working the hotels you could conceivably wear a swimsuit because most radio calls are simple pickups and dropoffs, so you don't even have to get out of the driver's seat. However if a radio fare is going to DIA you are forced to climb out and load luggage if you want a tip. But even if you don't want a tip you still have to load luggage. There's an art to it. A trunk loaded by a civilian is a catastrophe just waiting to happen.

But I reminded myself that I was a taxi driver and not a man seeking legal help, so I didn't have to worry about fashion statements. I gave the mayo stain one last dab, then sacked my trash and carried it to a waste can outside the grocery store. I climbed back into my cab, started the engine and pulled out of the parking lot. I headed for 10th Avenue making a mental list of all the places I would hate to be seen wearing a swimsuit. DIA was at the top of the list of course. Then there were grocery stores, as well as hotels. If I showed up at the Brown Palace wearing a Speedo, William might not slip me any more Aspen trips.

I parked in front of the lawyer's building, got out, and went up to the porch.

"You arrived here so quickly, Mr. Murphy," Mr. Heigger said as soon as I entered his office.

"I was just a couple minutes away when I got the call," I said, making another of the pointless explanations that beleaguer my life.

A man wearing a slightly rumpled suit and clutching a briefcase was seated on a chair next to Heigger's desk.

"This is Mr. Weissberger," Heigger said. "We have just now completed our business. He needs to go to an address up north."

Mr. Weissberger hoisted himself out of the chair. He appeared to be in his mid-sixties, and had the affable demeanor of a furniture salesman. I say this only because I once delivered furniture for a living. All of the young salesmen wore snazzy suits and were pushy. The older salesmen wore rumpled suits and were affable.

"This is Brendan Murphy, the taxi driver whom I spoke to you about," Heigger said.

"Oh yes," Mr. Weissberger said. He reached out to shake my hand.

"Mr. Weissberger was a friend of Mr. Zelner," Heigger said. Suddenly I felt awful. But I smiled and shook Mr. Weissberger's hand. His posture was rather stooped. He had an odd way of hunching his shoulders and raising his chin when he looked at me. "I understand you were with Mr. Zelner when he passed away."

"That is correct, sir," I said.

"Terrible thing—for both you and my old friend."

I nodded while simultaneously scouring my mind for a mature response. I drew a blank.

"I don't want to keep you any longer than necessary," Mr. Heigger said to Mr. Weissberger, relieving me of the responsibility of pretending to be mature on short notice.

"Yes, well, thank you very much," Mr. Weissberger said, reaching out and shaking Heigger's hand. "I think we can have this matter settled by Monday."

"I'll stay on top of it," Heigger said. "I might give you a call over the weekend."

Mr. Weissberger began nodding, adjusting the briefcase, tucking it under one arm, hunching his shoulders, raising his chin, and smiling at me. "I am ready," he said.

I led him out of the office and down the hall toward the front door, grateful that Mr. Heigger had not said anything more about the trip from Union Station to Diamond Hill. It was only as I was holding the door open to allow Mr. Weissberger to step out to the veranda that I thought about telling Mr. Heigger about my inadvertent "lie." I also wanted to ask if he had found Mr. Zelner's luggage.

I looked back and saw Heigger standing in the hallway watching us leave. It was the part of my brain that I sometimes refer to as "insane" that made me want to rehash a subject that so far I had managed successfully to avoid. I had been trying not to think about the lie. It was the part of my brain that I sometimes refer to as the "stranger" that caused me to keep my mouth shut and follow Mr. Weissberger outside. It seemed like every time I became involved in the personal life of a fare, the "stranger" was nowhere to be seen. I wished he would come around more often. I wanted to develop a deep and long-lasting relationship with him. Perhaps he could be permanently coaxed out of his hiding place if I got some goddamn therapy.

CHAPTER 10

"Where to?" I said, falling into cabbie patois as soon as I got seated behind the steering wheel.

"Do you know Wadsworth Boulevard?" Mr. Weissberger said from the backseat.

"Yes I do."

"Well this address I am going to is west of Wadsworth, up near a town called Broomfield."

"All right, sir," I said, starting the engine, hitting the meter, and pulling away from the curb. I made the quick calculation that all cab drivers make when they are given oddball addresses. The mental map of Denver that resides inside my head quickly told me that there was no fast way to get from here to there. I would have to work my way over to Interstate 25, then connect with the Denver-Boulder Turnpike, then get off at Wadsworth and head north into what amounted to farm country. It was a zigzag sort of route, the kind that makes a customer mutter "scenic route" under his breath. Believe me, I've heard plenty of those mutters, and they always make me bristle because I don't do scenic routes—the sign of either a newbie or a loser. Newbies do it because they don't know the territory. Losers do it for the same reason losers do all the things losers do: they think they will earn lots of money. But you don't make money driving people all the hell over town trying to drag out a single ride. You make money by getting people in and out of your taxi as quickly as possible.

Ergo, I glanced back at Mr. Weissberger and began the step-by-step process of convincing him that I was not a loser. "Do you know a good route to the destination?" I said.

The ball was in his court.

"I'm afraid not," he said. "I've never been there before."

Word of advice: never say that to a cab driver—you may be in the presence of somebody I'm not.

"There are different ways to get there," I said.

"Take whatever route you feel is best," he said, smiling and settling himself in.

As I drove toward Park Avenue to make the I-25 connection near the baseball stadium, I started thinking about the fact that Mr. Weissberger had an interesting voice. It was slightly muted and hollowish, like the voice of a man talking into an empty paper cup. I did not detect any note of a foreign accent, nor did it contain any sort of midwestern twang. You hear a lot of twangs in Colorado. I was raised in Kansas but I do not believe my voice has a twang. I blame television. I spent so much of my childhood watching newscasts originating in New York City that I developed the denuded, lifeless accent of a TV anchorman, a robotic voice totally devoid of character, a voice so banal that I could pass myself off as a Swede in any country south of the equator. Big Al tells me I talk like a chipmunk. You be the judge.

We came to the on-ramp at I-25. I adjusted my grip on the steering wheel, settled into my seat like an astronaut, and glanced at the rearview mirror. I played the acceleration game. I played it fast and I played it hard. I slapped my left blinker on and became a gate-crasher looking for an invitation to the party, a Johnny-come-lately who wanted to join the dance. I spotted an opening behind a diesel truck. I hit the afterburners, wedged in front of an Oldsmobile, and became part of the great steel snake slithering toward the North Pole, a piston-jockey burning with the fury of white line fev …

"Pardon me?"

"How long do you estimate it will take to arrive at my destination?" Mr. Weissberger said.

"It depends on the traffic," I said. I glanced at my wristwatch for no particular reason, then said, "It could take as long as forty minutes from where we're located right now."

He nodded but didn't say anything else.

I settled back and quit pretending that I was doing anything except driving up the highway. The Oldsmobile passed me on the left and disappeared, probably because I was doing the same thing the diesel driver was doing: the speed limit.

I won't bore you with a description of the various interchanges I had to negotiate on our trip to the North Pole. If you have a "need to know," check the map in your glove compartment. It took twenty-five minutes to get to Wadsworth, and when I rolled down the off-ramp I made the attitude adjustment that all human beings are forced to make after they exit a highway. I have never understood why driving slowly gives you the bends after driving fast, since you are always sitting motionless in the driver's seat. I blame Albert Einstein.

"I have a map," Mr. Weissberger said.

"What's that, sir?"

Mr. Weissberger leaned forward and held a piece of yellow legal paper near my right shoulder. "Mr. Heigger was kind enough to draw this map showing me how to get to the address," he said.

I let go of the steering wheel with my right hand and plucked the map with my fingertips. I glanced at it then set it on the seat beside me. "I'll have to pull over to take a look at it," I said.

"That's all right, that's fine," he said in his affable, paper-cup voice.

I began looking for a spot to pull over. We were at the edge of the suburbs, approaching farm country. The foothills of the Rockies loomed a little larger than they normally do in my life. I rarely go into the mountains. I'm like a person who lives in New York City but never visits Coney.

I pulled into the parking lot of a 7-11 store and stopped near a phone booth. I hardly ever see booths anymore. The modern phone "booth" is designed so that the telephone has a small canopy that protects it from violent rainstorms, leaving the customer to get soaked.

I picked up the map and studied it. It was hand-drawn but not "crude," the most common adjective used to describe pencil maps.

Heigger had a very precise line, and the block lettering was clear and easy to read. Heigger would have made a good comic-strip artist.

There was a country road that intersected with Wadsworth. An arrow pointed west, indicating the direction I was to drive. A small square had been drawn to indicate the house. The phrase "3 miles" was printed above the arrow.

"We're almost there," I said. "It should take only five minutes or so." I handed the map back, started the engine, and pulled onto Wadsworth.

"That's wonderful," Mr. Weissberger said, rearranging himself on the seat.

He turned his head and looked out the side window. He reminded me of a rich lady. A silence settled over the cab. I did not have my Rocky radio or the AM radio on. I often use one or the other to create a kind of "wall of noise" between my customer and myself, depending on the situation. You can usually sense when a customer does not want to converse, and the static from a radio fills the empty space. I prefer to use the Rocky radio when I feel the need to hide behind sound because I like to think that the never-ending voice of the dispatcher makes the customer think I am "working."

"A terrible thing about Mr. Zelner," Mr. Weissberger suddenly said. I glanced at the rearview mirror.

"Pardon me, sir?"

"Terrible business, Mr. Zelner dying like that. I was one of his oldest and dearest friends."

I nodded.

"Mr. Heigger told me that you were inside the taxi when he died, yes?"

"Yes, sir."

"Terrible thing. Just terrible."

I looked at Mr. Weissberger in the mirror. He was gazing out the front windshield with his arms crossed. He raised his right hand and began gently rubbing the tip of his nose with his index finger.

"There is quite an irony involved in this situation," Mr. Weissberger said.

"Irony?" I said—not for the first time in my life. I glanced at the mirror.

Mr. Weissberger was nodding. He lowered his hand and adjusted his position on the seat. He hunched his shoulders and raised his chin and looked at my eyes in the mirror. "Yes. You see, my friend Mr. Zelner was involved in the business I am taking care of today. Had he not died, he would be seated alongside me on our way to this address."

I felt my entire body seizing up. Suddenly I wished the Stones were blasting from my dashboard.

"Fate is strange," Mr. Weissberger said.

"It sure is," I said.

"You know ... Mr. Zelner and I went back a long ways. We were in the same fraternity together at university." He inhaled deeply, then exhaled. "But that was long ago."

I wanted to ask what university they had attended but I stopped myself. The "stranger" inside me had nothing to do with it. I sometimes rise to the occasion and take charge of situations myself, although I do like to leave that to the many underlings who live inside my head. Any time a customer says anything to me, I have a stockpile of responses that I can use to create a generic conversation. My voice is like an AM radio. I often use it to fill what I call "dead air." Disk jockeys call it that, too. Most of the responses are questions. I like to get the customer talking so

I can talk as little as possible. I also use this technique when I'm a guest at weddings, funerals, and checkout lines where little old ladies have decided that I came into their presence to act as a sounding board for their complaints about the inefficiency of bag boys. But I chose not to respond to Mr. Weissberger's statement.

"I will miss Heinrich," Mr. Weissberger said. "He was a very good friend. We didn't see much of each other over the years, but we kept in touch by mail."

I nodded. Normally I would have followed the thread by asking who Heinrich was. That would have eaten up thirty seconds of dead air. But I pretty much knew who Heinrich was. I usually know the answers to all the generic questions I ask. But I have found that most people enjoy "educating" me. Win-win, as executives say.

"The art of letter writing has faded from the world," Mr. Weissberger said wistfully.

I nodded. This was a perfect opportunity to tell him about the books I had read which consisted of the collected letters of famous authors. I love reading those collections. It's like digging through garbage cans. But I remained mum.

I came to the intersection and waited for traffic to pass, then turned left onto a gravel road that led straight toward the Rockies in the distance. I glanced at my odometer and fixed the number 3 in my mind. I ignored the "tenths" to the right of the 3. I have enough trouble with math without battling the horror of rolling digits.

Mr. Weissberger leaned forward on the seat. I could hear the springs creak, and I'm not certain Rocky seats have springs. He placed both hands on the back of the front seat. I glanced to my right. He was approximately two feet away. His head was craned to the left and he had a slight frown. "I wonder," he said, peering up at me from his hunched posture. "Would it be possible for you to tell me his last words?"

I swallowed hard. "Last words?" I said.

"The very last thing you heard Mr. Zelner say. I realize that since the place of his demise was a taxicab, any conversation may have consisted of nothing more than innocuous small-talk, but it would please me greatly to know the very last thing he said before he departed. I know that his wife and children would also be pleased to hear his last words from the gentleman who was with Heinrich when he passed away."

I began nodding, which is a last resort in the dead-air department. It ate up five seconds. A few cars coming from the opposite direction rolled past us. I slowed a bit, pretending to drive safely on this narrow two-lane gravel road, but I was just buying time. The nodding and the safe driving gave me time to decide whether or not to tell the truth—meaning whether to let him know that I had lied to Mr. Heigger. The situation called for a frantic meeting of everyone who lived inside my head, but the meeting was dominated by me. I decided that the very last thing on the planet earth that I wanted to do was to get involved in the personal life of anybody living or dead. In two miles this man would be out of my life forever.

I frowned as if I was thinking, then glanced at Mr. Weissberger. "We didn't talk much," I said. "He gave me the address that he wanted to go to ..."

"On Diamond Hill?"

"... Yes, on Diamond Hill. In fact he had it written down on a piece of paper. He asked me if it was very far. I told him it would take five minutes to drive there."

"What else did he talk about?"

I frowned again. But I wasn't pretending to think. I really was thinking. I was thinking that if later on my back was to the wall and I was absolutely cornered, I could always tell Heigger that I suddenly remembered that Mr. Zelner had said, "Can you elude him? I am late for an appointment." After all, on Thursday afternoon I didn't even remember what Zelner had said until I sat down to fill out the trip-sheet, so it wasn't as though I was lying to Mr. Heigger about not remembering. I was simply not telling the truth.

"You know … I think Mr. Zelner did say something else," I said.

"Something else?" Mr. Weissberger said.

"We were halfway across the viaduct when he spoke. But you know … it was raining … and there was a lot of thunder … and the windshield wipers were going back and forth, so it was difficult to hear what he said."

I looked at Mr. Weissberger's face. It was riveted on mine. His fingers seemed to dig into the top of the seatback. He moved perhaps four inches closer to me. "Do you think that he might have made some sort of statement, or perhaps asked for help?"

I called another meeting and asked for a volunteer to take over the conversation. I don't who he was, but somebody stood up and started talking. "Whenever I drive my taxi," "he" said, "I always keep my ears attuned to anything the customer might say. Customers sometimes make sudden suggestions about which way to turn … you know, turn left here, or turn right there … things like that. So I have to stay alert to the slightest sound coming from my backseat. The customer is always right in this business and I'm pretty good at picking up on what people say. But as I said, it was raining and there was a lot of outside noise … plus, it seemed to me that Mr. Zelner had a cold."

"Why is that?"

"When he got into my cab and spoke to me, his voice was hoarse."

"Is that zo?"

Did I hear a "Z" or was I just projecting?

I glanced at Mr. Weissberger. "It was a bad night. Anybody could have caught a cold in that weather." But I knew this wasn't true. Colds aren't caused by rain. They are caused by viruses that attack the lining of the sinus cavities, usually viruses pushed up there by a finger.

"So the last thing that you understood my friend to say was 'Is this very far?'"

I glanced down at my speedometer and then up at the visor for no particular reason. Perhaps he misinterpreted this as a nod. He sat back in the seat and looked out the side window.

We passed a few residential homes. The farms thereabouts were destined to be plowed under by condos and inhabited by Californians. I glanced at my odometer. A 6 had rolled halfway out of sight and a 7 was halfway in sight. I began to think of an odometer as a clock that measured space instead of time—a device that worked only when you moved. I may have been onto a Nobel Prize winning theorem, but fortunately a brick house came into sight, which I suspected was our destination. This was proven true when the 3 positioned itself in the exact center of the odometer at the precise moment that I pulled up in front of the house where the address was plainly visible beside the doorway.

The house had a refurbished look, as if it had been a home converted into offices. We were way the hell out in the middle of nowhere. Twenty years from now the house would probably be in the middle of a rundown neighborhood. Rundown neighborhoods are another kind of clock, but don't get me started on the Nobel Prize.

"May I ask you a personal question," Mr. Weissberger said.

"Sure."

"I have taken many taxi rides in my lifetime, and a great many of the drivers I have encountered are pursuing their work on a part-time basis. Many of them turn out to be students. I was just curious to know if this is a vocation you intend to stay with, or if you have other aspirations in life?"

As he spoke he reached into his coat pocket and pulled out a billfold. The meter read thirty-two dollars.

I sat at a fork in the road. I rarely confess to fares that my real aspiration in life is to do nothing, and to achieve that goal I intend to write a bestselling novel. But since we were way out in the middle of nowhere, and no other people were around, and Mr. Weissberger would soon be out of my life forever, I decided to come clean.

"This is sort of a part-time job with me," I said. "I'm trying to become a novelist."

His eyebrows arched. "Is that a fact?"

"I've been writing novels since I was in college."

"That is a wonderful aspiration," he said, as he shuffled through the bills in his hand. "I was acquainted with aspiring novelists when I was at university. Many of them went on to become English professors."

He reached across the seat and held out four ten-dollar bills. "If you write as well as you drive, I am sure that you will be a very successful author," he said in his paper-cup voice.

I started to give him change, but he smiled and lowered his head, splayed his fingers and waved it off. "You may keep it," he said.

He gathered up his briefcase, opened the door, and climbed out. "Good luck, young man," he said. He shut the door and walked toward the house.

CHAPTER 11

"Forty bucks an hour," I said aloud, as I drove east along the gravel road. Then I said mentally, Forty times twelve equals four hundred and eighty dollars. Then I said, If I could earn five hundred dollars a day I could retire from cab driving within ... but I never made it to Nirvana because I saw a car up ahead parked along the side of the road.

The hood was raised. A woman wearing a short skirt was leaning over the fender looking into the engine. I took my foot off the accelerator and slowed. I didn't do it because the woman was wearing a short skirt, I swear. I did it because raised hoods trigger something in men, although I am willing to admit that mini-skirts do that, too. But I drive an automobile for a living and whenever I see a car with its hood raised I think of all the hoods I have raised preamble to waiting for a tow truck to arrive and haul my taxi back to the motor. An immobilized automobile is the curse of modern man, along with missing TV remote controls. I really do not understand why the human race has allowed itself to become enslaved by things that make life pleasant.

The woman stood upright and looked at my taxi, then stumbled to the middle of the road and began waving frantically. As soon as I came to a halt the woman hurried around to my door and said, "Can you help me? My car broke down and I'm supposed to be at a civil service test this afternoon!" She was frantic. I immediately felt her pain. I've already mentioned that I often dream that I'm late for tests in high school, and the dreams always give me a panic-stricken feeling that makes no sense because being late for a test that I knew I was going to fail had never bothered me. On the other hand, I once arrived at a liquor store one minute after it closed, but let's move on.

"Is the car out of gas?" I said, reciting the first item on the list of frequently-asked-questions that all Good Samaritans refer to before they move on to Phase 2: electrical systems.

"I filled the tank this morning," she said.

I pulled over to the shoulder, got out, and approached the upraised hood. I peered at the engine for no particular reason, then said, "What happened?"

"The engine started losing power, then it just quit, so I coasted over here and parked."

"Would you like me to try to start it?"

"Please," she said.

I climbed into the driver's seat and took a surreptitious peek at the gas needle. Full. The keys were dangling from the ignition. Since the transmission was automatic, I made sure the gearshift was in P for park, then I twisted the ignition and tapped on the gas. Deadsville. I did the same thing a few more times because doing things a few more times often produce a different result, in spite of what the nickel-psychologists say. I cannot tell you the number of times I have done the same thing over and over again until I got a different result. Applying for jobs comes to mind.

I pulled the light switch on. I flipped the blinkers. The electrical system seemed to be working. I climbed out and took a second look at the engine. Everything that could be plugged in seemed plugged in— I'm talking spark-plug wires and all the other rubber spaghetti. I took a look at the fan belt and various other belts. If external evidence had any relevance to the situation I would have been forced to say that the engine was fine. I felt like a politician insisting that school uniforms would solve the problem of juvenile delinquency.

"I have no idea what's wrong with your car," I said. "But I can radio the cab company and have them send a tow truck."

"Oh my God, oh my God," she said. She staggered over to her door and sat down on the driver's seat and put her face in her hands. "I can't wait for a tow truck. The civil service test starts in an hour! I got up early, I filled the gas tank, I did everything to make sure I would get there on time, and now this!"

She wasn't crying but her facial features had collapsed somewhat. She looked the way I felt when the liquor store was closed.

"Where is the test going to be held?" I said.

"At the Hyatt."

"At I-25 and Fox?" She nodded.

"Well listen," I said. "I'll drive you there. It's right off the highway. We can be there in no time. You won't be late."

"I can't afford a taxi," she said.

I almost laughed, but I put a lid on it. Anybody can afford a taxi if they get the right driver. A taxi meter might be the most meaningless machine ever invented. Without going into detail, the amount of money that appears on the face of a taxi meter has about as much significance as the word "NEW" on a box of detergent. A cab driver can give away rides for free if he wants. RMTC doesn't care what I do after I give them my seventy bucks.

"Don't worry about it," I said. "You can pay me whatever you can afford."

"I have ten dollars," she said, only she said "doll-urs," as if she was revealing a shameful secret. That's when she started to cry. I knew right then that I was going to give her the ride for free. This would chip away at the forty bucks I had earned in the past hour. But to put things into perspective, on an average day I earned eleven dollars an hour, so right at that moment I felt like I was "in the chips."

"I won't charge you for the ride," I said. "This is what we cab drivers call pro bono work. We're like lawyers. We have to be nice once in a while."

She frowned, then stood up. "Are you sure about this?"

"Let's just get you to the test," I said. "I'll call the company and have them send a tow. Do you have any friends who can pick you up when the test is over?"

She nodded, then said, "Forget the tow truck. I don't ever want to see this pile of junk again. This isn't the first time it's stalled on me."

"What are you going to do?" I said.

"Do you have a screwdriver?" she said.

Let's jump ahead five minutes. She put her license plates into her purse, then handed the screwdriver back to me and said, "I'm ready to go."

I told the woman I would have to turn on the meter because it was a violation of PUC regulations to carry a fare with the flag up and the meter off, but I was not going to charge her for the ride. She nodded.

I dropped my flag and pulled out onto the road. As I guided 123 east, the woman lowered her head and covered her face with both hands. I glanced at the rearview mirror and decided she was crying. She didn't remind me of myself though. On the night the liquor store closed I just took a cab to Sweeney's.

Now that I have her in my backseat, I might as well describe her. She was pretty. She did not at all resemble Mary Ann from *Gilligan's Island*. I don't know why I bring that up. Her hair was short and dishwater-blonde, and she had freckled cheeks, but rather than try to describe her face in detail let's just say that her entire head was more in the ballpark of Gidget than Sophia Lauren. Not that it mattered. She looked about thirty, although her wedding ring did not appear quite that old.

After a while she raised her head and looked out the side window. By then I was rolling down Wadsworth toward the Denver-Boulder Turnpike, which would take us practically to the front door of the Hyatt. I glanced at the woman, then decided to start a conversation. Silence can be unnerving in a taxi, but I wasn't unnerved. Women never do that to me, unless they're rich, or I'm on a date.

"What kind of test are you taking?" I said.

"Post office," she said.

"Oh yeah, I did that once," I said. This was true. I took the test when I first arrived in Denver, before I went to college. I took it at the Denver Federal Center out on Alameda Avenue. I scored about as well as I ever do on tests. I received a couple of extra points on the final score for being a veteran, but that was a waste of ink. I'll admit it. My heart wasn't broken when I received the federal equivalent of a rejection slip. I've seen postal employees work. The operative word there is "heavy boxes."

I told her my sob story. She laughed.

"If I get this job I'll be making better money than I do now," she said. "Then I can quit my current job and move down to Denver."

"What do you do now?" I said.

"I'm a waitress. I have a kid to support."

Without any encouragement from me, she began telling me her life story. But this was not unusual. Even though I have always asserted that a taxi is a terrible place to have an epiphany, a lot of fares treat a taxicab as if it was a confessional. I was raised Catholic so I have a lot of first-hand knowledge of confessionals. I probably know more about the ins-and-outs of forgiveness, absolution, and backsliding than your average truant.

Let's cut to the chase.

The woman told me she was divorced and had a six-year-old daughter. I gave the gas a little more toe. I calculated that we would arrive at the Hyatt with twenty minutes to spare. I have a special affinity for waitresses. Waitresses and cab drivers have a lot in common, such as tips. Waitresses are the best tippers in the world. Young males are the worst, but don't get me started on cultural illiteracy. I am aware that by the age of twenty-five most young men have wised up and joined the human race. Okay. I'll admit it. I didn't achieve economic puberty until I was twenty-eight. It happened in a strip-joint, but let's move on.

We connected with the highway and began the long fast cruise toward Denver. I kept glancing at my wristwatch. I felt the same as I always feel in dreams when I'm late for a test, even though this was reality. I tried to fight the feeling but I couldn't do it because I had made a promise to this woman that I would get her to the test on time, and me and promises don't always see eye-to-eye. The part of my brain that I call "normal" was waiting for the glitch, the roadblock, the disaster up ahead that would prevent me from fulfilling my promise, but who doesn't feel this way when trying to meet a schedule, a deadline, an airplane departure? I try to avoid the "normal" part of my brain as much as possible because it inevitably makes me uneasy—or to put it more accurately, "fills me with dread." We connected with Interstate 25 and headed toward the skyline of Denver. Pretty soon I could see the roof of the Hyatt in the distance. The normal part of my brain scowled and went back to wherever it hides when I'm driving a taxi—I felt it leave my body like an evil spirit. My whole being became tranquil. It felt great. I was abnormal again.

"I really do want to thank you for doing this," the woman said. "Let me give you ten dollars for your trouble."

"This was no trouble," I said. "You don't have to give me any money. I had to come back to Denver anyway. It's where I live."

By then we were coming up on the exit. I drove down the off-ramp, braced myself for the bends, and began making my way over to the Hyatt. My heart soared like an eagle. She had twenty minutes to spare.

I pulled into the parking lot and stopped at the front entrance to the hotel. The meter read $28.60. I climbed out, walked around to the passenger side and opened the door. The woman got out and dug into her purse and pulled out a ten-dollar bill.

"I really do want you to have this," she said.

"I can't accept it," I said. I reached into my T-shirt pocket and pulled out a twenty-dollar bill. "Here, take this. You can't walk around Denver broke. I tried that once and it didn't work out so well. You might need to take a cab home."

She stared at the money as if I had pulled a rabbit out of my pocket. "I can't take money from a cab driver," she said in an incredulous voice.

"Why not?" I said. "Our money is as inflated as everyone else's." She gave me a wistful smile.

"I mean it," I said. "You've got a six-year-old daughter at home and you don't want to find yourself waiting around for friends to show up. I tried that once and it didn't work at all."

"Can you afford this?" she said.

"Cab drivers can't afford anything," I said. "If we were in this for the money we would get out as fast as possible."

"I suppose I could pay you back later," she said.

"No need to do that," I said.

"I could mail it to the cab company."

I decided to give up. Have I ever mentioned the fact that I never argue with women? Meaning I never win arguments with women.

"You don't have to mail it, but you can do that if you want," I said. I was starting to get impatient. Bickering about money bores me. I prefer to bicker about important things, like who gets the last donut.

She finally relented and accepted the money. Then she did something that took me by surprise. She hugged me.

Okay. I'll admit it. I hugged her back. People were watching. I didn't want them to know I was abnormal.

"Thanks for everything," she said.

"Good luck on the test," I said.

She headed for the door to the Hyatt. I watched her enter the lobby. By the time I got behind the steering wheel I was thoroughly depressed. I had never seen anybody go to so much trouble just to get a job.

CHAPTER 12

I picked up my trip-sheet and began filling in the rectangles for Mr. Weissberger's trip. I also had to fill in the $28.60 meter fare for the trip that cost me twenty bucks. My profits were plummeting as usual. I was scribbling this meaningless information when the back door opened and a man with a briefcase climbed in and said, "DIA."

I tossed the trip-sheet aside and said, "Yes, sir." I started the engine and got the hell out of there before the Yellow Cab that he had probably called for showed up.

I never park and wait for fares at the Hyatt cabstand. The Hyatt is on the west side of Interstate 25 where business is slow, so this trip was a windfall. It was like something out of a Horatio Alger book. I once read part of an Alger book when I was a kid. It had one of those optimistic titles like *Pluck and Luck*. It was about this boy who goes to the big city to make his fortune and happens to see a runaway carriage with a girl in it, so he stops the carriage and discovers that the girl is the daughter of a rich man, who thanks the boy by giving him a job. That took care of page one. I was so filled with ambition by then that I quit reading and scoured my neighborhood asking people if I could mow their lawns.

No luck.

I often wondered how that book ended.

Happily, I supposed. Alger used a lot of adverbs.

After we arrived at DIA the man handed me sixty dollars and told me to keep it. I filled out a receipt and gave it to him. There was a time in my life when I sometimes handed blank receipts to businessmen and let them fill in the cost of the ride, but the police taught me to stop doing that. It's a long story that involves kidnapping, murder, and suicide, but it ends happily.

I drove down to the DIA cab-staging area, which is way the hell out in the middle of nowhere. It's an asphalt island where taxis wait to be called to the terminal to pick up airline passengers. But I didn't get in line. I parked in front of a small cinderblock building where DIA personnel work and which also has a small snack bar where cabbies can sit around and not play poker. There are pop and food machines in there. I wanted to grab a soda before deadheading back to Denver, and I also wanted to fill out my trip-sheet and count my gross for the day. During the past two hours alone I had taken in one hundred dollars but had given away twenty, so I was forced to make some calculations with a pencil. Subtraction does that to me.

The rich novelist woman had given me twenty, plus I had earned about thirty bucks making Capitol Hill runs. Then there was the Weissberger forty, minus the Hyatt twenty, plus the DIA sixty. As far as I could tell I had hauled in one hundred and thirty dollars total, but don't hold me to that. The upshot is that I had achieved my normal take for the day, which is one hundred and thirty dollars. I still had four hours left on my cab shift, which meant I could easily earn another forty or fifty dollars clear profit. This sent me spiraling into a blue funk. If it had been six o'clock at night I would have been elated because I would have felt as if I had landed a helicopter with precision.

Let me explain:

When I was in the army, a helicopter pilot once told me that the proper way to land a chopper is to make certain that your velocity and your altitude both reach zero at exactly the same time. If your altitude is zero and your downward velocity is thirty knots an hour, you're in trouble. If your altitude is thirty meters and your velocity is zero, you haven't quite completed the mission and you shouldn't step out of the chopper. Don't ask me what the hell an army officer was doing explaining anything to an enlisted man, but I was fascinated by the simplicity of the mathematical concept of velocity and altitude reaching zero at the same time. It made me want to apply for flight school. Instead I went to the enlisted men's club.

At any rate, whenever I arrive at Rocky Cab at seven p.m. with one hundred and thirty dollars in my pocket I feel as if my altitude and velocity have reached zero at exactly the same time—a perfect landing. Yet here I was with four hours left on my shift and no reason to go on working because I had earned my fifty bucks minimum profit for the day. I have always felt that as a cab driver it is incumbent upon me never to get ambitious. No matter how much extra money I earn on a single day, I also have bad days when I go home with only ten bucks profit in my pocket. Believe me, it happens. Yet on April 15th I always pay the same taxes to Uncle Sam. You never win and you never lose in the taxi game.

I have to tell myself these things whenever I start to feel the dark tendrils of pluck wrapping themselves around my heart. To continue driving that day would have been tantamount to blasphemy. It would have demonstrated an egregious form of hubris found only in Greek mythology and Las Vegas.

But I always know that I am going to quit early whenever I make my minimum because there is a vaporous and rarely seen person who lives inside my head similar to the "stranger." For lack of a better name I call him "conscience." He tries to make me feel guilty about quitting early. He has been following me around like a stray cat ever since my childhood. I first met him at Blessed Virgin Catholic Grade School in Wichita. Every time I smoked a cig or peeked at a *Playboy* he threatened to tell my Maw. I figured he was out of my life forever when I left home to make my fortune in the big city, but when I arrived in Denver, there he was standing in front of my new apartment. I felt him enter my body like an evil spirit ... but ... perhaps it's best I not speak of these things.

I went into the cinderblock bunker and bought a soda. Cabbies from other companies were sitting at the tables in the room listening to portable radios and talking about women or the international conspiracy by a group of wealthy industrialists to take over the world. As I bought my soda I kept my back to everyone in the room, especially the Yellow Cab drivers. Some of them had not quite gotten over the fact that they had once put their faith in me.

As I drove out of DIA and headed toward Denver I glanced at my wristwatch. I now had three hours and forty minutes of free time on my hands. The clock was being eaten away like a riverbank eroded by the ol' Mississip in flood time.

I gave the gas a little toe. I wanted to sign out at Rocky Cab, go home, and start doing nothing as quickly as possible. I hate to waste free time in a cab when I normally waste it at home. When I'm at home I use the free time to wrestle with the decision of whether to start a new novel or watch TV, and you can't do either in a taxi. It gives me such a feeling of helplessness.

I arrived at the motor and turned in my key and trip-sheet to Rollo who gave me a "knowing" look, i.e., he knew I was flush but he didn't say anything. And I knew why. He was afraid I was quitting early because I had made a ton of money. It's the rare driver who quits early on a Friday. After we finished our business I turned away and sauntered out of the on-call room acting as if I had hit the mother lode. Of course after looking at my trip-sheet Rollo would have been able to deduce that I had simply made my quota of profits for the day, the Fabulous Fifty. But I knew that my cocky exit would eat him alive for a minute. I treasure those minuscule moments of victory in our never-ending battle of the intellects.

Just before the door closed, I heard him burp.

I climbed into my Chevy and wheeled out of the lot. On the way home I stopped off at a Burger King for my Friday feast. I hate cooking on Fridays. It takes five minutes to cook a hamburger at home, and

I need those five minutes to prepare myself psychologically for doing nothing.

When I pulled up behind my apartment building I saw the manager dragging his ten-speed bicycle out of the cellar. The manager is a kid who goes to a free school where he studies macramé and yoga. He's twenty-five years old but he's so goddamn healthy that he looks twenty. He giggles a lot. He seems happier than me even though he doesn't own a car.

"Hi Keith," I said, as I climbed out and shut the door without bothering to lock it. I had given up locking my Chevy long ago. Car thieves weren't impressed.

"Hey Murph!" Keith said, his eyes lighting up as he hoisted the bike over the last cellar step and set the wheels on the ground. He was wearing a teardrop-shaped helmet and tight black racing clothes. I figured he was headed for either school or France.

"Where are you going?" I said.

"I'm taking a ride around City Park."

I almost said, "Why?" but managed to stop myself in time. It was a learned thing.

"Have a nice trip," I said, as he hopped onto the seat and began squeezing the hand brakes—testing them, I assumed. I once rode a friend's ten-speed when I was a kid. That was back in the days when ten-speeds were not so common. The hand brakes struck me as pretentious if not downright un-American. I was somewhat of a xenophobe at the age of eight.

Keith jammed his toes into the pedal brackets and wobbled around the parking lot, then got his groove and headed for 13th Avenue. I trudged up the fire escape with my sack of dinner trying to decide whether the guy who had invented the shift mechanism on a ten-speed was a genius or a madman. By the time I reached the top of the stairs I no longer cared.

When I entered my apartment I glanced at the light bulb hanging from the kitchen ceiling. I knew that I would have a psychological tic for a few days. I would become obsessed with making certain the light was turned off each time I left my apartment, and then, like all things that I feel are important, it would fade from my mind. I looked forward to that day. I estimated Monday.

I set my sack on the kitchen table, then went into the living room and withdrew my copy of *Lolita* from the bookshelf. I opened it and hid my taxi profits and put it back on the shelf. I went back into the kitchen to get eating out of the way, one of the few irritants that I have learned to accept as a fact of life or death.

After dinner I sat in my easy chair staring at the TV and thinking about writing a novel. I now had two and a half hours of free time before my regular free time started, and it seemed to me that if I started writing a novel right now, I could get twenty-five hundred words written before my time was up and I could start doing nothing for real.

I write an average of one thousand words a day when I do write novels. It takes an average of an hour to write a thousand words, provided I have thought about the plot ahead of time. If I haven't thought about the plot it can take all day just to write a paragraph, although that was a problem that I generally outgrew after college.

When I got my degree in English from the University of Colorado at Denver I realized it was time to buckle down. I'll admit it. I took the romantic approach to crass commercialism when I was in my twenties. I used to stand at the window of my apartment, smoke a cigarette, and stare at the cloud-blasted landscape trying to compose profound sentences in my mind. This was because I didn't have a plot to fool with. But it wasn't just that. I felt like a visionary artist staring out the window, smoking a cigarette, and waving at the garbage collectors as they made their runs. On top of that, I was getting paid three hundred bucks a month on the GI Bill so I didn't take the writing of novels very seriously in terms of money-making. During my college years I felt like I was "in the chips."

But then I graduated and the money ran out and I had to find a job, which really shook me up. I realized that I ought to have been writing books with plots rather than profound sentences. Even though I was given four year's worth of money by Uncle Sam, I managed to stretch it out to seven years, which I don't want to delve too deeply into, but the point that I do wish to make is that I felt I had wasted seven years staring out windows when I should have been reading how-to books. By then it was too late. I had an English degree and no marketable skills.

Eventually I went to work as a corporate writer for a company down in the Denver Tech Center called Dyna-Plex. They made things or traded things or whatever executives do, but I worked there only a year, and then I started driving a taxi for a living. By that time I had secretly read a couple of how-to books so I had a loose grasp of plotting. I had already seen about ten thousand movies, so this helped me to visualize things like flying saucers and werewolves. In fact it was the combination of how-to books plus Hollywood that helped me to write my very first novel rejected by a real publisher, the aforementioned "Draculina." It was about a swinging stewardess who was transformed into a vampire during a trip to Eastern Europe—it was written before the word "stewardess" was transformed into "flight attendant." I know absolutely nothing about Europe, and I know even less about vampires than I do about women, so it was the combination of these factors that aided in the shaping of my first significant rejection slip. I still have it. I know you're not supposed to save rejection slips—that's what the how-to books say—but I enjoy collecting souvenirs of New York City.

Anyway, if things are going well I can write a thousand words an hour, which means that if I had started right then I could have written twenty-five hundred words before getting around to writing my regular one thousand words for the day, which would have added up to three thousand five hundred words, which would have been a new record for a Friday, which it wasn't. I never got around to writing because the goddamn phone rang.

I stopped making the mathematical calculations that are so crucial to my writing career and looked at the telephone. It rang again. After the third ring I automatically leaned a bit toward the phone. I have never quite divested myself of the intimidation that machines evoke in all human beings. Even though I hate that aspect of my own humanity, I am not ashamed of it. Whenever inanimate objects do things automatically, my senses go on alert and I brace myself for the worst, as would anybody with half a brain.

It rang a fourth time.

The only thing I hate worse than telephones is not knowing who is calling me, and more importantly, why. I am intrigued by the idea that there exist people who—at a specific point in time—have a need to communicate with me, since I never have anything to say to anybody at any time about anything.

On the fifth ring I picked up the phone, pinched my nose, and said, "Yeh."

I was using my "sorry wrong number" voice.

There was a silence at the other end, followed by a few clicks, then the dial tone poked my eardrum. But the clicks were the sort of clicks that always make a guy like me think my phone lines are being tapped. Illegally of course—I mean, if the cops ever wanted to know what I was up to, all they would have to do was ask. I would disappoint them real fast because I'm never up to anything. I would be hard-pressed to name anybody I've ever met who has never been disappointed in me.

I hung up and peered at my AudioMaster DeLuxe and thought about turning it off. But I always made a point of never turning the thing off. The AudioMaster may have been the only machine I ever encountered that actually aided and abetted my sanity. It was like owning an invincible robot butler—when Robbie was on the job, the Krell couldn't get me.

As long as I'm on the subject, do you want to hear something sort of funny? One time I called my apartment from Rocky Cab and left a message just so I could go home and hear what I sounded like on the AudioMaster. I was hoping I would sound like Morbius, the ruler of the planet Altara, who had a deep, crisp, resonant voice—he was played by Walter Pigeon in *Forbidden Planet*. Instead I sounded like Betty Boop. That's where I got my "sorry wrong number" voice.

I stared at the phone for a little while then turned the auto-answer off. But this made me feel nervous. I knew that I would have to pick up the receiver again if I wanted to know who was calling.

I switched the recorder back on and waited for the phone to ring. I always do this after touching my telephone. Again, it's the machine/intimidation thing—sort of like touching a sleeping grizzly and then waiting to see what happens.

I won't bore you with the result.

I went back to thinking about writing a novel, but my concentration kept being interrupted by the expectation of a phone call. The fact that the phone had already rung once fragmented my ability to concentrate, so the odds of my thinking up a plot for a novel was teetering on the edge. But I stuck with it. I came up with an idea for a novel about a gang of punk Martians who come to earth in a flying saucer for no other reason than to commit mayhem. Martians usually come to earth to study the habits of mankind and report back to Mars for reasons that are never made very clear, or else they give mankind scientific devices that will turn the earth into a paradise. But I had never read a book about serial-killer aliens. It seemed like I might have found a niche market, assuming there were science fiction fans hungry for police procedurals.

This got me to wondering if I could pull in some other genres in order to "play the field" and capture as many different audiences as possible. I'll admit it. This was no less than a crass marketing strategy designed to earn as much money as possible. But then I wondered if I might be making a mistake. Instead of milking money from one large group of specific genre readers, I might be spreading myself thin by getting only a little bit of money from the few people who might enjoy reading a science fiction homicide romance spy western high-seas adventure. I suddenly pictured the critics using the phrase "disjointed mess" rather than "charming blend."

I finally gave up and turned on the TV. I came across an episode of *Gilligan's Island* broadcast out of Chicago, but it was one I had never cared much for. It involved a dream sequence where Gilligan plays a Sherlock Holmes character. I dislike dream sequences because any ludicrous thing can happen, and this fragments my willing suspension of disbelief. I want my Gilligan stories grounded in raw realism.

Ergo, I did something that I rarely do, which was turn off Gilligan in the middle of the episode after getting a good look at Mary Ann.

It was only after the TV was off and a pristine silence had invaded my apartment that I realized something was bothering me. It wasn't the telephone and it wasn't the lack of realism on my boob tube, it was the ride that I had given to Mr. Weissberger that afternoon. He had said something that I tried to forget as soon as he had said it. But the vaporous entity that lives inside my head remembered, and it went like this: "I know that his wife and children would also be pleased to hear this from the gentleman who was with Heinrich when he passed away."

I had been trying to put out of my mind the fact that I had lied to Mr. Weissberger by not telling him the very last thing that Mr. Zelner had said to me. And I remembered my excuse for lying to him, which went like this: "The very last thing on the planet earth that I wanted to do was to get involved in the personal life of anybody living or dead. In two miles this man would be out of my life forever."

I started to feel badly. Mr. Zelner had a wife and children. I assumed that the children were grown because Mr. Zelner had seemed pretty old, so they weren't like "little" children, but they were still biological children. And then there was his wife, who probably wished she could have been with him when he died. She would have wanted to hear his very last words. I thought about me ol' Dad, who died eight years ago. Maw was with him in the hospital when he passed away. I thought how badly she would have felt if he had died in the backseat of a taxi.

I have met three people who were born in the backseat of a taxi. I delivered all three of them. That's how I met them.

I finally decided I would get in touch with Mr. Heigger and tell him that I did remember, after all, that Mr. Zelner had said something to me as we crossed the 14th Street viaduct. Having decided this, I then did something that I rarely do, if ever. I leaned over to the table where the telephone resides, reached underneath it, and pulled out the dustiest phone book you ever saw.

I had to get up and go out to the fire escape to shake the dust off the book. Before I shook it I made certain there weren't any topless women sunbathing on the second-floor landing of the fire escape. A woman who once lived in the apartment below mine used to sunbathe topless out there. It caused a psychological tic that I have never quite outgrown, even though she moved away four years ago.

I went back inside and sat down in my easy chair and opened the phone book. I have more experience with books than telephones since I'm an aspiring writer and have a degree in English, but my pagination skills didn't do me much good because I could not find "Heigger & Associates" among the aitches. Did you know that the letter "H" is spelled "a-i-t-c-h"? Don't ask me how the dictionary writers got away with using a lower-case "h" in the spelling of the letter's name—to me that's like defining a word by using the word in its own definition. I did that once in high school and got away with it, but let's move on.

After failing to find the lawyer's office in the business section of the white pages, I began the drudgery of searching for it in the yellow pages under every conceivable synonym for "lawyer." I won't put you through all that, except to mention that the word "shyster" does not appear in the Denver telephone book. I can't speak for Washington D.C.

I finally closed the book. Heigger's office was not that far away from my apartment so I decided that the following morning I would drive over there, even though he might not be working on Saturday. I preferred to speak with him in person, but if he wasn't in, I would slip a note under the door asking him to call me.

By the time I went to bed I even had a plausible explanation worked out—to wit: Mr. Weissberger had asked me if Mr. Zelner had said anything to me during the trip, and it was only after Mr. Weissberger had gotten out of my cab that I remembered what Mr. Zelner had said. I would tell Heigger that it had been such an inconsequential remark that I simply had not remembered it. However Mr. Weissberger had started me thinking along those lines, and it all came back.

I've had quite a lot of experience making up long-winded explanations wedded with duplicity—usually when talking to nuns. But for the most part it had to do with my complete and total disinterest in getting involved in the lives of other people or homework assignments—although my conscience never got involved in long-winded explanations when it came to my failure to hand in homework. Normally the nuns didn't find out I hadn't done my homework until I was out the classroom door and on my way to the drugstore for a creamy thick milkshake before heading home to supper.

CHAPTER 13

I woke up Saturday morning feeling terrible. I had something to "do." Having anything to do automatically makes me feel terrible. I didn't look at the clock. I knew it was ten o'clock. Either my body or my brain is such a finely tuned instrument that I automatically wake up at ten o'clock on my days off. I wake up at 6:00 a.m. on workdays but I don't feel terrible because I have never thought of cab driving as "doing" anything.

I ate a cheese sandwich and had a quick soda while I surfed the TV, but I knocked that off because I was afraid I might accidentally run across an episode of *Gilligan's Island* and end up postponing my self-imposed chore. I try not to drink beer, smoke cigars, or look at Mary Ann before noon. One morning I did all three and my day was shot to hell.

The mansion that housed Heigger & Associates was less than fifteen minutes away so I figured I could get shut of this chore and be back in my crow's nest and continue to do nothing within thirty minutes, unless I stopped off to buy beer, which was not beyond the realm of possibility. I considered stopping at a video store that was down on south Broadway. It was an off-the-beaten-track video store that sold specialty tapes—independent if you get my drift—where you could find movies that you would never find in the homes of decent people. I'm not talking spicy movies, but rather Ed Wood films, early Roger Corman, and any other kind of bizarre, noir, or avant-garde film produced by small companies where "production values" is a concept dismissed as self-indulgent if not entirely irrelevant. Some people call it "art."

But I would worry about beer and art later. Right now I had a confession to get through. I found it ironic that I was making a confession on a Saturday since I had gone to confession every Saturday between the ages of seven and seventeen—I'm talking the Catholic church of course and not a lawyer's office. I rarely confess anything to lawyers unless the cops are on my case.

I arrived at the redstone building, parked, went up to the front porch and entered. When I got to the office door I raised my fist to knock, but my curled fingers paused a few inches from the spot where there was supposed to be a sign that said "Heigger & Associates." It wasn't there.

I went ahead and knocked. There was no reply. I reached down and twisted the doorknob. As I pushed the door open I heard a voice say, "Can I help you?"

I turned around and saw a small man wearing grubby clothing. By "grubby" I mean he was dressed like me, except he was wearing an ugly maroon knit shirt, whereas I was wearing a white T-shirt almost fresh from the laundry. We were both wearing blue jeans and tennis shoes. His jeans were a bit baggy, whereas mine were tight, like that worn by a man in denial of his beer gut. He was holding a broom with its bristles planted on the floor and gazing at me with his head tilted in a position that I had long ago come to label "suspicious."

"I'm here to see the lawyer," I said.

"Who?"

"Mr. Heigger."

He looked me up and down without moving his head. He used only his eyes, like a wary man who was ready to use the rest of his body for something else and I don't mean sweeping.

I was still holding onto the doorknob. The door was halfway open. I pointed at the opening with my other hand and pushed the door all the way open so Mr. Heigger would see both me and the small man whom I felt was associated in some way with building maintenance.

The room was almost barren. There was a desk but no chairs, no wall hangings, and most significantly, no people.

"That room is empty," the man said.

I started to say "I can see that" but I didn't. I closed the door and looked farther down the hallway. There were no more doors. "I'm looking for Heigger & Associates," I said.

"There's no business here by that name," he said. When he spoke he barely moved his lips.

"Did they vacate?" I said.

He didn't reply. He pulled the broom a little closer to his body. Then something happened that I had no control over.

I chortled.

"I drive for the Rocky Mountain Taxicab Company," I said. "I picked up a fare at this office on Wednesday."

A flicker of humanity crossed the man's face. I think it was the word "taxicab" that did it. For some reason people respond positively to the word "taxicab."

"I don't know nothing about it," he said. "Maybe you got the wrong building. Maybe you should try next door." Then he backed up against the wall. I realized what he was doing. He was giving me room to walk past him and go out the front door.

"Are there any other lawyers who work in this building?" I said.

"No," he said. "Maybe you should call your company and ask for the address again. Maybe you got it wrong."

I realized that he thought I was on duty. I also realized that if he saw me walk outside and climb into my Chevy he would think I was lying. Maybe he would think I was some kind of a burglar. He probably had been thinking that from the get-go, and might still be thinking it. The word "taxicab" can carry you only so far.

My inherent inability to control my chortles suddenly left me. I started to get annoyed. I don't mind being suspected of things when I am actually "up to something," but when I'm innocent it makes me bristle. I reminded myself that I was a professional taxi driver, so I decided to start acting like one even if I was off-duty. In other words, I decided to treat this like a no-show.

"All right, thanks anyway," I said with a confident and slightly disgusted tone of voice that did not reflect my inner being. My inner being was baffled and uneasy. I was familiar with that dynamic duo.

I walked past him. Then I turned and looked at him. "The dispatcher might ask me who I talked to—do you work in this building?"

"I'm the supe."

"Thank you, sir," I said.

I walked outside and went down the steps, debating whether to climb directly into my heap or to turn and walk along the sidewalk as if my cab was parked farther down the block.

But by the time I got to within five feet of my heap I was no longer concerned with pretense. I turned and looked up at the mansion, then I looked at the mansions farther along the street. Right at that moment I was willing to concede that a mistake on my part was not beyond the realm of possibility. But it was only a fleeting doubt. This was the same mansion that I had visited on Wednesday. The only reason I entertained a doubt was because I had made plenty of mistakes in my life and I had come to accept the fact that my brain was not the most reliable map printed by Rand McNally. But I had passed this mansion enough times during my years in Denver to know that I had come to the right place.

I glanced at the front door. The "supe" was standing behind the glass watching me. Now that I was outside and beyond his territorial imperative I didn't care what he thought. I walked around to the driver's side of my heap and climbed in, started the engine, and drove away.

CHAPTER 14

S o much for beer and art. I hate it when my nebulous plans are interrupted by tics, but I wanted to know what had become of Heigger
& Associates. Here's the thing though: I myself had packed up and fled
enough cities to know that sudden disappearances were not implausible.
Did I ever tell you about my "incident" in Albuquerque?

No?

Let's keep it that way.

I drove west to Broadway, then tried to go south, but I couldn't do
it. Twenty minutes earlier I had made the mistake of putting myself in
the mood for really bad movies, and I had calculated that I could visit
Heigger & Associates, confess my sins, receive absolution, then head
straight for the video store that is called—and I'm going to say this only
once—Gandalf's. It seemed like every week the store stocked at least one
new cinematic atrocity that was waiting to burn a hole in my VCR. And
if there was nothing new, I could always rent *Plan 9 From Outer Space*, a
reliable substitute for everything.

As I drove down Broadway though, I couldn't bring myself to commit blasphemy by renting a movie that I knew I would only half watch
because I would be pestered by the psychological tic of wondering where
Mr. Heigger had disappeared to. I once tried to watch *Glen or Glenda*
while waiting for a phone call from my Maw. Total washout.

I finally turned left off Broadway and cut east along 6th Avenue. I
headed back toward my place. I didn't even stop to buy beer. I started

thinking that if I was a lawyer who wanted to get out of town fast and leave no footprints, I just might consider bribing a man who made a living sweeping office buildings. Maybe the "supe" had lied to me.

As I turned left and headed up Downing Street I thought about that guy. Except for the jeans with the practical fit, he didn't look all that different from me. We were both blue-collar workers, and if his annual income held any resemblance to mine, there was a good possibility that he had about as much willpower as I did. Maybe Heigger had paid the superintendent a hefty sum to keep mum if anyone came nosing around. Heigger may have figured that the supe would hold out long enough to give him time to flee across the border, either north to Canada or south to Mexico—it's irrelevant when the IRS is on your tail, believe me.

Five minutes later I pulled into the parking lot behind my crow's nest. As I climbed out of the car I glanced at my wristwatch, but this was just a cabbie habit. On weekends I never care what time it is, especially in the daytime. I measure time on weekends like a caveman—if the sun is in the sky, the bars are open.

It was noon.

I was golden.

I climbed the fire escape and unlocked my door, stepped inside and glanced at the kitchen lightbulb as I knew I would for at least two more days. The bulb was off. I passed through the kitchen without stopping at the fridge for a beer.

I went into the living room and sat down in my easy chair and stared at the wall above my TV. That part of my wall gets a lot of attention when I have things on my mind. You would be surprised at the number of times I have had things on my mind. Or perhaps it might be better to say that you would be surprised at the things themselves—like stealing one hundred thousand dollars. But that's all in the past and some day I might have a good chuckle over it.

I stared at the wall until I saw movies taking shape on the flat surface.

One of the movies showed me meeting Mr. Heigger in his office, and then leading him to Diamond Hill.

The next movie showed me meeting Mr. Weissberger in Heigger's office and driving him to Broomfield.

Before I shut down the projector I watched the movie about the woman whom I had driven to the Hyatt for the post office exam. I laughed when I watched her remove the license plates from her car. I was certain she had aced the letter-carrier test.

I shut down the projector. I was now engulfed in a psychological tic of mammoth proportions. Mr. Zelner had died in the backseat of my taxi, and now his lawyer had disappeared—and according to both the supe and the Denver telephone directory, Heigger's office didn't exist. Let's see you watch *Plan 9* with those bees in your bonnet.

I finally did something that I consciously and deliberately tried not to do very often, which was to make a phone call to Rocky Cab. Maybe Hogan could get Heigger's number through RMTC's insurance company. I was grasping at straws, my standard approach to everything.

I dialed the cage. The cage is like Step One in the board game of Rocky Cab. You start there and then get shunted on to other squares. You can't just call Hogan directly, for the same reason that you can't call me without going through my AudioMaster DeLuxe.

"Rocky Cab ... this is Stew."

"Stew, this is Murph. Can you put me through to Hogan?"

"No can do, Murph. He's gone for the weekend."

I had forgotten that. Whenever the weekend arrives I try to forget everything that ever happened in my entire life. I have a success rate of only 17 percent, but I'm not giving up.

"Listen Stew, I have a kind of small ..." I started to say "problem" but I wasn't really sure what to call it. I didn't think Stew would have truly grasped the phrase "psychological tic." "... question," I finished, fielding my own fungo.

"Shoot."

"I picked up a fare named Weissberger on Friday from a lawyer's office called Heigger and Associates and I wanted to get in touch with this Heigger fellow, but I can't find his office in the phone book. I drove over to Heigger's office just now but the place is empty. I need to talk to Mr. Heigger. It has to do with the death of my fare last Wednesday, and I wondered if Hogan could tell me how to contact him."

"You'll probably have to wait until Monday, Murph. Hogan gets in at six a.m."

"Yeah," I said dolefully, the way you say yeah when the inevitable has firmly established its presence in your life.

"Listen," I said, "could you check the records and see if there's a phone number for Heigger and Associates on file somewhere."

"I can't check but I can put you through to the dispatcher."

I won't drag you through the entire quagmire—we'll take the magical bridge. I talked to the Channel 4 dispatcher and explained about my personal on Friday. He checked the records and found a phone number. He said he would try it. He put me on hold. A minute later he came back and told me he had gotten the world-famous woman's voice that said, "We're sorry, but the number you have dialed has been disconnected."

I thanked the dispatcher and hung up thinking about the deluded optimism of Alexander Graham Bell.

I felt exceptionally doleful now because Monday was the day I had scheduled to recover from the psychological tic related to my kitchen lightbulb. But now I had at least one other tic lined up in the queue: I wanted to find out where Heigger's office had disappeared to. The way things were shaping up I was destined to suffer psychological tics clear into the middle of next week.

I sat there staring at the wall above my TV. Unfortunately I still had my hand on the telephone and it suddenly rang, which scared the hell out of me.

I yanked my fingers away from the jaws of the grizzly and immediately entered the panic mode. I didn't want to answer it, yet I did want to because I felt there was the thinnest chance that it might be Heigger—I know what you're thinking: save it for the Colorado lottery.

On the fourth ring I snatched up the receiver and said, "Yeh" without pinching my nose.

I heard a few clicks, but otherwise silence.

Have I ever told you how little it takes to make me go ballistic? It's not something I'm proud of, and I don't like to talk about it much because it not only causes me embarrassment, it sometimes scares me. But if somebody pushes the right button, my entire brain seems to fly right out the window.

"Hello!" I said loudly.

I was tired of hearing clicks and silence coming from the plastic delusion in my hand.

"Who's calling!" I barked. Nothing.

I slammed the receiver onto the cradle and sat there fuming. I don't know about you, but I like fuming. I also like WWI movies with aerial dogfights.

The next thing I knew I was unhooking the AudioMaster from my phone. Then I disconnected the telephone itself from the cord that led into the wall. I set the two bastards on the phone book beneath the table. I sat back in my chair, took a deep breath, and exhaled with pleasure. I felt like the WWI ace who had shot down the Red Baron. Baron von Richthofen had an uncle who once owned a large estate in east Denver. The mansion is still there. It's called the Richthofen Mansion. The guy who named it was a goddamn genius.

I suppose it's not necessary to explain to you that I now felt like I had completely disconnected myself from the entire planet earth. Nobody could get at me. The earth would have to wait until I plugged it in on Monday, assuming I decided to do it again. As I sat there fuming I began to wonder why the hell I owned a telephone. After I left Wichita and began traveling around the country, I rarely had telephones in the apartments and rooms that I rented. I made calls over pay phones more often than private phones. But back then I was young and stupid and thought it was cool when I did have a phone of my own, although nobody ever called me—not in Cleveland anyway. I do remember getting a few phone calls in Cincinnati, and one in Philadelphia, although that was a wrong number.

The more I thought about it, the more I wondered why I bothered to waste money every month paying a bill for an electronic device that I loathed. There was a pay phone down the block from my crow's nest—I could use that whenever I needed a pizza.

But I remembered that my Maw called me every now and then. Believe me, brother, that did not motivate me to plug the phone back in. But I foresaw something even worse than a phone call from Maw, which was a longwinded explanation through the mail. I already knew what Maw would write to me about not owning a phone: "Supposing yeh accidentally slashed yer wrist on a broken window and needed to call an ambulance, boy-o?"

"Hey Maw, the day I slash my wrist it won't be an accident," I would write back—but she probably wouldn't laugh. There are two things that my Irish/Catholic mother takes a very dim view of: suicide and gold-digging floozies. These have to do with shadowy events on her side of the family that date back to the Potato Famine.

To hell with it. I would leave the phone unplugged until Monday and then decide whether or not I wanted to continue paying loathsome bills. I had learned long ago that it was not a good idea to make a crucial decision after going ballistic. It takes a few hours for my brain to come back through the window, and by then I'm usually watching TV and don't even notice its return.

I put a final flourish on my ballistics by going into the kitchen and unscrewing the lightbulb and placing it in the cupboard next to my plate. I did this to pull the rug out from under the psychological tic that made me glance "up" whenever I entered the kitchen. Maybe it wouldn't stop me from glancing "up" in the future but at least I would have the satisfaction of wiping the smug smirk off its bulb.

As I closed the cabinet door I whispered, "Have a nice life, Rollo." I cannot tell you how good that made me feel.

I walked back into the living room wondering if there was a method to my madness, assuming that "personification" could be defined as an "element" of a method. I don't have much experience with methods. I'm more of a "wing-it" personality. I often incorporate winging-it when I write novels, go on dates, or avoid responsibilities.

But maybe "winging-it" itself was a method. I hoped not. I would hate to think that my rejection slips were the results of volition, not to mention my dates. Rejection was frequently an "element" of my dates, although I had never received a formal rejection from a woman. Conversely, I had never been kissed by a book editor. And the future wasn't looking very bright.

CHAPTER 15

I woke up at six o'clock on the dot Monday morning. I liked that. It proved to me that my brain was still the way it always is. I had gone to bed on Sunday night worried that all the tics would bollix my mental wiring and I might not wake up on time. Not that it mattered. My alarm clock was always set to go off at 6:01. It was the rare Monday when I didn't Beat the Clock.

I got up and went into the kitchen and forgot to glance at the light socket. As I was standing in the bathroom shaving I realized I had forgotten. I finished all the onerous jazz you have to do in a bathroom before entering the public arena, then I stepped into the kitchen and looked at the dangling socket. It was relatively dark in the kitchen but the ambient light from my living room bulb—as well as the blazing TV screen—allowed me to see quite well in the kitchen. I gazed at the empty socket until I felt like I was engaged in a battle of the intellects. It was as if the socket was saying, "Well ...?"

I smirked and opened the fridge where the light of the 40-watt illuminated my stack of American cheese. I proceeded to make a one-layer sandwich. I grabbed a soda and opened it and walked into the living room and stood watching TV while I ate breakfast. It was 6:25 and the kitchen socket kept saying, "Well ...?" but I ignored it. I decided to play a little mind game of my own. I wanted to test the parameters of my existence and see how long I could survive without a kitchen light. It was a game that I knew I was destined to lose, insofar as I would eventually replace the bulb, but I was curious to find out how long it would take for me to capitulate. This was an adjunct to torturing myself with exquisite anticipation while watching TV commercials.

When I was a kid I sometimes held an M&M on my tongue to see how long it would take before I lost control and gulped it down. I lost that battle many times, but then one night while guarding the ammo dump I beat the little red bean. I accredited my endurance to the P.O.W. training I had received in basic. Unfortunately the mastery of my tongue did not result in a promotion to corporal. Nor did it inspire me to continue holding M&Ms on my tongue for extended periods of time. I had beaten the enemy once, and it told me everything I wanted to know about myself.

I gathered my plastic briefcase and toolbox, took my starting pay out of *Lolita* and tucked it into my T-shirt pocket. I put on my deep forest green Rocky jacket and cap, and headed out the back door.

I was halfway down the fire escape when I froze. My car was gone.

The choice V-spot where fence-meets-fence was vacant. I recognized the vacancy. I had seen it many times during the past fourteen years. I turned and climbed back up the steps fuming—not because my car was gone but because I would have to call Gladys, which would be embarrassing. Of course getting my car stolen did give me an awful feeling, but I was a professional taxi driver so I was used to awful feelings.

I plugged the telephone back into the wall and dialed. "DPD."

"Hello again, Gladys," I said.

"I'll put out the call, Murph," she giggled.

I ate up one minute of her workday by asking Gladys about her kids and husband. I figured that the city taxes I paid entitled me to one minute of the government's time. Gladys had a fifteen-year-old daughter who was a cornerback on the high school football team, which had taken the championship two years running. Her son's talent lay in basketball. Her husband drove a forklift in a furniture warehouse. I did that once. "Once" is the operative word there.

We rang off. I put away my cab accoutrement and got down to the serious business of doing nothing. There was no telling how long it would take before the police came by to tell me where the thief had abandoned my rolling dump. The record was fifteen minutes but the circumstances had been unusual. This took place ten years ago. I'll tell you that story while we wait for the police:

One afternoon I drove to a liquor store five blocks away to buy some beer, even though it was so close that I usually walked. I shot the breeze with the clerk for a while, then stepped outside and walked home and discovered that my car was gone. Infuriated that I had been the victim of a daring daylight robbery, I called Gladys. Fifteen minutes later Officer Lafferty knocked on my door. He worked the Capitol Hill beat so I had gotten to know him pretty well. He had returned 62 percent of my stolen cars, so to speak. He told me that my Chevy had been found in the parking lot of the liquor store. He then saw the six-pack on my kitchen table. He gave me "the eye" and politely asked if I would be willing to give him a sobriety test. I said sure. I made him walk a straight line, then told him to recite "rubber baby buggy" three times real fast. He passed. We both laughed. Then he drove me to the liquor store. That was one of the most pleasant embarrassing moments of my life.

I know four other policemen fairly well. I don't want to go into detail explaining why I know four detectives. Let me just offer some key words and phrases: kidnap, murder, bank robbery—actually there were something like four kidnappings and maybe five murders, I've sort of lost count. There was also one highly suspicious suicide, and a couple of assault-and-batteries, although I want to make it abundantly clear to you that I had no connection with any of those cases, beyond the fact that I was the prime suspect. But they all turned out to be ridiculous misunderstandings that were easily explained, except for the bank robbery that—well, maybe I've said too much. Let's move on.

I seriously considered calling the detectives who worked the Robbery

Division. I got along pretty well with them because they didn't know me as well as the other detectives. The other guys were named Duncan and Argyle. They had grown sick and tired of seeing me, I could tell, although they never came right out and said so. But I have an instinct for these things.

The Robbery Division detectives were named Ottman and Quigg. They investigated the bank heist that I somehow got mixed up in. Basically, I drove the getaway car. But that's not what it sounds like. The thing is though, I knew Ottman and Quigg, so I felt like I had an "in" with the DPD and might get some quick action. I'll be honest though. I have never felt very comfortable talking to the police. But who does? Any American who feels cool, calm, and collected while talking to a policeman needs some kind of goddamn therapy. I don't know about you, but the sight of a polished badge and a well-oiled revolver makes me think of things that I would rather not think about. Not crimes exactly but ... you know ... things.

I began to wonder if Ottman and Quigg would come over to my apartment if I called them about my stolen car. I didn't know much about federal crimes, but it seemed to me we could be talking a felony here. I had never thought about it before because my car was always found so quickly. Given my predilection for getting roped into jams, I suppose I ought to keep a small law library in my apartment. But most of the books on my living room shelves consist of unpublished novels that I have written. The published novels are kept on a shelf in my bedroom. I did not write them. They were written by people that do not live in Denver. Okay. I'll admit it. One of them lives in San Luis Obispo.

I ultimately decided not to report the robbery to my connections down at DPD. I could just see Ottman and Quigg giving me "the eye" as their investigation into my charges against unknown street punks or junkies was interrupted by the quick return of my Chevy. I would feel like an idiot if my frantic "felony" phone call took Ottman and Quigg away from a barbecue with their families. They would probably get tired of seeing me real quick.

By the time 8:45 rolled around I had resigned myself to the fact that I would not go to work that day. I would be forced to work on Tuesday to make up for my lost fifty bucks. My days off are voluntary, but I have so many of them that I don't mind jettisoning one in a pinch. As I have demonstrated, it's not like I do anything important on my days off, although the word "important" is open to debate—to certain people who shall remain nameless, doing nothing is important. But even if I had retrieved my car within the next half-hour I still would not have gone in to work. I intensely dislike playing catch-up in terms of earning money. I could have gone in at noon and still earned my fifty-dollar profit for the day, but that would have entailed working hard, and I did not sign up to become a cab driver in order to work hard. I signed up because I was broke.

There seems to be a lot of people in this world who do not understand the point of having money. I don't know about you, but it bugs me whenever I read articles about guys who earn fifty million dollars a year and still go to work in an office every day. Who are they trying to impress? Me? I ought to market a self-help tape for rich people who do not grasp the direct link between money and not working. And I know just what I would say: "You, sir, obviously have been brainwashed by society into believing that all work is noble. But my question to you is: why would anybody want to be noble? What is this obsession with civic virtue that fills intelligent people with a manic desire to wear suits? You say you want nobility? Toss a goddamn cape over a mud puddle, then buy yourself a solid-gold hammock, you deluded bastard!"

There just might be a pretty penny in a self-help tape like that.

Aaah, why bother? Trying to help people is a problem I've been grappling with every since I began driving a taxi. It's one of the reasons I have come to within a hair's breadth of having a rap sheet a mile long. I sometimes wonder if there are any felonies left on the books that I haven't been mistakenly suspected of committing. Smuggling, I suppose. But I credit that to geography. Colorado isn't close enough to a U.S. border for me to get roped into an international jam.

These are the kinds of thoughts I have when I'm waiting for the police to knock on my door.

I felt sort of trapped because I couldn't leave my apartment. It was like waiting for a cable man to show up, or a plumber, or a telephone lineman—or even a taxi. I'll be honest. Whenever I call a taxi I feel a compulsion to get my things together quickly and prepare myself for the horrifying moment when the driver arrives. What if he gets impatient? What if he honks and scowls at me? What if he drives off in anger leaving me standing at the door? You wouldn't think I would feel this way since I drive a taxi and know the score—which is to say, cab drivers live with a constant fear of no-shows. They are so grateful to see the front door of a house open that they become putty in a passenger's hands.

Well … perhaps I shouldn't speak of these things.

I thought about killing some time by digging out my Rubik's Cube and trying to solve the mystery. It had been a long time since I had thrown the cube against a wall. But I finally did the only thing a man can do after his car is stolen. I watched TV. Normally watching TV is a happy occasion for me but I kept waiting to hear a knock at the door. The police rarely call on the phone to report that my car has been found because it's always tracked down within walking distance, and they are so close to my apartment when they find it that they just drop by. It's very chummy. But it still detracts from my viewing pleasure, waiting for the sound of someone climbing the fire escape and knocking on my door. I know cop knocks. Their knuckles are different from anyone else's—although perhaps I am being a bit disingenuous when I say that because the only other individual to knock on my kitchen door during the past five years was a guy named Harold. Harold is a bartender at Sweeney's. That's all I want to say about Harold, except that he wasn't bringing me a beer. A S.W.A.T. team once hammered on my door. Not even my friends used to do that.

Around noon I was channel-surfing the soap operas. I once saw a documentary where the literary critic, Leslie Fiedler, admitted to having gotten hooked on a soap. This worried me. If an intellectual could get dragged down that rabbit hole, imagine what *The Edge of Night* could do to a cab driver. My Maw once got hooked on a soap called *Dark Shadows*. The main character was a vampire. But I wasn't able to get hooked along with her because I was in school at the time—high school or college, I really don't remember, and I'm willing to bet it doesn't matter.

I kept surfing back and forth between the soaps looking for something that might be worth getting hooked on. I refer to this activity as "tickling the dragon's tail." Nuclear physicists used that term in reference to bringing the first atom bomb as close to critical mass as possible without an explosion. They did it in a laboratory in Chicago. I was in Denver, but other than that, the risk was about the same.

Then I heard footsteps on the fire escape. By this I mean my apartment began to subtly vibrate the way it does when cops and bartenders drop by. It was with mixed feelings that I shut off my TV. I heard a knock. I set the remote on the table, got up and went into the kitchen to stand and wait for the second knock on the door in the same way that people stand motionless next to a telephone waiting for the second ring before answering it so the callers won't think their days are so empty that they snatch up a phone on the first ring just to break the monotony of their pointless lives.

Been there.

I heard a second knock.

I opened the door and saw the pink and shining face of a man my own age, but who had more money and prestige. This describes almost everybody in Denver over the age of thirty-five.

"Top of the morning," said Officer Lafferty. I glanced at my wrist-watch. It was 11:59.

"Good morning, Officer Lafferty," I said, feeling foolish being polite to someone who probably had been a sophomore when I was a junior.

"Well, this is an interesting one," Lafferty said. "We got a call fifteen minutes ago from a woman who lives at Tenth and Madison. Your car is blocking her driveway."

"What makes it interesting?" I said.

Lafferty removed his snappy hat and ran his fingers through his red hair. "She said she had gone grocery shopping an hour ago and the Chevy wasn't there. So whoever stole it must have parked it some time within the last half-hour."

"That certainly is interesting," I said. "Why would anybody drive my car for more than five minutes?"

"It's one for the books," Lafferty said with a shake of his head. "Can I give you a lift?"

I nodded. Lafferty drove me to 10th and Madison. My Chevy was still blocking the driveway. Lafferty waited while I started the engine. I gave Lafferty the traditional thumbs up. He saluted and went back on patrol.

As I watched his black-and-white grow small in the distance I thought about becoming a cop. As I have said, cab drivers and cops lead similar lives. They work in cars, they have two-way radios, and they lead lives of danger. The big difference is that cops carry guns. I had learned how to fire pistols in the army, as well as machine-guns and grenade launch-ers, and I knew more about Military Police work than the average GI. I couldn't begin to tell you the number of MPs that I became personally acquainted with in various army towns that turned out to be off-limits. I got into the habit of using the same excuse whenever the MPs hauled me in: "I'm a new guy, I was transferred here last week, I didn't know!"

Lafferty's cruiser disappeared along with my brush with ambition. I may have known how to use a pistol, but there were other aspects of military life that I could not say in all honesty that I had mastered. The word "discipline" springs to mind.

I pulled away from the driveway and headed for 13th Avenue. As I cruised west I started thinking about calling the phone company and telling them that I was going to drop my phone service forever. That ought to shake up a few executives at Ma Bell. Heads might roll. This made me feel powerful. I was as high as a kite by the time I pulled into my parking lot. Which is to say, all the warning signs were present, yet I failed to see them. Any time I feel ambitious, optimistic, or hubris, it's time to yank the covers over my head.

I climbed the fire escape and entered the kitchen. My telephone rang.

I went into the living room and peered at the AudioMaster. "Please leave a message after the beep."

That was me—a cappella.

"Mr. Murphy? My name is Melanie Donaldson. If you're there could you please pick up the phone? The man at the taxi company said that sometimes you don't answer the phone even if you're at home."

There was only one man I knew of who was vile enough to reveal that information—Rollo!

I did not touch the receiver.

"I'm sorry to call you at home, but I really want to pay you back the money you loaned me. I'm the woman whom you drove to the Hyatt Hotel last Friday. I called the taxi company this morning and they said you would be working, so I came by at seven to see you, only you didn't show up for work, so I asked the man …"

I grabbed the receiver and lifted it to my ear. "Hello?"

"Hello?"

"Hello?" I said again. I hate telephones. "This is … Mr. Murphy."

"Oh! You're home!"

"I was in the tub." I blurted that out and regretted it immediately. Not a first for me.

"Oh I'm so happy I got in touch with you," she said. "I'm down in Denver today and I wanted to come by the taxi company and pay you the cab fare plus the loan you gave to me."

I slumped against the wall, raised my left palm to my face, and began rubbing my closed eyes.

"I appreciate that," I said, in a voice that did not reflect my inner turmoil. "But you didn't really have to do it."

"That's what you said on Friday, but I want to pay you back. Please don't let's argue. I hate bickering about money."

That pulled me up short.

"You're right," I said. "We won't. I'm sorry that I didn't make it to work." That was the first time in my life I ever said that. "I mean I'm sorry I made you drive all the way down here for nothing."

"I didn't come to Denver just for that," she said. "I have other business to take care of. I scored well on the post office test and I'm going to be moving down here. I'm already looking for an apartment."

"That's good to hear," I said. "Congratulations."

"Thank you. It makes me feel ecstatic!" she said. "Do I sound ecstatic?"

"Er … yeh," I said. David Niven couldn't have said it with more aplomb.

"The thing is, Mr. Murphy, I wanted to see you in person because I wanted to ask if I could buy you dinner at a restaurant tonight. If it hadn't been for you I never would have made it to the test on time, and I would really like to show you my appreciation."

This brought me to a screeching halt. Let's cut to the chase:

I didn't have a thing to wear—unless you counted a pile of T-shirts. But the only thing that kept me from turning down her offer was the fact that Melanie was pretty. I'll admit it. When she was in my taxi on Friday afternoon I kept glancing at my mirror and thinking how much more pretty she would be if she wasn't weeping, miserable, and frantic, which describes 28 percent of all my dates since college.

"You don't really have to buy me dinner," I said, then I bit my tongue because she had asked me not to bicker about money, and money is what people hunt for instead of buffalo in this modern plastic world.

"I have been told that taxi drivers always know the best places to eat," she said, driving right past my faux pas. "So I thought I would let you recommend the restaurant where I am going to buy dinner for you tonight."

I surrendered. I hope I don't have to explain that again. "Well … okay," I said. "I guess I could go for a free feed. But I'll let you buy me dinner under one condition."

"This is non-negotiable," she said.

"Okay. I promise to swallow my food under one condition—that you call me 'Murph'."

"That's acceptable, Murph. Where do we eat?"

I knew of only one restaurant in town where the waiters felt comfortable serving me. A little out-of-the-way bistro on the east side called Bombalini's.

"Do you like Italian food?" I said.

"Everybody likes Italian food," she said.

I had never considered that before. But she was right—anybody who doesn't like pizza is out of his gourd. What an insightful woman. "I know a nice place on east Colfax," I said. "They serve pizza and spaghetti."

"Is that all they serve?"

"That's all I ever order," I said. "But I think they sell other stuff, like lasagna and Rice-a-Roni. I've never fully examined the dinner items on the menu. They also serve wine and soda."

"Are we talking Denver or Rome?" she said.

"We're practically talking Aurora," I said. "It's out toward Fitzsimmons Army Hospital where President Eisenhower recovered from his coronary."

"You're making my mouth water, Murph. Would you like me to come by this evening and pick you up? I've already got a new car."

"Uuuh ..." I said, as cool as James Bond. "I have some things to do this afternoon so I'm not sure about my schedule." Now there was something I hadn't said in half a lifetime. "But I did get my car back, so I could drive to the restaurant and meet you in the parking lot."

"What do you mean, you got your car back?"

I bit my tongue again. "It was out for repairs but it's back now," I said, lying to a woman as usual. What is it with us guys?

"Okay, Murph. It's a date. Why don't I meet you at the restaurant around ... say ... sevenish?"

Sevenish. I hadn't heard anybody use that kind of language since the last time I was out in Hollywood. I wasn't making a movie though. I was looking for a teenage girl whom I had been suspected of murdering. I made a mental note not to mention that to Melanie.

CHAPTER 16

After we rang off I went into the bathroom and looked at my face in the mirror. I do this every time I have a date. I also do it when I shave. The two events sometimes coincide.

I stared at the mirror trying to remember the last time I had been on an "official" date. But I knew this wasn't an "official" date. It was more of a "virtual" date. It was still a date though, because Melanie had said as much. When it comes to splitting hairs I'm the demon barber of Fleet Street. As I said, I try to forget everything that ever happened to me during my life so I had trouble conjuring up my last official date. Unfortunately my 17 percent success rate included all my dates. I did remember a number of dates that I had in the army, mostly in the towns that were off-limits, but they weren't "official" dates, take my word for it.

I once dated a girl named Mary Margaret Flaherty, but that was long ago and in another town: Wichita. I once asked her to marry me but she turned me down. I do remember that. It's the main reason I live in Denver. After she said no, I fled Wichita and traveled around the country for a few years trying to "find" myself. I found myself in Cleveland, Pittsburgh, Baltimore, Philadelphia, Kansas City, Los Angeles, St. Louis, and Philadelphia again because I fell asleep on the bus. I passed through Seattle once but didn't stick around. I have never been to San Luis Obispo, and how many writers can say that? I know of one lucky bastard who can't.

It took me a long time to recover from Mary Margaret's refusal to marry me, though. I got over it when I went back to Wichita at Christmas and my brother Gavin gave me a word processor. I don't really understand the connection between my PC and Mary Margaret, but I have never questioned it. All I can say is, thank God for Bill Gates. If he hadn't parlayed DOS I would still be moping around.

I gave up on my face and went into the bedroom, opened my closet and looked at my taxi uniforms. I own multiples of everything. Not everything in the world, just in the taxi game. T-shirts, jeans, underwear, socks. That's everything. But I knew it was time to break down and do what I never had any reason to do before, which was to buy some decent clothes. The waiters at Bombalini's didn't mind serving me when I came in dressed like myself, but I think a lot of that had to do with my ponytail. The owner of the Italian restaurant is also my barber. His name is Gino Bombalini.

Every month I go to Gino's Barbershop for a free haircut. Gino is a man in his sixties, he's from the old country, and I once did him a favor— I helped his nephew overcome a chronic gambling problem. The odds of my success were slim, but that's Vegas for you. Ergo, Gino won't let me pay for haircuts or spaghetti dinners. I don't even know why I work anymore.

Suddenly the Heigger business faded from my mind. I couldn't have cared less what all that crap with the disappearing office meant, because I had a date with a pretty woman.

I calculated that I had six hours to get ready for the date. I could have been ready in six minutes except I had to buy some clothes. It had been so long since I had been on a date that I literally had to stop and think about the things that women expected of a man on a date, and clothes was one of them.

I also remembered something about corsages. I couldn't recall going to any proms in high school or college, but what has that got to do with my memory? Maybe the corsage flashback had to do with the job I once had delivering flowers. I got suspended from Rocky Cab after I became the main suspect in a kidnap, murder, and suicide deal that I really don't want to go into. As you can see, I have better success remembering my murder charges than my dates. While I was waiting around to be exonerated by the boys down at DPD, I delivered flowers for a living. I might have delivered some corsages to a few boys who got roped into wearing tuxedos, unless I'm thinking of movies about teenagers who dress up like adults and go to proms where terrible things happen. Proms are bellwethers of the future.

I decided to go to Cherry Creek Shopping Center to buy some clothes, but I won't drag you through the entire mall. When I arrived at Cherry Creek I parked as far away from the cabstand as possible and went in by a rear entrance. Taxi drivers hate to be seen "on the sidewalk" by other taxi drivers. It's like seeing your school teacher at a grocery store when you were a kid. If I have to explain that, then you were never a kid.

I got back to my crow's nest and unloaded my packages in the bedroom. I had bought a pair of what my Maw used to refer to as "trousers." By this she meant "pants." They were gray. From my perspective they were elegant yet subdued. I also bought a matching sports jacket. I almost bought a shirt that was blinding white, but for some reason a salesman stopped me from doing that. He was young and resembled George Lazenby. If you don't know who he was, consider yourself lucky. He looked as bored as hell wandering around the department store, which was virtually empty. But I knew that he was "keeping an eye" on me. This I was used to. Water off a duck's back. I had just draped the trousers across my left arm and was picking up the blinding white shirt when he came out of nowhere like James Bond and said, "May I help you, sir?" He had an anxious look on his face.

"I'm buying some clothes for a date," I said.

It was only after I walked out of the store that I realized he had virtually taken over my shopping trip. He asked me to try on the "slacks" as he called them. When I came out of the dressing room he folded his arms and started chewing on a thumbnail. Then he hurried over to a clothing rack and began picking out various shirts. He held them up to my chest like I was a mannequin. He didn't frown as deeply as dog-track security guards do, but there was a resemblance. He finally raised a pale-blue shirt and said, "This."

That's all he said.

Then he asked me if I intended to wear "those tennis shoes" on the date. I told him no. He asked me if I would mind telling him what I intended to wear. I thought he was getting rather familiar, but I told him I had a nice pair of brown dress shoes at home. The next thing I knew we were in the shoe department and he was holding up a pair of black shoes that were subdued yet inexpensive. I was sold.

The clerk was wiping his forehead with a handkerchief when I walked out of the store.

But here's the funny thing. After I took all the clothes out of the sack, a pair of black socks that I hadn't bought tumbled onto my bed. George must have accidentally stuffed them into the sack along with my shoes during the flurry at the cash register. I thought about taking them back to the store, but then I realized I did not have a receipt for the socks. What an ironic situation—it almost had the quality of a moral quandary. What was I to do? Try to return a pair of socks that I hadn't paid for? People went to jail for trying that.

But when it came to a toss-up between moral quandary and false imprisonment, I would take guilt any day. I kept the socks.

Let's jump ahead a few hours.

I went down the fire escape and approached my two-tone '64 Chevy—and suddenly I didn't want to climb in. I didn't want to sit on the seats wearing my new slacks. It was at this point that I started thinking it was time to buy a decent car. Maybe George would help me to buy a car that matched my shirt.

Well, there was nothing I could do. My date had already started. I climbed into my Chevy, pulled out of the parking lot, headed down to

Colfax Avenue and drove east toward Aurora. I arrived at Bombalini's with fifteen minutes to spare, but Melanie was already there. I hate being both early and late simultaneously. It throws off my metabolism.

Melanie was sitting in a late-model Plymouth when I pulled into the parking lot. I had an urge to ask how long she had been there. I recognized the urge though. Or perhaps I should say, my internal Univac recognized the urge and quickly analyzed it. It had to do with a desire to know how late I had arrived. The purpose of this analysis was to ameliorate the feeling of inferiority that I experienced at not arriving ahead of her. This urge did not apply only to racing women to parking lots, it had other applications in my life that were equally meaningless. I really did need some kind of goddamn therapy. But instead of bombarding Melanie with questions about her driving habits, I smiled and waved.

She climbed out of her car and said, "Hello, Murph!"

I heard that exclamation point. It had been a long time since I had heard a woman express delight at my arrival. Long, long time.

"Hello, Melanie," I said. "It's nice to see you again."

She was wearing a tight dress and carrying a small purse that matched her high-heeled shoes, but I don't want to get into a long-winded description of clothing—you probably had your fill of that during my shopping spree. I know I did.

Instead I'll give you a thumbnail sketch of Bombalini's. It was a small restaurant that seated perhaps thirty people maximum. The carpeting on the floor was a deep, dark red. The walls were wood-paneling halfway to the ceiling and the rest was red velvet wallpaper that always made me think of spaghetti sauce. There were booths along one wall, and tables in the center of the room. Small, lit candles rested in red glass cups on the tables. The overhead lighting was dim. Gino Bombalini is a romantic. He wasn't on the premises that night, but whenever I show up and he's there, he always asks me why I "no bring a date." So I felt a mild form of chagrin at the fact that he was not there to see me escort a pretty lady into his beanery.

Whenever I go for a haircut at his barbershop he tells me to look at the girly magazines on the table while I wait for my turn at the chair. The magazines are wrestling magazines that occasionally show pictures of women in bikinis. Gino thinks the bikinis will make me want to get married.

"Murph!" said the combination cashier/maître d' as Melanie and I entered the restaurant. His name was Luigi. He was a nephew of Gino. "Welcome to Bombalini's!" he chirped. Luigi was a good-looking kid in his early twenties, but I don't want to get into another long-winded description—let's just say he looked like that twenty year old in *The Godfather*.

He started to turn his face toward Melanie, but then his head jerked back toward me. He looked my wardrobe up and down, and his face went blank. He looked up to my head, and while I cannot say with certainty, I had the feeling he wanted to double-check my facial features in order to ascertain that it was actually me wearing tasteful attire.

"It is so good to see you back, Murph my friend. And what is the name of this lovely young lady?"

He gave Melanie that quick, subtle once-over that Italian males are so adept at. I knew right away that Uncle Gino would be getting a phone call later in the evening. I tried not to have mixed feelings about this, but all of a sudden I wasn't looking forward to my next haircut.

"Her name is Melanie," I said. "She's my date."

The second statement slipped out before I could bite my tongue. I really ought to get out more often.

Luigi escorted us to an interesting booth in one corner of the restaurant. It was a table for two, and interesting because it was built at a right-angle so the occupants practically sat on each other's laps as they chowed down. A number of large potted plants more-or-less hid the table from the view of the other customers. For obvious reasons, I had never been seated there before.

I remembered to wait until Melanie was seated, then I slid into the other 90-degree seat and managed not to bang her knees with mine. The upholstery was super soft. I felt like I was seated in the first-class section of an airliner headed for Reno.

"First things first," Melanie said. She opened her purse and reached in and pulled out two twenty-dollar bills and a ten. It took all of my will-power not to bicker with her, and I don't have much willpower to begin with. She had pretty much used it all up.

"Thanks," I said, automatically reaching toward my breast pocket. "You've got a dollar-forty coming."

"Keep it, cabbie," she said with a smile.

I'll admit it. I had felt tense and uncomfortable up to that point, but after Melanie tipped me I felt like I was sitting in the front seat of #123. I was in my element. I couldn't have been more cool, calm, and collected if I was parked in front of the Brown Palace eating a Twinkie.

Luigi brought us menus then discreetly evaporated.

I opened my menu and began perusing the dinner section. I felt like a phony. I knew I was going to order spaghetti even though I really wanted a pizza. I noted that Rice-a-Roni was not on the menu. I prayed that Melanie would not be annoyed.

"What would you like ...?" I said. I almost added "to eat" but stopped myself in time.

"I'm eating what you're eating, Murph," she said.

"Do you have a preference?" I said.

She closed her menu, set it on the table and looked me right in the eye. "Pepperoni pizza," she said.

I almost died right there in the booth. Who was this woman?

"Would you care for some wine?" I said.

"Thank you, but no," she said. "I never drink and drive. And I'll bet you don't either, do you cabbie?"

"That is correct," I said nonchalantly, as I closed my menu. "It is against the law to drink alcohol while driving a taxi."

Luigi took our order. After he brought us sodas he faded into the shadows.

That was the signal for The Dreaded Small-Talk to begin.

Melanie told me that the postal test was much easier than she had expected. She said she had received a letter in the mail telling her that she had passed, which she credited to the fact that she had studied. "There are books you can buy that have samples of previous tests," she said.

"I did not know that," I said. Had I known it when I had taken my own postal test I still would not have bought a book. I'll admit it. I did not really want to work for the post office. I only took the postal test for the same reason that I do everything: I exist.

"Do you enjoy driving a taxi?" she said.

By the time the pizza showed up, I had Melanie in stitches. I was telling her cab driving stories. I may have already told you a few of them. The interesting thing about my funny stories was that none of them were funny when they were happening to me. This was also true of my cab stories that weren't funny. I felt like I was homing in on an insight into the nature of storytelling, but then Melanie asked how I happened to be out in the boondocks when I came across her stalled car.

I set my crust on the plate and looked at her.

"I was taking a man to an address west of Wadsworth," I said. "You may have seen my cab go by on the gravel road."

"I didn't really notice," she said. "My car had been stalling on me for five minutes. I was freaking out."

"I know the feeling."

"Where was your fare going?" she said.

I shrugged. "It was just a house about a mile beyond the spot where your car broke down. I guess it was some sort of … office."

A lightbulb went on inside my head. I began to wonder the same thing that Melanie was wondering. What exactly was that building where

I had dropped off Weissberger? Not that its function mattered. What did matter was that I had dropped him off there. Maybe I could drive out there and see if I could track down Weissberger, and ultimately Heigger.

"Why are you frowning?" Melanie said.

I looked at her, then tried to remove the wrinkles from my face without using my hands.

I cleared my throat and said, "I was just thinking about something. I had a strange experience on Saturday."

"If it's anything like your other strange experiences, I want to hear it," she said giggling.

"No, it's nothing much, it's just that … on Friday I picked up that fare and took him to Broomfield, and then on Saturday I went to the place where I had picked him up but it was gone."

"What do you mean, gone?"

"It was a lawyer's office. But … the office had been cleared out. The lawyer wasn't there anymore."

"Where did he go?"

"I have no idea. The janitor told me …" I stopped abruptly.

"Told you what?" she said.

I raised my head and looked around the restaurant at the people who were eating real dinners. The place was packed but quiet. They were the kind of people I always think of as "clientele" rather than "customers." I didn't turn my head so much as my eyes. I was starting to get a funny feeling.

I cleared my throat again. "He told me that nobody was leasing the office. The lawyer must have moved out on Friday."

"Did the janitor say where the lawyer went?" she said. I shook my head no but didn't say anything more.

I picked up my napkin and dabbed at my lips, then said, "Would you excuse me for a moment, Melanie?"

"Certainly."

There was no need for further explanation—I think we both knew what I was getting at.

Bombalini's has a great men's room. It's down a hallway and around a corner and can accommodate only one occupant at a time. The door has a lock on it. When you use the can at Bombalini's you feel like you're flying first class.

I entered the room and locked the door, closed the lid on the toilet and sat down. I had to think. As I was talking to Melanie about the disappearing lawyer's office, a thought had come to me all at once. Melanie had said that she'd received her test score in the mail even though she had told me that she'd come to Denver at seven this morning—which meant she could not have received her mail unless she had driven back to Broomfield during the day, which I had no reason to believe she had done, since she told me she was in Denver on business other than buying me dinner. I glanced at my wristwatch. It was getting toward eight p.m.

I began to suffer from what is known in the world of big business as "creeping doubt." I had learned about that when I worked for Dyna-Plex. It has to do with business plans, but let's move on.

As I sat there on the lid of the can, events from the past few days began swirling around inside my mind like psychedelic background colors in the opening credits of half of the Roger Corman movies produced in the 1960s. Mr. Zelner's death, Mr. Heigger's disappearance, Weissberger's and Heigger's questions about Mr. Zelner's last words, the clicks on my AudioMaster, my stolen car, and most inexplicable of all, the fact that I was on a date.

Why would Melanie tell me she had read a letter that she could not have received?

I pictured Melanie leaning over the fender of her car out in the boondocks. And now we were in a restaurant and she was asking me questions related to Heigger.

The intensity of my funny feeling increased. Someone knocked on the door.

Startled, I stood up and flushed the toilet. I glanced around the restroom and noted that it did not have a window that a man could crawl out of if for some reason he wanted to.

I washed my hands at the sink, made a racket of yanking paper towels and drying my hands, then tossed the wadded paper into a wastebasket that had a pedal-operated lid. I braced myself and opened the door.

It was Enrico the dishwasher.

"Hey Murph!" he chirped. "That is some beautiful lady you are with tonight. Where did you meet her?"

"Broomfield," I said, as I strode past him.

CHAPTER 17

"Would you like dessert?" I said after I slid into the booth. "That's not the question," Melanie replied. "The question is would *you* like dessert."

"No," I said. "To me, pizza is dinner and dessert all rolled into one. I never eat dessert after dessert."

She smiled as if she was truly amused. This troubled me. I could not say for certain, but I could not recall ever getting along this well with a woman for such an extended period of time—four days, if you looked at The Big Picture.

"What were you doing out on that gravel road where your car broke down last Friday?" I said.

"What do you mean?" she said.

"I mean your car broke down out in the middle of nowhere. How come you were driving down that particular road on Friday?"

"I live in Ramblewoods," she said.

"What's that?"

"It's a subdivision west of Broomfield. I lived there with my husband for three years before we got divorced. I ended up with the house and Barbara."

"Barbara?"

"My six-year-old daughter," she said.

"Oh. I see. Is the gravel road the access to Ramblewoods?"

"No. A Hundred and Twentieth Avenue is the main access but I like to take the gravel road. It's one of those little-known shortcuts in the suburbs. There's less traffic. You must know what I'm talking about, being a cab driver."

"Yes I do," I said. "During the past fourteen years I have learned every shortcut in the Denver-metro area. I even invented a few of my own."

"I'll bet you did."

"So … did you go back home today to check your mail?" I said.

"Pardon me?"

"You said you got the results of your postal test in the mail today. Did you drive all the way back to Ramblewoods to check your mail?"

"No. Mrs. McNeary told me about it."

"Who is Mrs. McNeary?" I said.

"She babysits Barbara when I'm gone. I called her on the phone and she told me I had received a letter from the post office. I asked her to open it and read it to me. That's how I found out I passed the test."

I nodded. I had been thinking the worst thoughts I had ever thought about a pretty woman, I had been surreptitiously grilling her about her activities last Friday, and letting my imagination run away with me, when all she wanted to do was to buy me a meal in gratitude for helping her get a decent job to support herself and her six-year-old daughter. I began to feel like the walking embodiment of pure evil. Not a first for me.

I gazed down at the pizza crusts on my plate. I never eat the crusts. This bothers a lot of people that I don't eat pizza with anymore.

I sighed. "It must be great to pass a test," I said.

"Haven't you ever passed a test?" she said.

I looked up at her. "That's open to conjecture. I suppose I must have passed a few tests. I graduated from both high school and college."

"Where did you go to college?"

"Oooh … let's see … Kansas Agricultural University in Wichita, and UC Denver. That's where I got my diploma."

"What was your major?"

"English."

"Did you plan to become a teacher?"

"No. I've never planned to do anything."

"Have you been driving a taxi for fourteen years?"

"What?"

"You told me that you learned a lot of shortcuts during the past fourteen years. I just wondered if that was how long you have been driving a taxi."

"Yes. I've been driving for fourteen years."

"Well since you say you never plan anything, can I ask if you intend to do anything other than drive a cab?"

"No. I have no other intentions."

She nodded and looked down at her plate. Not a crust in sight. A silence fell over the booth.

I decided not to tell Melanie about my plans to become a rich novelist. I decided I would never tell that to anybody again as long as I lived— possibly even myself.

"Murph?"

I looked up at Melanie. "Yes?"

She sat up straight in the booth and scooted a little closer to me. I felt her knee touch mine. She reached out and placed a hand on my forearm. "I really do appreciate what you did for me last Friday."

I nodded. I no longer trusted my mouth to do anything except eat. She squeezed my arm and said, "I'm staying in Denver overnight. I have a room at the Hyatt. If you don't have anything to do after we leave here, I was wondering if you would like to come back to my place for a ... cup of coffee."

Roger Corman suddenly sat down in the booth next to Melanie. His face was a mass of swirling psychedelic colors. The notion that a beautiful woman would ask me to come with her to a hotel was so off-the-charts ludicrous that it completely destroyed my willing suspension of disbelief.

It was at this point in time that something else peculiar about Melanie's story occurred to me. I began to feel uneasy again.

"It's not that I don't want to," I heard myself saying, "but my fiancée probably wouldn't like it."

"Are you engaged to be married?"

"Yes."

"What's her name?"

"Mary Margaret Flaherty."

I felt the pressure ease off my arm.

I looked down at the tabletop. Melanie had clasped her hands together. "She's a lucky lady," Melanie said.

"Luck of the Irish," I replied.

"When is the wedding?"

"That's open to conjecture," I said. "Irish men have a great deal of difficulty, you know."

"With what?"

"You name it."

Melanie clasped her hands tighter and her shoulders drooped perceptibly. "Tell Mary Margaret I envy her."

"That would probably not be advisable."

Melanie started laughing with her mouth closed. Women are good at that.

"Thank you for the dinner, Melanie," I said. "I appreciate the gesture. When you get back home, say hello to your daughter Barbara for me."

"I will."

"Well, I have to get up at the crack of dawn to work tomorrow, so I guess it's about that time," I said.

She nodded.

We both arose from the angle-iron. We went to the front counter where Luigi was manning the cashier.

"One large pepperoni pizza and two sodas," I said to him.

Luigi laughed and shook his head no. "Your money is no good in this place, you know that, Murph."

"This meal is on me," Melanie said. Luigi's hair almost stood on end.

"I am sorry, Miss Melanie, please forgive me, but ... did I hear you correctly?" Luigi said. "Do you wish to pay for this meal?" His Italian accent seemed to increase threefold as he said this.

"I'm buying dinner for Murph," Melanie said, opening her purse.

I could see confusion in Luigi's eyes. On the one hand I always got free meals at Bombalini's. On the other hand a female wanted to pay for a male's dinner. Luigi was just a kid. He didn't know how to deal with this. It was like an Italian moral quandary. I would have felt sorry for him except it struck me as funny. For some reason it made me think of exploding tires.

After Melanie paid, I escorted her outside to her car. She dug through her purse and pulled out the keys, then looked up at me with a smile. "Thanks again for helping me get to the test on time," she said.

I had the feeling she wanted to hug me like she had at the Hyatt. As much as I wouldn't have minded that, I nevertheless didn't want to hug her. Consequently I incorporated body language to indicate that I was not available for a hug. I know what you're thinking—I must have been out of my gourd. But I had a funny feeling about Melanie and for some reason I didn't want to give her the idea that I didn't. My body language apparently worked because she unlocked her door, got in, and shut it.

I would have been surprised if my body language hadn't worked because I had been perfecting body language most of my life, specifically the language which indicates that I do not want to do something. This involves slack facial muscles as well as backing away from an individual without actually moving my feet. It's difficult to communicate the subtle nuances ... as difficult as trying to explain how to ride a unicycle. Believe it or not, I know how to ride a unicycle. But I don't do that anymore. The unicycle is a young man's game.

Melanie rolled down her window and smiled up at me. "Maybe I'll be seeing you around, cabbie," she said.

I nodded. "See you on the asphalt."

She rolled up her window. I waited as she backed out of the slot and drove toward the exit. She stopped to let traffic pass on Colfax. I glanced at her rear window and noted that it did not sport a paper license plate indicative of a newly purchased car. Ergo, I glanced at the license plate on the rear bumper, and although I was standing motionless, what I saw stopped me even colder. The license plate indicated that her car was a rental. Interpreting license plates is somewhat of a cabbie thing, and to a certain extent, a guy thing.

I watched her pull onto Colfax and head west. I had the urge to hop into my Chevy and follow her.

I fought the urge successfully. Tailing anyone in my two-tone junk heap would have taxed the skills of the most surreptitious private investigator. I almost laughed at the thought.

But I didn't laugh.

Melanie had told me she'd gotten a new car, and yet the car she was driving was a rental. This dovetailed in an abstract way with the uneasy feeling I had when she squeezed my arm and asked me to come to the Hyatt with her. Melanie had explained that her babysitter had read the letter over the phone. This was plausible except for one thing—I had taken the post office test twenty years earlier and I remembered receiving a letter containing my score a few weeks after the test was over. There must have been two hundred people in the auditorium that day. It was like taking a college entrance exam. Yet Melanie claimed that her results had arrived by mail in three days, which included a weekend when nobody in the government works.

I had spent two years in the army so I knew a little bit about the functioning of the federal government, and one thing we soldiers never did was work on weekends unless there was a big inspection coming up, or else the commanding officer was a fanatic who believed the communists couldn't take over America as long as we mopped the latrines for three hours every Saturday morning. His name was Captain Gertler. I lasted six weeks under his command.

But even if there had not been two hundred people at the Hyatt on Friday, how could the postal authorities have graded the tests and mailed out the results in so short a time—and over a weekend?

I watched Melanie's rental disappear down Colfax Avenue, then I looked around the parking lot. My car was thirty feet away. I began casually moving toward it. All of the thoughts that had been bothering me when I was seated on the can in Bombalini's began coming back: Zelner's death, Heigger's disappearance, the subtle questions, my stolen car, my phone, and the fact that I was on a date with a woman who had told me lies.

I got into my car fast. I didn't have to unlock it. I think I have a subconscious hope that it will get stolen permanently and I will never have to deal with it again. This ties in with my perpetual reluctance to make decisions that I might regret, i.e., every decision I ever make.

I took 13th Avenue back toward Capitol Hill. I felt uneasy during the entire ride. When I pulled into the parking lot behind my building I looked up to see if the kitchen light was on. If it had been on I would have driven to the nearest phone booth and called Ottman and Quigg. But my place was dark. I got out of the Chevy and climbed the fire escape as lightly as possible. I didn't want my crow's nest to vibrate—my first line of defense against visitors.

I stood in the darkness above the rooftops of Denver and pressed my ear against the door and listened for a little bit. I didn't hear anything. I inserted my key in the lock and quietly opened the door. The ambient light cast from a distant street pole lit my apartment. I wished then that I had embraced the habit of most people and made a point to leave a light on in my place whenever I left, but until recently I'd never had anything worth stealing. I admit that this is a skewed form of logic, because burglars obviously wouldn't know that I wasn't sitting on a fortune up there in the sky. But junkies probably aren't particular—they could doubtless pawn an AudioMaster DeLuxe answering machine for a couple of bucks to feed their vile craving for a quick fix in needle park.

I left the back door open, stepped inside, and opened my refrigerator to put a little light on the matter—40 watts to be exact. I entered the living room and quickly turned on the overhead light and backed up into the kitchen, but I won't drag you through the 12 Steps of Paranoia upon which I based my recovery from optimism, a disease that I had suffered from during the first five years of my life.

After every light in my crow's nest was blazing, I took an inventory and found that everything appeared to be the way I had left it when I went on my date. I closed the kitchen door and ratcheted closed a deadbolt affixed near the bottom edge of the door and which had never been used during the years that I had lived in the apartment. It was an eight-inch length of steel that was rusted stuck. I had to get a hammer to loosen the thing.

I looked at my wristwatch. 9:15.

It was at this point that I stepped back and took a long look at all of the jams I had gotten into as a cab driver, and suddenly the solution to my paranoia came to me. I would just pretend that none of this had ever happened. So what if Heigger's office had disappeared and Weissberger had asked me questions about Mr. Zelner's last words and Melanie had lied to me—I stopped making a list then because I was beginning to talk myself out of my plan. But one thing I had learned during my fourteen years as an asphalt warrior was that you could not solve a problem that refused to show its face.

As far as Melanie was concerned I would take her at face value—a divorced woman with a six-year-old daughter, an ex-waitress who had gotten an early report on a postal test and who simply wanted to thank me for helping her out. Hell, maybe she had lied about the rental because she was too embarrassed to admit that she couldn't afford to buy a car. I could understand that. While I myself did not invent the practice of lying about being broke, I can say with a certain amount of humility that I raised it to an art form.

Pretend none of this had ever happened. That was the essence of my "plan."

Buoyed by the fact that I was once again descending into the opium den of denial, I went into the bedroom, kicked off my dancing shoes, and collapsed into bed.

CHAPTER 18

I woke up Tuesday morning in a state of total pretense. It felt great. I made a breakfast of cheese, bread, and soda, then went into the living room and watched a little TV before starting out the day. As far as I was concerned this Tuesday was no different from all the other Tuesdays of the past few months, except that I was working. Tuesday was my normal day off. This helped to enhance the feeling of pretense that I knew would buoy my spirits throughout the day.

There are few feelings in the world quite as good as pretending that everything is fine. As numerous people have said to me during my lifetime, "It's all in the mind, Murph." While I understood that "it" was not all in the mind, I also understood that most of it was. For instance, taxes are not all in the mind, but if you pretend you're making a down payment on a pet snail darter, it can get you through April 15th with a feeling of personal empowerment unrivaled by any brand of beer.

I put on my jacket and cap, pulled my starting cash out of *Lolita*, grabbed my briefcase and toolbox, and headed out the door. When I got to Rocky Cab I walked into the on-call room still pretending that this was just another typical taxi Tuesday. I do drive on Tuesdays during what I call "rent week"—five days in a row of driving to make enough dough to pay Keith. But I do that only once a month unless my life is going to hell in a hatbox.

The jury was still out on this week.

I played it cool. I smiled at Rollo and handed him seventy bucks. He handed me a trip-sheet and the key to #123. I didn't explain what I was doing there on a Tuesday. I felt that this would adequately stick in his craw.

I went outside, found 123 in the parking lot, and checked it for dents and dings. Everything was copacetic. I drove to my usual 7-11 and bought my usual Twinkie, joe, and gas, then headed for the Brown Palace Hotel. I cruised to 18th and Tremont and turned left. There were three taxis at the cabstand: a Rocky and two Yellows. I always figure a ten-to-fifteen minute wait per cab, so my waiting time would have topped out at forty-five minutes—if I had pulled in at the end of the line.

It was at this precise moment in time that I stopped pretending that it was a typical taxi Tuesday. Instead, I drove past the cabstand and began working my way toward the Valley Highway.

Destination: North Denver.

I linked up with Speer Boulevard and crossed the valley via the same viaduct that I had driven on the previous Wednesday when Mr. Zelner had died in my backseat. As I passed the middle of the viaduct I heard Mr. Zelner say, "Can you elude him?" I was just pretending of course, although I did look into the rearview mirror to make certain I was pretending.

After I crossed over, I made my way up to the business park of Diamond Hill. I pulled into the same slot where I had parked on Wednesday. After I shut off the engine, a silence fell over my cab, not counting the roar of traffic on I-25.

I climbed out and looked around at the office buildings on the hill. They looked like Tech Center buildings, as do all office buildings constructed in America nowadays. I could have designed those buildings.

Architects.

Give me a break.

I pulled my Rocky cap tighter on my head, zipped my Rocky jacket up to my neck, and entered the nearest building. I stopped in the foyer to peruse the names of the businesses posted on a large framed rectangle on the wall—black background, white letters, you've been there. I searched for Heigger & Associates. No dice. I walked up to the receptionist and pinched the brim of my cap. I told her I was from the Rocky Mountain Taxicab Company and I was looking for a lawyer named Heigger, who had an office called Heigger & Associates. She told me there was no such business in the building. I believed her. When I had worked for Dyna-Plex there was a receptionist in our office named Linda. She knew everything that was going on in the office. To my knowledge, she was the only person who knew what was going on, although it had never occurred to me to ask her how Dyna-Plex made its money. To this day I still don't know. And I care even less.

I asked the receptionist if a lawyer named Heigger had come into this building on Thursday to make an inquiry about a man named Mr. Zelner. She said she did not recall any such visitor.

I walked into all the office buildings on Diamond Hill and pulled my cabbie act. Again no dice. As I headed back to my taxi empty-handed, I wondered what made me think this was an "act." After all, I really was a cabbie—and I really was looking for Heigger & Associates. The situation had the quality of a brain teaser. I almost got distracted trying to figure out the answer.

I tried to focus. That rarely works, especially when I'm entering the last stages of giving up on my Rubik's Cube, but I managed to climb into my cab and start the engine without staring vacantly at nothing.

I drove away from Diamond Hill.

I had been hoping that Heigger might have moved his office up there, even though the hope was the size of a molecule like most of my hopes—it wasn't even big enough to possess the quality of a hunch. But I had given it a shot because I had learned long ago not to assume that something wasn't true just because I had thought of it.

Next stop: the Hyatt.

I drove to the hotel and pulled into the parking lot. There were no cabs at the stand, but I didn't park there. As I said, I never park at the Hyatt because it's not very active. I was no Mr. Vegas but I knew enough about odds to know that a businessman would probably come rushing out the door if I pulled up at the cabstand. I had some business of my own to take care of, so I parked as far away from the stand as possible, hidden behind a panel truck.

I climbed out of 123, gave the bill of my cap a tug, touched the zipper of my jacket for no reason, and walked toward the entrance. When I got inside, I walked up to the man at the front desk and introduced myself.

"A fare named Melanie Donaldson called for a taxi twenty minutes ago," I lied. "I expected her to be waiting outside but she isn't there. Can you tell me if she's checked out yet?"

"Let me look at my register," he said.

It's amazing the doors that a taxicab uniform will open. If I had walked in looking like I normally do, he probably would have called the house dick.

"I'm sorry, sir, but I have no record of a Melanie Donaldson staying at our hotel," he said.

I nodded and began pulling at my chin with my right hand, holding it the way you do when you want to create a shadow-show of a quacking duck: fingers together, thumb extended. I can also do a silhouette of Richard Nixon, which is always a crowd-pleaser at parties, but that takes two hands.

"I brought her here in my taxi last Friday," I said. "But maybe she didn't actually register. She came here for the post office test."

He gave me a blank look and said, "There was no postal test here last Friday."

"Pardon me?"

"There was no … postal test … held here … last Friday," he said, as if he was talking to someone who didn't speak English. I am acquainted with people who seem to think that if they holler their sentences, foreigners will magically comprehend English. I call that "Blitzkrieg Berlitz." But this guy's approach was to speak very slowly and distinctly.

It worked.

"No post office test?" I said.

He frowned at me and said, "Yes sir, that is correct." He sort of talked like Franklin Pangborn—but what desk clerk doesn't? He picked up a sheaf of papers and pretended to work with them so that I would go away. I recognized the move. I patented it.

"Were there any tests at all held here last Friday?" I said.

He set the papers down, tilted his head back slightly, and rolled his eyeballs to the one o'clock position. Franklin Pangborn patented that one.

"No, sir. No gatherings of that sort took place here last Friday, although there was a wedding reception held in the ballroom." He rolled his eyes downward and gazed at me in the same way that a person might look at an uninteresting tree.

I had the urge to say something sarcastic that would bring his world crashing down around his shoulders. But then I thought of William, and of all the palace guards in Denver with whom I got along well. Pangborn here was kind of like a distant relative of those doormen. I began to empathize with him. It was obvious that he was forced by the immutable laws of hostelry to deal with people like me every day. "Thank you for the information, sir," I said. I turned and walked out of the Hyatt.

I crossed the parking lot toward the panel truck knowing full well that a businessman would be standing next to my cab looking around with an impatient frown and wondering what a driverless cab was doing in a real-person slot when it should be parked obsequiously at the cabstand.

I was wrong.

I like being wrong when I'm expecting the worst—but that's just me, Mr. Negative.

I climbed into 123 and sat there for a moment wondering why Melanie would lie to me about a postal test. I considered the fact that she had invited me to the Hyatt on Monday night, which meant that she must have been staying here. Unless—unless she had registered under a different name. But why would a woman not use her real name when registering at a hotel, and then invite a man …

I stopped thinking then. The answer was on the tip of my tongue. I didn't like what that tongue was about to say. I decided to go back to my original plan and pretend that none of this had ever happened. I didn't know what else to do. But the one thing I did know was not to get involved in the personal life of a fare. As far as I could remember, I had never actually applied that knowledge to a real-life situation, but I "knew" about it in the way that I "knew" algebra was a form of mathematics.

I backed out of the slot, swung around the parking lot, and cruised past the front of the hotel hoping a businessman would come running out waving frantically with his coattails flying. I've always wanted to see that outside of a comic strip.

CHAPTER 19

I had wasted more than an hour of my normal driving day. This meant I would have to work hard in order to avoid toppling the delicate balance of my monthly finances. Of course this didn't mean much. After all, I could earn a fifty-dollar profit in eight hours if I took calls off the radio. I could net ninety dollars in eight hours if put out a little more effort. And if I busted my hump, the potential was wide open. But I hadn't busted my hump in a long time. The last time I did it, the situation involved The Dreaded Weekend Lease—I drove virtually non-stop during a three-day weekend in order to avoid a sense of guilt. The upshot of that hump was a lifetime of free haircuts and spaghetti dinners, but let's move on.

I drove to the Brown Palace and got in line at the cabstand. There were four taxis ahead of me, which gave me plenty of time to take care of one last thing before I dove into the asphalt fray. I had to prepare myself mentally for taking calls off the radio. Whenever I waste an hour or more I get nervous and try to play catch-up by using the radio. The prep includes shifting my mind into a mode of thought similar to Transcendental Meditation except I keep my eyes open while I think about absolutely nothing. It is incumbent upon me to think of nothing when I have a hard day, otherwise I am nearly crushed flat by the realization that I am working hard.

Since I was fourth in line I didn't have to worry about getting a trip from the hotel. I was able to sit there for five minutes dolefully wishing I hadn't wasted an hour. But I was merely pretending that I was in line at the cabstand, even though I actually was in line at the cabstand, but not really. I was simply prepping. I don't know why it's called "prepping"—it's just a modified form of denial. I understand that pole-vaulters prep before an Olympic jump. I have no idea what Olympic athletes are denying prior to picking up that fiberglass pole, and I don't want to know.

I finally sighed and started my engine, pulled away from the Brown, and started listening to the radio.

I jumped one bell after another. I didn't think about the paperback lying in my briefcase, or stopping off for joe and Twinkies, or *The After-noon Movie* that I was missing on a Tuesday. I had gotten pretty good at thinking about nothing when I was in high school—as soon as the nun said, "Open your arithmetic books," my mind went blank.

"Care if I smoke?" a fare said. "Go right ahead, sir."

Some drivers don't let fares smoke in their cab. I call these drivers "tip destroyers." I let fares do whatever they want in my backseat as long as it doesn't involve firearms. I once let two hippie girls smoke pot in my backseat, but not on purpose. They sort of slipped that one past me. That was another one of those kidnap/homicide deals that had a happy ending. When it comes to happy endings my life is a regular Andy Hardy movie. Have I ever mentioned the fact that I once saw Mickey Rooney in person? If so, I promise not to bring it up again.

But I like the smell of cigarette smoke. I know you're not supposed to admit to a fondness for cancer-causing carcinogens, but the odor of burning tobacco takes me back to the days when I earned twenty grand a year writing brochures. I smoked a pack a day at Dyna-Plex. My lungs dread the day when I will finally wise up and get another job utilizing my English degree. Sometimes I think about becoming an English teacher, but this gets me laughing so hard that I don't see how I could possibly stand in front of a classroom full of young people and talk seriously about the subjunctive case, whatever the hell that is.

Once in a while I get a cigar or pipe smoker in my backseat, but mostly it's cigarettes, and even then it's only a couple times a week.

And I would say that the majority of the smokers come out of bars, but don't get me started on meaningless statistics. That's the government's job.

At six-thirty that evening I dropped a fare off at a bar on Larimer Square. I noticed that he had a pack of cigarettes in his breast pocket. It was uncracked. Maybe he smoked only when he drank. I once played that game. Let's move on.

I earned seventy-two dollars in profits that Tuesday. I was hoping to earn only fifty. That would have made me feel like a chopper pilot. I had been steering a steady course—not too fast, not too slow, keeping my velocity and altitude in check and planning to set 'er down on the landing pad at 0+0. But then a couple of easy calls came over the radio, the money was fast and good, and I subsequently lost sight of my mission. I came out twenty-two dollars ahead. I felt ashamed of my inability to control my craving for money, but I'm used to shame.

I arrived at the motor at ten minutes to seven. I finished filling out my trip-sheet, then took a minute to clean up the cab so it would be in good condition for the night driver. I yanked the metal ashtrays out of the backseat armrests and carried them to the trash barrel by the garage and began shaking them out. I heard a "clink." The only time my ashes clink is when a fare slips unwanted pennies into an ashtray. I looked into the trash barrel to see if they might perhaps be quarters, but instead I saw a key.

My hands froze.

The key was covered with cigarette ash.

I started shaking the ashtrays again, glancing surreptitiously to my left and right. I carried the trays back to 123 and placed them into the armrests, then got into the front seat and pretended to fiddle with my trip-sheet. But in fact I was staring at the trash barrel inside my brain. I was picturing what I had just seen at the bottom of the barrel.

How many smokers did I have in my taxi today?

That's what I asked myself. There were at least two smokers, a guy dressed in jeans and wearing a red cap that a long-haul truck driver might wear. He had come out of a bar. The other was a woman who had come out of Saks at the Cherry Creek Shopping Center. A lot of cab drivers don't bother cleaning ashtrays at the end of a shift. They are like me when I was a kid—they leave the mess for someone else to clean up. You may have experienced this yourself, either as a kid or a parent.

I also recalled that Mr. Zelner had smoked a cigarette on Wednesday night. When the cop stopped me, Mr. Zelner had put out the cigarette in the ashtray and snapped the lid shut.

I sat in my cab staring at the trash barrel and thinking about a time in college when I was walking home from a bar and saw a cellophane baggie filled with white powder lying in the middle of the street. It took five minutes of wandering up and down the block to work up the nerve to pick up the baggie. I waited until there was no traffic. I was in pretty good shape in those days because I had recently spent two years in the army drinking beer, so I figured I could run away from whoever had planted the powder in order to illegally entrap an innocent sucker. I could jump fences pretty well in those days—and take my word for it, there are plenty of fences on army bases. But the baggie turned out to be filled with powdered plaster of Paris that must have been dropped by a customer who had come from a hobby shop farther up the block. I subsequently was relieved to know that I would not be compelled to carry a baggie full of raw skag to the local police station and explain to a narc what I was doing helping to clean up the neighborhood at midnight like a good citizen.

I looked around the parking lot to make sure it was deserted. Given the fact that there were dozens of taxis that a mugger could hide behind, my caution was as moot as ever. I finally got out of my cab and walked over to the trash barrel. I leaned down and grabbed the key. I raised it

and blew the ash off the "crang" or the "bozart," or whatever the nomen-
clature of the round part of a key is—I'm sure a locksmith could tell me.
Engraved in the metal was the number "96." It was the kind of key that is
used for public lockers that are found in airports and bus stations—and
railroad stations. I had used keys like that during my drifter years. I rode
a lot of buses in those days. I would stuff my duffle bag into a locker
before desperately seeking a bar.

I knew that there were probably lockers of that type all over Denver,
possibly including the YMCA, although I had never worked out at the
Y—but don't get me started on people who jog, swim, or eat smart.

I went back to my cab and picked up my accoutrement then walked
into the on-call room. Rollo was still on duty. I placed the key into my
T-shirt pocket and stepped up to the window.

"Hi, Rollo," I said in as friendly a tone as possible in order to fi-
nesse any mind games that might have occurred to Rollo the moment
he saw me.

"Hello," he replied enigmatically.

I slid the trip-sheet and key to 123 beneath the window. Rollo placed
the key on a hangar. The wall to his left has scores of tiny hangers for
taxi keys. The wall behind him holds the shotgun. The wall to his right
has a calendar that depicts scenes from *Stars Wars*. I always suspected
that it belonged to Rollo but I was afraid to ask. He had the personality
characteristics of someone who collected comic books. This troubled me
because I had them, too. I own a mint condition Indiana Jones #1, but
let's move on.

"Is Hogan in his office?" I said.

"He went home an hour ago," Rollo said.

"Did he leave any messages for me?"

"Not that I know of."

I heard the door to the on-call room open.

I glanced quickly to my left. It was Stew. He was coming in to take over the graveyard shift. I realized I had a rare opportunity to see Rollo "outside the cage." I was usually gone by the time Rollo and Stew traded chairs. But I had too many things on my mind to take advantage of the situation. What the advantage might have been I could not say, but I didn't stick around to find out.

"See you later," I said to Rollo. That was the feeblest parting volley I had ever hurled, but I wanted to get home.

As I walked toward the door, Stew saw me and stopped dead in his tracks. "Murph!" he said.

But did he exclaim it? Or did I merely imagine the exclamation point. My nerves were raw. "What?" I replied.

"Did you get that problem solved?" he said.

"What problem?"

"The problem you called about on Saturday night."

"Oh that problem."

I hesitated to say no because if he found out I hadn't solved the problem he might become further involved—he might even go so far as to try to "help" me. I hate it when people try to help me with my problems because their "help" always takes the form of advice. It never involves large sums of money.

"Yeah," I lied. "Thanks for the help."

"No problem."

I walked out of the on-call room and headed for my Chevy. I climbed in, started the engine, and drove straight home. No stopping at a burger joint. I had to think. This meant I would have to cook my own burger. This would give me five minutes to think while the meat sizzled on the grill. I just prayed that I didn't start thinking so hard that I forgot I was cooking a hamburger. Been there. Doused that.

I pulled into the parking lot behind my building and looked up to see if the kitchen light was on. It wasn't.

I climbed the fire escape and didn't bother being paranoid. I unlocked the door and walked into the kitchen and opened the refrigerator. The 40-watt gave me enough light to see my way into the living room where I turned on the overhead light. I stashed my profits and accoutrement, then pulled the locker key out of my T-shirt pocket and stared at it.

Beneath the light of the living room bulb I could see that it was still dusted with fine ash. I blew on it, then went into the bathroom and grabbed a square of toilet paper and washed the key as well as I could. My fingers were slightly blackened from the ash, so I took a moment to wash my hands. I set the key on the sink and scrubbed. After I dried my hands I picked up the key and noted that there were a few drops of water on it, so I began drying it with a towel.

Suddenly I stopped.

I realized I was developing a psychological tic.

What the hell was I doing washing and drying everything in sight when I might have in my possession the key to a mystery that had been plaguing me since Wednesday? It reminded me of college. Whenever I had a bad hangover I would do my laundry. I think it had something to do with symbolism. Did I ever mention the fact that I majored in English?

"Okay Murph, settle down," I said out loud.

I might as well admit it. I frequently talk out loud when I'm alone. I do it when I'm walking through shopping malls, too—also in my cab. To be honest, I doubt if I have ever been any place alone where I didn't say something out loud—with the exception of police stations. Whenever the police leave me alone in a small room I make a conscious and deliberate effort to say nothing out loud. My success rate is 100 percent.

I set the key on the kitchen table, then went to the fridge and started to pull out a pre-shaped hamburger patty. But I stopped myself. I had been forgetting a lot of things lately, and the last thing in the world I wanted right now was to forget a hamburger browning over an open flame. Oh sure, when I was younger I liked a challenge and enjoyed measuring the capacity of my mind to juggle two concepts at once. But who isn't like that when he's in his twenties, when he's footloose and fancy-free and doesn't have a care in the world? A guy in his twenties likes to push the envelope, take chances, ask women out on dates when he knows he hasn't got a snowball's chance in hell or a dime in his pocket. Okay. I'll admit it. Asking a woman for a date when I was broke entailed no risk because of the snowball deal, but still, it was exciting to walk up to a woman at a party and say, "Do you live alone?" Nine times out of ten her husband would lean in and say, "No she doesn't," which only added to the thrill of sipping scotch from a tin flask and barking lines from John Garfield movies.

I seem to have gotten off the track here.

I closed the refrigerator and walked into the living room holding the key in the palm of my hand.

I thought back over the events of the past week, of the death of Mr. Zelner, who must have put the key into the ashtray before he died. Was he afraid the police might find it on him? I didn't know, but there were people in this world who might be able to give me a glimmering of an idea, such as Mr. Heigger with his questions about valises and his disappearing law office.

"What law office!" Burt Reynolds hollered.

And that supe with his sensible pants—sure, he had given me straight answers to my questions, and had even admitted who he was. But I had gotten enough straight answers in my lifetime to know that telling the truth was one of the most effective evasive maneuvers ever invented. Whenever anyone gives me a straight answer to a question, a little bell goes off inside my head that makes me wonder what he's up to. Sure, nine times out of ten he's hoping a straight answer will cause me to go away, but what about reason number ten?

I began walking in circles in my living room, which was easy because I own practically no furniture. A TV. A chair. Plenty of room to think. To think about Weissberger with his fond memories of his old school chum, Heinrich. He had inquired about Mr. Zelner's last words, just as Mr. Heigger had. And what about Melanie? Somehow during my free feed she had worked the conversation around to the business of Mr. Heigger and the missing law office. How had she done that?

I began tossing the key up and down in my hand, bouncing it off the stretched skin of my palm. I tried to trace our conversation back to its beginning. How in the hell did Melanie and I get onto the subject of Heigger and Weissberger and the disappearing law office? Was she in on this, too? Were all three of them working together? What in the hell was going on?

I stopped bouncing the key. I was kind of enjoying it and I was afraid I might develop a tic that would lead me to invent a toy that could entertain children for hours on end like the hula-hoop, or that goddamn Rubik's Cube. How in the hell did Rubik think up the Cube anyway? Forget the idea of matching the colored squares, I could have thought that up, but how did he design a toy that could be twisted in any direction?

I suddenly had the urge to get my Rubik's Cube and rip the damned thing apart and find out the real mystery.

I tried to focus.

I walked into the kitchen and looked out the window. It was dark. Storm clouds were brewing. It was starting to rain. There was nothing I wanted more right at that moment than to go down to Union Station and try to open locker #96 to see if Mr. Zelner had stashed something in there on the night he had died. The part of my brain that I sometimes referred to as "insane" made me want to do that. You wouldn't believe some of the insane things I have done in my life. For instance, one time I spent Christmas with my family. I don't want to talk about it.

It was the part of my brain that I sometimes referred to as the "stranger" that caused me to step away from the window and drop the idea of driving down to Union Station in a night so rainy it could have been a Xerox of the night Mr. Zelner died.

I walked back into the living room and stared at the key in my palm. I was beginning to develop an awful lot of psychological tics and if I didn't eliminate them one by one in the near future I was in for a big fall. I decided there was only one thing to do. The "stranger" started to say something but I told him to clam up and amscray. I wanted to find out what the hell was happening here.

On the one hand, I had something working in my favor: nobody knew I had the key to locker #96 at Union Station—or perhaps I should say a key to a locker #96. I didn't know for a fact that it was a Union Station key, but we've had that conversation.

On the other hand, out of four of the strangers whom I had encountered since Wednesday night inclusive, one of them was dead, number two and number three had disappeared after asking me similar questions, and the fourth one had told me peculiar lies. I'm talking Melanie Donaldson—or "Octavia Brandenburg" for all I knew. Her and her rental car and her splendid test score. I now regretted not going with her to the Hyatt on Monday night—though not for the reason that might pop into the minds of crude people, but because it might have clarified for me her role in this mystery. What had she really wanted from me? But if I had gone with her, I might have ended up regretting it for reasons other than the reasons crude people regret things. In other words—again—of the four strangers I had encountered since Wednesday night, one of them was dead.

I thought back over the encounters with Heigger and Weissberger and "Octavia," which I now preferred to call her because "Melanie" was just too damned wholesome. Nobody named Melanie would date a guy like me.

Both Heigger and Weissberger had asked if Mr. Zelner had said anything to me before he died. And the only reason Octavia had not asked might have been due to the fact that my paranoia caused me to cut short our date. If I had gone back to the hotel with her, she might have plied me with drink. She might have worked the conversation around to the conversation that I'd had with Weissberger, and I might have mentioned what Zelner had said about eluding the police because he was late for an appointment. I could just see myself doing that, especially if Octavia offered me a glass of wine and then said she wanted to "slip into something more comfortable."

Fer the luvva Christ.

I had been around plenty of comfortable clothes before, and believe me, they can get mighty interesting.

I went back to the kitchen and looked out the window. It was raining buckets, the kind of buckets that farmers use to milk cows—I'm talking big-assed galvanized tin. It was the kind of rainstorm that a man could get lost in. By this I mean the kind of storm that could camouflage a man's moves, especially at night—especially if he was being followed.

I slipped the key into my T-shirt pocket, then went to the closet and pulled out my "big" coat. It was a goose-down ski parka, but don't let that fool you, although it occasionally fools women who are into skiing.

Rather than leave my crow's nest by the fire escape, I took the less-appealing interior stairwell route. I hated walking down the stairway inside my building because it increased my chances of running into another tenant. Aside from the woman who used to sunbathe topless on the fire escape, I had not seen or spoken to another tenant in four years. I had never spoken to the sunbather either, but let's not get into that. I avoided the fire escape that night because it was made of metal and it got as slippery as hell when it was wet. A learned thing.

I stepped outside into the storm, tugged my cap tighter on my head, and hurried around to the backyard, or "parking lot" as it had come to be known after the grass died.

I climbed into my Chevy and started the engine. I pulled onto 13th Avenue and headed west toward the lights of downtown Denver. The windshield wipers slapped back and forth like desperate hands wiping a glass forehead and tossing the cloud-sweat into the gutters.

I promise not to use similes like that again.

I came to Lincoln Street and turned left, made my way to 18th, and drove through downtown Denver in the direction of Union Station. I kept glancing at my rearview mirror, looking for tailgating headlights. I didn't know what was going on, didn't know if somebody was watching my every move, tapping my phone lines, following me at a discreet distance, or trying to probe my mind through innocuous questions asked from the backseat of a taxi or a corner booth in an Italian restaurant.

I came to Wynkoop and stopped at the intersection. Union Station was two blocks to my left. I decided to park close to the intersection. No matter where I parked I was going to get wet when I headed for the terminal but I didn't want anybody to see where I had come from. My decision also had to do with my distaste for paying a fee in a parking lot, but mostly it had to do with the idea of parking in a spot where I could make a fast exit. This, too, was a learned thing. I learned it in Albuquerque.

I pulled over to the curb and shut off the engine. I sat for a moment watching the street. I couldn't see much of it. The rain was falling fast and hard. I zipped my coat up to the neck, yanked my Rocky cap tighter on my head, and got out. I ran across Wynkoop and headed for the marquee that hung over the front of the terminal.

I didn't loiter outside. I was in this deal all the way and there was no turning back. I shoved open one of the big wooden doors that led into the terminal and it occurred to me that I had been there before. Not in Union Station but in places from which there was no turning back. I can't list them all right now—just start with the concept of birth, and follow the drooping shoulders.

The terminal was crowded with people who had arrived on trains and people who were prepping to leave. Redcaps were shoving dollies stacked with luggage toward the doors that led out back where the tracks were spread across the flat earth. I could hear a voice from the PA echoing off the ceiling announcing arrivals and departures. I heard the word

"Zephyr." People were seated on high-backed wooden benches with suit-cases crowding their legs—men, women, the elderly, even children who appeared too tired to run and scream for the fun of it the way kids are wired to perform when their world opens up to long journeys. But even without their squealing contribution to the melee, the place was noisy. I've always said that the backseat of my taxi is like Grand Central Station, and this was the living exemplar. Relatives greeting relatives, friends meeting friends, strangers saying goodbye to strangers. Ships passing in the night. Hail and farewell. The lonesome lives of American Bedouins.

I made my way through the crowd toward the lockers where people were opening tin doors, inserting carry-ons, slamming the doors, and removing the keys. I could see locker #96 near the far end. No key in the lock. It made sense. My personal brand of logic dictated that the key was in my pocket.

I edged past a redcap with his rolling dolly, then worked my way close to the lockers. I casually reached into my pocket and withdrew the key as if I was just another passenger getting ready for a night journey by rail. I sidled in front of locker #96, raised the key, and inserted it into the cylinder. It fit. Then I heard a voice say, "Very good. I vill take over from here."

CHAPTER 20

I looked around and saw Mr. Heigger standing behind me. He was wearing a trench coat and a hat. They were soaking wet. Standing beside him was Mr. Weissberger. He was wet, too. The men had positioned themselves to form a close blockade that prevented me from walking past them without making bodily contact.

"You vill step away from zee locker," Mr. Heigger said, in a voice that was subdued but loud enough for me to hear above the crowd noise.

My fingers were still gripping the bozart. I pulled the key back out and lowered my hands to my sides.

Heigger raised his right hand palm-upward. He was wearing black gloves. He smiled. His lips were compressed flat and level, but it was still a smile. It held a superficial resemblance to a cop smile. "Come now, Mr. Murphy. Hand it over. Ve do not want any trouble."

"Trouble?" I said. "What are you talking about?"

"The key, Mr. Murphy. Please give it to me and our business vith you shall be concluded."

I stepped back and felt the locker bump my spine. I looked at Mr. Weissberger whose face was devoid of emotion, unlike the previous Thursday when he had chatted amiably from the backseat.

"Who the hell are you guys?" I said. Heigger raised his palm higher.

"The key, Mr. Murphy."

My years of experience as a cab driver kicked in at that moment. Whether standing outside a hotel or the terminal at DIA, I had become extremely efficient at pocketing tips with a discreet flick of the wrist.

Which is to say, the pocketing of the key to locker #96 was a learned thing. It was over before either of the men realized what I had done. But they did realize it.

My gripped fist made a bulge in my jeans pocket.

Heigger lowered his hand and closed his eyes. His level smile evaporated. "So Mr. Zelner did not say anything to you on the night he died, eh?" he said.

I looked at Weissberger. He flexed his cheeks, raised the corners of his lips, then let them drop.

The key slipped out of my enclosed fist and fell to the bottom of my pocket. My fist then wrapped itself around a squeeze-bottle containing ammonia. Have I ever mentioned the fact that I carry a squeeze-bottle when I drive a taxi? During my fourteen years as a cab driver I had never drawn my ammonia in the line of duty, but as far as I was concerned I was on duty that night. I was hauling a piece of luggage that had belonged to a fare who had never made it to his destination. Mr. Zelner had taken possession of this key the previous Wednesday night and I had found the key in my taxi—and in my book that meant the meter was still ticking.

"First of all let's get something straight," I said, my eyeballs quickly scanning the crowd for a sign of a cop, a security guard, or a familiar cabbie—even one who worked for Yellow. But I didn't see any friendlies in the vicinity. "I'm under no obligation to reveal my conversations to anybody."

"That is a commendable attitude," Heigger said. "I hope that after ve have concluded our business here, you vill continue to adhere to that philosophy."

Then something happened that I had no control over. I may have mentioned this before. It happens to me when people say absurd things. By "people" I mean "cops."

I chortled.

"We don't have any business at all," I said. "I'm going to call the police now so I suggest that you get out of my way." I started to move forward. My "plan" was to muscle my way between them.

With a flick of the wrist worthy of a cab driver, Mr. Weissberger reached beneath his lapel and pulled out a small-caliber pistol. It had "shoulder holster" written all over it.

His back was to the crowd and my back was to the lockers. Nobody could see the pistol but the three of us.

"Ve do not want to harm you or anybody in this terminal," Heigger said. "There are innocent people who might get hurt if you do not do as ve say."

Fer the luvva Christ.

This was a ploy as old as the battle between good and evil. It's hell having an Achilles heel—some people call it a "conscience." As good a name as any, and better than most.

I don't remember if it was in the army, or else during training to become a cab driver, but one of the things our instructors had taught us was to cooperate if a man pulled a gun and gave us an order, usually to hand over money. Logic leads me to believe it was during taxi training because the army had taught us to lock-and-load. I say "logic" because the cab company doesn't supply us with guns, and enemy soldiers rarely demand money during a firefight.

"Perhaps it vould be best if you accompanied us outside," Heigger said. "Ve shall conclude our business there."

He stepped back and pointed at the big glass doors that led to the trains.

I looked at Weissberger. He discreetly slipped the pistol inside his coat. He withdrew his hand but kept his palm splayed against the place where a normal human's heart would be.

I hesitated, glancing back and forth at the two men's faces. Then I stepped forward. Heigger and Weissberger walked alongside me, jostling my arms with their shoulders.

"This vill all be over in a minute," Heigger said.

I nodded, but I wasn't paying much attention to what he was saying because I was busy working the cap off my squeeze-bottle with a thumb and forefinger.

We exited the terminal. A motionless train was chuffing on the track nearest the station. I couldn't tell if it was the Zephyr. Call me a Philistine but all trains look alike to me. I could hear the slow rumble of other trains in motion. Railroad trains move slowly in a station, especially in the vicinity of passenger-loading. Probably a learned thing.

It was still raining but the passengers who were on the platforms were not getting wet. The platforms at Union Station have the standard T-shaped roofs that run the length of the concrete walkways. There was little conversation among the passengers. The loudest sound was the rain sweeping across the flats. Beneath that, the rolling rumble of southbound boxcars moving slowly along a set of tracks farther out on the flats. Heigger touched my shoulder. I looked at him. He pointed to the right, indicating that I should walk toward an area where luggage had been stacked on dollies, where the light from inside the station did not quite reach. A place where our transaction could take place without witnesses.

We stopped in the shadows. I was scared. Would they shoot me? How much noise would a small-caliber pistol make in all this muffling racket of trains and rain?

"The key," Heigger said.

I looked at Weissberger's empty hand pressed flat against his coat, then I looked at Heigger's extended glove. I pulled my fist out of my pocket and raised the bottle and squeezed it harder than any plastic bottle had ever been squeezed in the history of pharmaceuticals. The stream of ammonia hit Weissberger in the face. Before he had a chance to scream I swept the spray toward Heigger's face. I shoved Heigger backward and ran into the rain.

I don't know if you have ever been hit in the face with ammonia—

my guess would be no. I might as well admit it. I have. It happened during a high school chemistry class while the nun was out of the room. A bunch of us guys were horsing around with a beaker. It's a long story that ends with a roaring faucet and a frantic janitor, so I will say only this: it felt like someone had shoved an icicle up my nose clear to the top of my cranium. I subsequently lost control of practically all of my bodily functions. I'll leave the rest to your imagination.

I dashed across the tracks toward the string of slow-moving boxcars. The last car was passing at a walking pace. I skirted to the far side and began running alongside it, pacing it, looking for the rungs that led to the roof. I grabbed a crossbar and hoisted my feet to the bottom rung and hung on like a monkey.

The boxcar continued to trundle at a walking pace. I turned my head so I could see back toward the terminal, but I couldn't see much of anything, and I was willing to bet neither could Heigger or Weissberger. If the ammonia in my plastic bottle was as strong as the ammonia they used in high schools, I doubted they could even walk, much less aim guns. But I'd never had much faith in my doubt. I had greater faith in my ability to retreat, and I clung to that faith as tightly as my fists clung to the vibrating rung.

Word of advice: never horse around with boxcars, not even when the sky is sunny with temperatures in the high seventies. My tennis shoes kept slipping on the bottom rung. The train passed out of the rail yard and entered the dark back lot of old Denver, the broad bleak undeveloped Platte River Valley behind the warehouses that had been converted into fern bars. I looked toward the engine far, far ahead but the rain kept plastering my face. I could barely see, and I realized I had lost my Rocky cap.

I looked back toward the terminal but could see nothing through the downpour, not even the glow of lights from Union Station. The train was picking up speed. I estimated its velocity at a trotting pace with my altitude at four feet. The boxcar crossed the intersection of a road where a streetlight gave me a glimpse of blurred asphalt. I wanted to let go, but the boxcar passed into darkness. I held on and kept swiveling the soles of my tennis shoes, which felt like they were sliding backward due to centrifugal force. Or was it centripetal force? I should have stayed awake in science or English class. My guess was neither. The sliding felt like it was caused by the vibration of a boxcar combined with the tendency of wet rubber to slide all the hell over wet metal. I wanted to hop off the rungs, but at the same time I wanted to stay on.

I pulled myself closer to the ladder, flattened myself, closed my eyes and waited to hear a gunshot. I heard nothing except the sweep of rain and the grinding rumble of iron wheels beneath the car. I felt like I was riding a motorcycle through a hurricane. The fact that I have never ridden a motorcycle somewhat diminishes the verisimilitude of my analogy, but I have seen plenty of biker movies. I kept opening and closing my eyes but it was all darkness and wind and rain. I couldn't see anything, didn't know how far I had traveled, had no bearings, and didn't know where I was going, except south. "Going south"—I had heard that phrase somewhere before and something told me I wished I hadn't.

The iron wheels made the "clickety-clack" rhythm so familiar to movie audiences as they sit safely in their velvet seats munching popcorn. The boxcar crossed another intersection. In the quick flash of a streetlight the answer came to me: it was "centrifugal." The train was making a long sweeping leftward curve on tracks that were laid out in a southeasterly direction. I suddenly realized that we would be making a crossing at Sante Fe Drive near Alameda Avenue. I had traveled almost twenty blocks.

I knew the intersection because I had made the mistake of getting caught at the railroad crossing both in my taxi and in my Chevy. When I was in my taxi my fares got impatient waiting for the trains to pass. When I was in my Chevy I went ballistic for being stupid enough to take Santa Fe during the rush hour.

As the train approached the intersection I knew that after it crossed Sante Fe it would begin to pick up speed and start highballing toward Colorado Springs. I had seen it do that plenty of times in my rearview mirror.

I saw the glow of the Alameda streetlights up ahead. The lights of Interstate 25 were at my back now. There was a short crossroad that linked I-25 with the Sante Fe crossing. The intersection came into view. Automobiles were lined up on Sante Fe waiting impatiently for the train to pass. The earth by the railroad tracks was sandy. Wide puddles were strung along the berm that supported the tracks. Raindrops were hitting the sheets of water like hail. I could see the entire tableau in the light from a streetlight, like the interior of a circus tent. Beyond the glow of light was a canvas wall of blackness, and highballing, and Colorado Springs. The curve of the track became more pronounced and my shoes kept slipping. The phrase "now or never" blossomed in my mind. I hate that phrase. It's like a fuse connected to an explosive device known as "adrenaline"—the word "choice" disappears from the universe and Charles Darwin stands there tapping his toe and saying "Well ...?"

The boxcar was traveling at a running pace, but I knew I was not going to hit the ground running. Never had and never will.

I waited until the boxcar crossed Sante Fe Drive, then I shoved my body away from the rungs. The ensuing chaos reminded me of a traffic accident I was once involved in near Salinas. When the laws of physics stopped toying with me, I found myself lying on my back in a puddle looking up at the cloudburst while automobiles honked their horns. Were they honking at me? Or were they honking at the drivers who had seen me leap and were still stopped at the intersection gawking at my sprawled body?

I heard the sounds of traffic starting up. The line of autos moved northward and disappeared. I slowly sat up in the puddle and did these "wriggly" motions with my body until I had ascertained that nothing was broken, with the possible exception of my heart. Could not one Denverite have stopped to at least rifle my billfold? I was in shock of course. In all probability nobody had seen me, which was how I usually liked things.

I worked myself up out of the puddle and stood staring southward, but the train had disappeared. I was alone. In Salinas there had been people all over the place but nobody got hurt. Fender-bender. My Chevy did get bounced into a ditch. A tow-truck driver charged me fifty bucks to drag it onto the asphalt. I don't want to talk about it.

I was near the railroad tracks so there was nothing but warehouse buildings and fences all around. I could barely see through the rain. I trudged one block north on Sante Fe and came to a residential street that led toward Broadway, which was five or six blocks east. That was about all I knew. I was experiencing the lost and windblown feeling you get after a traumatic experience, when all of your senses have decided to make themselves as scarce as friends who owe you money. I've been on both sides of that fence.

I felt physically exhausted from holding onto the rungs. My hands ached. My arms had no strength. My legs were rubber. Broadway seemed six miles away. I reached up to wipe the rain from my eyes but my hand felt like a claw. I couldn't straighten my fingers. I lowered my hand and fixed my sights on the lights of Broadway, my goal the place where I would find whatever I was looking for. I didn't know what it was right then, but I did know that it didn't matter. I would take it one step at a time. That's what the self-help infomercials advise. First get to Broadway. Then start thinking. Maybe by that time my senses would decide it was safe to come back and pretend to be my friends again.

As I moved along the sidewalk I could not help but feel that this was the worst situation that I had ever experienced in my life. There was nothing that compared with it, not dental appointments and not the army, although in truth there was nothing difficult about the army aside from simply "being in" it. KP and pushups were just frosting on the cake.

The rain began to slacken. By the time I was two blocks from Broadway the only sounds were that of water dripping from the trees in front of the houses. I began to hear the hum of traffic along Broadway. This made me think of my Chevy.

There was nothing I wanted more at that moment than my Chevy. I felt completely out of my element trudging along the sidewalk. What was a professional taxi driver doing on a sidewalk anyway? Sidewalks were for pedestrians. I had to get to my car. It became a beacon in my mind, a suit of armor, a two-toned steel womb that I wanted to crawl back into. I wouldn't be able to think straight until I got behind a steering wheel, the geometric symbol of control, of independence, of power!

But mostly it just felt weird to be walking. I could not recall walking any great distances on purpose in years. The liquor store nearest my crow's nest was a five-block walk. Five blocks apparently was the measure of my willingness to do things on purpose. As far as I was concerned, if Man was meant to walk greater distances, Charles Darwin would have given him eight legs. Think how fast you could get to a liquor store if you had eight legs! These were the kinds of thoughts I had that night. I also have them when there's nothing good on TV.

By the time I stepped into the bright lights of Broadway, I had made my decision. I was going back to Union Station. I would get my car and drive to the Denver Police Department and go inside and walk up to the front desk and ask if Detectives Ottman and Quigg or Duncan and Argyle were on duty. I would ask them to place me in solitary for the rest of my life. I guess one of my senses had not yet returned. For all I knew it was seated in a bar on Broadway. I felt delirious. But the delirium did not come from the physical exhaustion of hopping a boxcar in a rainstorm. It came from anger.

As I said, never in my life had I drawn my ammonia in the line of duty, and I now resented the fact that those two men had made me do something that did not sit well with me, which was to panic and run. It made me feel cowardly. Even when I was dashing across the tracks I hated doing it, and I could only assume that the "stranger" had surreptitiously returned and advised me to do it anyway because there would be plenty of time later to wallow in self-reproach, one of my favorite pastimes.

I walked up to an intersection and crossed Broadway on a green light, then walked one block east and began looking up and down Lincoln Street for a bus stop. I saw one a half-block north. It had an open-fronted shelter made of Plexiglas with benches lining three sides. There was no one inside the shelter. This made me wonder what I looked like. I was soaked. But I doubted I was muddy. The irony of falling rain had seen to that. I began walking toward the stop and was immediately filled with the dread that all Americans feel when they walk toward a bus stop, i.e., what if the bus comes before I get there!!!

I entered the shelter and sat down. I began to experience a sensation like a deflating balloon. The last bit of strength and energy in my legs seemed to be running out the soles of my shoes. I immediately stood up. I felt that if I continued to sit I would not be able to stand up when the bus arrived. I could feel the weight of my soaked clothes. I feared for one moment that I might catch a cold that could lead to pneumonia, but I remembered that colds are not caused by rain, they are caused by viruses that get into the sinuses. My only hope was to keep my fingers out of my nose until I could get to a hanky.

I leaned against the shelter and looked south on Lincoln. I prayed that a bus would come soon—and I'm not much of a praying man. But my prayer was answered. Far down the street floated five tiny orange lights planted above the big front window of a bus. I reached into my jeans pocket to make sure I had change. I had no change. But I felt the cap of the nasal-spray bottle—and the key to locker #96. It was still with me. I had forgotten about it—and who knows, but maybe on purpose.

I reached into my back pocket and dragged my wet billfold out and removed a couple bucks. I didn't know what the current cost of a bus ride was—cab drivers try not to think about those things. But I was willing to bet a bus driver could be bought cheap.

The bus pulled up to the stop and the doors opened. I trudged up the steps and held out two dollars to the driver. "I don't have any change," I said.

"It's only a dollar," he replied, then pointed at a slot on the money box. I paid and began staggering toward the rear of the bus. There were five or six people in the seats. A thought passed through my mind: What are these idiots doing out on a night like this? Okay. I'll admit it. I can be a real hypocrite when the barometric pressure is right.

I sat down on the long seat beneath the rear window where street punks and junkies sit when they can afford bus fare. It made me think of the seats at the backs of classrooms where rowdies congregate. Rowdies are too chicken to sit at the front of a classroom. The back wall makes them feel safe. The only reason I sat at the back of a classroom was to be close to the door. When the bell rang I was gone. Ergo, I always sat by the rowdies. So I guess I could blame logistics for the "Ammonia Incident" in high school, assuming I had been the kind of teenager who blamed my problems on concepts too abstract for an angry chemistry teacher to grasp.

I got off the bus at Colfax and trudged one block to the 16th Street mall and took a shuttle bus to the end of the line. The end of the line was not far from Union Station.

When I stepped off the shuttle, the concrete made my feet hurt. It made my shins hurt. My heels ached as I made my way toward the station. I walked along a street one block east of the station. I wanted to stay as far away from the terminal as I could until I had to make the final push. The few fragments that remained of my ability to reason told me that Heigger and Weissberger would not be looking for me in front of the terminal, but I had long ago learned not to pay much attention to my ability to reason. I went with my gut instinct. I walked two blocks farther on so I could circle around and come at my car from behind.

I began hurrying. The vision of my car was like a magnet or a pepperoni pizza. Forgive my lame similes, but I was exhausted.

I made it down to Wynkoop and peered around the corner of a brick building. I could see the lights of Union Station two blocks south. I scuttled around the corner and began hurrying toward the space where I had parked my car. I say "space" because that's all I saw. My car was gone.

"Nohhh," I moaned, adding the aitches involuntarily.

My knees began to lose their strength. I leaned back against the building and gazed at the empty spot at the curb where I had parked my Chevy a thousand years ago it seemed. I almost slid down the wall to a squatting position, but I knew instinctively that if I did that I would never get up again. My life would end with a pair of dark glasses and a tin cup full of pennies.

It was at this point in time that things began to careen completely out of control. The next thing I knew I was running down the block toward the terminal. A final surge of strength grounded in victim umbrage had launched me toward Union Station. I left the last remnants of my ability to reason leaning against the wall. As I drew closer to the terminal I could hear the voices of people exiting the doors and hurrying toward the line of taxis waiting at the cabstand. Newbies, I was certain. What kind of cabbies would go to Union Station at this time of night except rank amateurs and me?

When I entered the glow of light cast from the terminal windows I slowed down. I was breathing hard. I approached the entry and reached into my pocket and clutched the key to locker #96. I no longer cared. I was going to open that box and see what was inside it even if I had to plow my way between two armed men wiping ammonia from their nostrils.

The terminal was as crowded as it had been when I hopped the freight. I didn't look to see if anyone was watching me. I made a beeline toward the lockers. I bumped into people. I was rude. I jostled a redcap who frowned at me. I stumbled up to locker #96 and pulled the key out of my pocket.

I inserted the key, turned it, and yanked the door open expecting the impact of flying lead to penetrate my spine. I reached into the box and slapped the metal, the hollow metal, the empty rectangle of echoing tin. There was nothing inside locker #96.

I turned and looked at the crowd expecting to see the familiar faces of Heigger and Weissberger grinning at me—just before they pulled the triggers.

I saw no familiar faces. I saw only blurs.

The redcap walked up to me. He was still frowning. He was standing so close that his frown lines came into focus. The crowd behind him was a blur. I was breathing hard. I was dizzy. I felt sick. I felt like I was going to faint. His frown changed from one of utter disgust to one of baffled concern.

"Are you all right, sir?" he said, examining my soaked clothes.

"I'm fine," I lied. It rolled easily off my tongue, as usual.

"Do you need help?" he said, apparently ignoring my reply.

But maybe he hadn't understood my reply. Maybe I had slurred my words. I could barely hear myself speak beneath the voices of the crowd. "I need a taxi," I gasped.

He seemed to understand. He took me by the arm and escorted me to the front door. I had the urge to tell him to be prepared to duck, but I could barely think much less give unsolicited advice to a man in uniform.

He walked me outside to the first cab in line. It was a Rocky Cab. For one moment I felt a surge of energy. I felt like I was coming home. The redcap opened the rear door. I climbed inside. He didn't wait expectantly for a tip. He seemed to understand that this was not a "gratuity moment." He shut the door firmly. The cab driver turned around in his seat and looked at me. I didn't recognize him. He was young. He had "newbie" written all over him.

That was the last thought I had before everything went black. I slumped sideways across the seat. I don't remember slumping. The newbie would describe it to me later. He would tell me that when he saw me fall over he was afraid that the Rocky Mountain Taxicab Company had another fare on its hands who had "exited en route."

CHAPTER 21

I don't know what the opposite of reality is, but apparently I spent two hours there after I slumped sideways in the taxi. That's how long it took before I fully recovered my senses. The phrase "fully recovered" is a ballpark estimate—take it for what it's worth. All I know is, when two shimmering obelisks finally transformed themselves into recognizable entities, I realized I was in the presence of detectives. They were standing at the foot of a bed I was lying on. At first they looked like Duncan and Argyle, but as I blinked a bit of ambient moisture from my eyes they seemed to change into Ottman and Quigg. By the time my eyes were clear they didn't look like anyone I recognized, beyond the crewcuts and inexpensive gray suits indicative of plainclothesmen.

When they saw me open my eyes, the men pulled out their badges and introduced themselves. Their names were Ferguson and Boyd.

They put their badges away and pulled small notebooks from their coat pockets. "Do you feel up to answering some questions for us?" Detective Boyd said.

I had seen cop notebooks before. I'm not going to say that cop notebooks make me uneasy, but they do make my entire universe shrink down to a point where my responses to questions become more focused than usual.

I nodded.

Boyd came around to the left side of the bed. Ferguson stepped around to the right side. I had been in this position before, although not horizontally. The last time I was surrounded by detectives I was seated comfortably on a chair in Hogan's office, a chair that I had come to think of as "my" chair. As I laid in bed looking from one detective to the other I wriggled various parts of my body. I wanted to make certain that I was not lying on what might end up becoming "my" bed. All my limbs seemed to be intact. I didn't know what was going on, but this was not unusual. So I simply did what I always did best. I "went with the flow."

"First of all, do you know where you are?" Ferguson said.

For all I knew I was in a cloud castle built by Lord Dunsany. "A hospital?" I said.

"That's right," he said. "You're in the emergency ward at Denver General Hospital."

I had been to DGH before. The first time I was there it was in the line of duty—I had delivered my very first baby in the backseat of the taxicab I used to drive, #127, and I subsequently decided to take a brief vacation from reality. I had no choice. I was unconscious.

"Could you please give us your full name?" Ferguson said.

I told him that my name was Brendan Murphy, although my full name is Brendan Aloysius Murphy. But I hate saying "Aloysius" because it sounds so … I don't know … goofy or something.

He asked for my address. I gave it to him. Then he said, "What do you do for a living, Mr. Murphy?"

"I drive a taxi."

Ferguson nodded. "Do you know how you got here?"

"In a taxi?"

Ferguson shook his head no. "According to our report, you lost consciousness in the backseat of a taxi approximately two hours ago. You were brought to DGH in an ambulance. "

I nodded. I was almost half-right as usual.

"Mr. Murphy," Boyd said, forcing me to rotate my head in the opposite direction. "We spoke to the medics who brought you here in the ambulance and they said you were …" he paused to consult his notebook "… babbling incoherently. Do you remember doing that?"

I cleared my throat. I was having trouble speaking. I was slightly hoarse. I hoped like hell I wasn't coming down with a cold. But I won't keep you in suspense. I wasn't.

"I have been known to do that," I said. "But you're talking about this evening, correct?" I was trying to be specific. I knew that detectives preferred specifics over vague generalizations. I can do both with élan.

"Yes," Boyd said. "During the ride in the ambulance."

I nodded for no specific reason then said, "I don't remember babbling incoherently this evening, but it is not beyond the realm of possibility."

Boyd frowned. "Are you saying you have no memory of the ride here, or of any statements that you made to the medics?"

"Yes. I don't remember doing either," I said. I hoped this didn't sound like a lie to him. It sort of did to me.

"We are concerned about a statement that you made to the medics that someone in Union Station pulled a pistol on you," Boyd said.

I stared at Detective Boyd with mounting horror. This surprised me. It normally takes six to eight minutes before mounting horror joins a grilling.

"That's true," I said.

"True that you said it—or true that it happened?" Ferguson said. He sounded like he was trying to be specific. This made me feel as if I had a like-spirit standing by my bed. I didn't like that. Whenever I encounter someone like myself, my senses go on red-alert.

"It's true that it happened," I said.

"According to your statement, this man made you walk outside where the loading platforms are located, and that you feared this man was going to shoot you," Ferguson said.

I nodded in response to my statement. Then I remembered where I was—in the presence of cops. I had learned long ago that detectives preferred that a "person of interest" respond verbally rather than through body language. I may or may not have mentioned this to you, but certain elements of body language are not admissible in court, such as, for instance, The Exasperated Glare.

I rolled my head on my pillow and looked at Ferguson. "Before I reply, can I ask you something?" I said.

"Certainly, Mr. Murphy."

"Could you please go stand on the left side of my bed? It's really cumbersome looking back and forth between both of you."

Ferguson nodded. He moved around to the other side and stood next to his partner. He didn't seem to mind. He had probably concluded that there was no danger of my acting violent or trying to escape. He may have been reassured by the fact that I had a rubber tube stuck into my body that acted as a kind of leash. When I had first awakened I noticed a transparent rubber tube dangling from a metal post overhead, but I didn't know what part of my body the tube was stuck in, and I didn't want to know. I knew only that it wasn't shoved up my nose.

"It's true that it happened," I said. "Two men approached me in Union Station and demanded that I give them a key to a locker."

"Do you know these men personally?"

"Yes. One is a lawyer named Heigger, and the other is a man named Weissberger."

"Do you know where they are right now?"

"No."

"It says here that you squirted these men in the face using a plastic bottle filled with ammonia. Is this true?"

Fer the luvva Christ.

I started to nod, but instead I closed my eyes to give my reply a moment's thought. The reason I did this was because I felt intuitively that squirting people in the face with ammonia was against the law. I tried to put myself in the position of a lawyer. It didn't take long. Believe it or not, I have a lot in common with lawyers, although I do not wish to delve too deeply into that aspect of my personality.

"I said that?" I asked.

"According to this statement," Ferguson said.

"I'll be darned," I mumbled. That was the best I could come up with. I hated talking that way but I could not help but feel that it might be best to "go with the flow" of vague generalizations until I had a chat with a lawyer. This, too, was a learned thing. It's amazing the things you learn after you leave home and go out into the world.

"The gun, Mr. Murphy," Boyd said. "What we are most concerned about right now is the gun. Did this man pull a gun on you inside Union Station tonight?"

"Yes."

"What time did this event take place?"

"Around eight o'clock."

"Why did he pull the gun?"

"Because I wouldn't hand him the key to the locker."

"Locker number ninety-six?" Boyd said, looking down at his notebook. Both of them kept referring to their notes as they questioned me.

"Yes," I said. "Locker number ninety-six."

I wondered what else I had said to the medics when my faculties were not intact. This may sound sort of crazy, but I began to worry that I had told them about my stalled writing career.

"Even though he was holding a gun on you?"

I paused and tried to think for a moment. Suddenly I was filled with the kind of glee that only madmen are said to enjoy. I actually couldn't remember.

"I don't think ... he didn't show me the gun until after I refused to obey him ... I think that's how it happened anyway," I said. I couldn't believe it. I was telling the truth. The continuity of events that had taken place at Union Station was jumbled in my mind. I felt like I had discovered a secret treasure-trove.

"But you do remember him pulling a gun on you?"

"Yes, I do remember that. He stuck his hand inside his coat and pulled out the gun and showed it to me. He did it to intimidate me. I do remember that very clearly."

"Did he have the gun in his hand when he escorted you outside of the terminal?" Boyd said, referring to his notes again.

"No," I said. "But he had his hand held against his chest. I think he did it so he could get to his gun fast, but I don't know for certain, although I believed that was the reason he held his hand there. I have a lot of trouble with the dichotomy of 'belief' versus 'knowledge.'"

"You're not alone, Mr. Murphy," Ferguson said.

I was astonished when he said that. I had never before encountered a law-enforcement officer who understood any of my prattle.

"Did this man fire the weapon?" Boyd said.

I started to shake my head no, but then stopped to think about it. One of the major problems I have in my life is telling people what they wish to hear. The situations are often related to their vaunted opinions, but right at that moment I didn't think these two cops were interested in opinions, just the raw facts. That did not bode well.

"I don't know if the weapon was fired. I didn't see or hear the gun being fired. I was too busy running away."

They both nodded.

"Is it nevertheless possible that the gun was fired?" Ferguson said. A strange question, from my point of view. It seemed to call for an opinion. I believe in court they call this "leading the witness." Or is it "badgering the witness"?

"There was a lot of noise in the railroad station," I said. "It was raining hard and there were trains moving on the tracks. It's possible that the gun could have been fired. But I tend to think it wasn't."

"Why is that?"

"Because I had squirted Weissberger in the face. It's almost impossible to do anything with ammonia in your face, especially if it goes up your nose."

Ferguson scribbled something in his notebook. He was using a snap-top ballpoint pen rather than the usual Bic that I was so used to seeing in the hands of detectives. But it still made the standard "skritch-skritch" sound. I would imagine that in the cloying and tightly knit world of ballpoint pen manufacturers, not a lot of thought is given to the sounds that pens make. I wondered who the genius was who thought up the tiny ball at the end of the ballpoint pen? And how did he make his first working model? I'll tell you one thing though. I'll bet a lot of people laughed at him—until he made his first million.

"That's probably true," Ferguson said, raising his pen and smiling at it.

I realized with horror that at some point I had begun talking out loud in reference to ballpoint pens. I hadn't even known I was doing it.

"Could you describe for us the events that took place out on the platform?" Boyd said.

I nodded. "After we got outside, they made me walk over to a spot that was in the shadows. There was a cart stacked with luggage. The location was dark enough that nobody in the station could see us very well. It was raining so hard that I could barely hear Heigger when he told me to hand him the key."

"Where was the key?" Boyd said.

"In my jeans pocket."

"Where is the key right now?" Boyd said.

I started to answer, then stopped. I already knew the answer, or at least I thought I did. That's why I stopped. Whenever I think I know something, I pause to double-check, in the same way that you're supposed to double-check your answers after you solve an arithmetic problem. I never did that even though the nuns advised us to do it. Frankly, I saw no point since I always got two different answers.

"I left it stuck in the keyhole of locker number ninety-six," I said. "That was just before I went outside and got into the taxi."

Ferguson stopped writing. He looked at Boyd. Boyd nodded at him, then looked at me.

"We don't want to tire you out, Mr. Murphy. So we think it might be best if you were to come down to DPD and make a more detailed statement after you are discharged from the hospital. But the thing we are most concerned about right at the moment is this business with the gun." He glanced at his notebook. "Let me just run over this again real quickly. A man named Weissberger pulled out a gun and showed it to you, and then he and a man named Heigger escorted you outside to the platforms and demanded that you give them the key to locker number ninety-six. At that point you squirted them in the face with ammonia, and then you ran away. Is that correct?"

"Yes."

"And to your knowledge the pistol was not discharged."

"Correct."

"Did you see these men again after this incident?"

"No."

"Do you know where they went, or where they might be right now?"

"No."

Boyd nodded. "All right. Thank you, Mr. Murphy. There are other questions we need to ask you, but we wanted to check into your statement that someone had displayed a weapon at Union Station. After we got word of this incident, we sent some people down to the station to investigate. Our people talked to a number of employees, but nobody seemed to know anything about it."

I nodded. "That's strange," I said. "You would think that the men would have run into a restroom to wash the ammonia off their faces. They might have even screamed. I know I di…would."

"Yes," Ferguson said. "Your story does possess a number of curious vagaries. That's why we would appreciate it if you would come down to DPD in the morning after you are released. The sooner we talk to you, the better. We're going to remain on duty until we get this cleared up."

"Before we shove off here," Boyd said, "I wonder if you could answer one last question?"

"Okay."

"Why were you carrying a bottle of ammonia?"

I swallowed hard. "It's … it's kind of a long story, but as I said, I drive a taxi for a living and … well … sometimes I carry a small, very little, hardly big at all nose-spray bottle that I fill with ammonia for self-protection."

The detectives glanced at each other.

Ferguson looked at me. "What company do you drive for?"

"The Rocky Mountain Taxicab Company."

He wrote something down in his notebook. I was willing to bet I knew what he had written. I was also willing to bet Hogan would find out what he had written. I was also willing to bet that my job was about to go to hell in a hatbox.

CHAPTER 22

They threw me out of the hospital at eight o'clock the next morning. I was feeling kind of shaky after having spent the night with a tube stuck in my body—my right forearm as I later ascertained. It was an I.V. drip. The nurse told me that I had been dehydrated, which I thought was ridiculous because on the previous night I had been running and jumping and wandering around in a rainstorm. But I didn't quibble. I just wanted to go home, take a shower, climb into bed, and pull the covers over my face. Standard operating procedure after doing anything. I wasn't even in the mood to channel-surf for a glimpse of Mary Ann.

Except I had something to do.

I was ambivalent about this. I had to go to the police department and talk to Ferguson and Boyd. I was ambivalent because I wanted to find out if they had discovered the whereabouts of Heigger and Weissberger. I also wanted to report my stolen car. Whenever I want something, I feel a burst of rejuvenation, partly because I never want anything, not counting a million dollars.

DGH is located near 8th and Speer so I decided to walk to DPD, which is only five blocks north. I could have taken a cab, or even a bus, but I felt like walking. Maybe it was all the physical exercise of the night before, but I felt good as I headed north. Maybe I was getting used to this walking jazz. Maybe I would buy myself a ten-speed bicycle and join my landlord Keith on his rides around City Park. These are the kinds of thoughts that seep into my mind when I haven't had a beer in twenty-four hours. But I knew the cure for that.

I arrived at 13th and Bannock and crossed the broad apron of concrete that fronts the DPD building. I had been there before, although I had never entered by the front door. I was always in the backseat of a police car that entered through the basement parking garage. This was in connection with the various murders, kidnappings, robberies, and so forth that the police thought I might know something about, which I did. Not that I was guilty of anything, although the police were never entirely certain of that. I suppose you could say from a technical viewpoint that I might reasonably be labeled a "suspect" whenever John Law invited me down for a grilling, but that's more semantics than anything else. The detectives had never come right out and told me that I was a suspect, although I wasn't certain if that was a "technique" that the police utilized to put a suspect at his ease, or just a "trick." At any rate, I was always able to make it quite clear to them that I was the victim of ridiculous misunderstandings that could easily be explained—especially after the murder victims turned up alive. One of them is attending college nowadays, and another one is apparently hiding out in Brazil, but let's move on.

I entered DPD, approached the desk, and informed the sergeant that I had an appointment with Detectives Ferguson and Boyd. He picked up a phone and mumbled a few things, then told me to go down the hall and take an elevator up to the third floor and go to the fourth office down the hall. I braced myself for another trip to what I call "a small room" where I would be required to fill out a witness statement and endure a lot of questions. There is a dull predictability to interviews with policemen, but I had accepted it with the same forbearance that I had accepted the existence of TV commercials and golf.

I stepped out of the elevator onto the third floor and walked down the hallway until I came to the fourth office. I peeked in before I knocked. This was a sort of "habit" that went back a long way and had more to do with nuns than cops. But the detectives saw me peek in at them, which rendered moot the knock on the doorsill that I was not able to brake in time. I went ahead and knocked even though they were looking right at me. Ferguson was seated at a desk and Boyd was standing near a window. As my knuckles rapped the frame, I grinned in the hopes that they would think my pointless knock was jocular.

"Mr. Murphy," Ferguson said with a smile. "Come on in." Ferguson's smile indicated that he believed it was a jocular knock.

I could not help but feel that we were once again on the same wavelength that we had shared the night before when he had demonstrated his uncanny ability to comprehend my tangential remarks.

"How are you feeling, Mr. Murphy?" Boyd said, crossing the room and shaking my hand.

"A little shaky," I said, then I realized he might have thought I was mocking our handshake. I don't usually make physical/linguistic puns until I've had a few snorts.

To my surprise, Ferguson and Boyd did not ask me to accompany them to a small room. Instead they offered me a seat in their office, which in fact was about the size of a small room, except it had two desks instead of a table. The room also contained filing cabinets, a coat rack, family photographs—your standard American detective office. I sat down on what I hoped would never become "my" chair.

"Are you feeling up to answering a few more questions?" Boyd said.

"Yes, sir," I said. I smiled with my lips closed.

Boyd remained standing. Ferguson remained sitting. Neither of them were wearing coats. They looked tired. I wondered if they had gotten any shut-eye but I didn't ask.

"Good," Boyd said. "I'd like to start off by letting you know that we did not find either of those two men whom you claimed pulled a gun on you."

I started to nod, then stopped. It would have made sense for me to nod if they had caught Heigger and Weissberger because it would have been a nod of confirmation. But since they hadn't caught them, the nod would have been superfluous. After all, what would I have been nodding at? Nothing? It might have made me look like I did not understand statements.

"We interviewed as many people as we could find who were present at Union Station during the time that you indicated the events took place, and we could not find anybody who was able to give us an eyewitness account."

I went ahead and nodded. I felt obligated to let Boyd know that I had heard what he was saying. I just hoped he didn't interpret it to mean that I understood what he was getting at. I couldn't recall ever doing a thing like that.

Boyd reached to Ferguson's desk and picked up one of two small notebooks. He flipped it open and studied it for a moment, then he looked at me. "Mr. Murphy, when we spoke to you in the hospital last night we were primarily interested in learning whether there was any danger that someone at Union Station might be carrying a gun, and that he might still be there at that moment, and that he might put other people's lives in jeopardy. But as I said, our investigators were not able to confirm any of your statements. You weren't in very good shape last night, so I would like you to describe again ... to the best of your recollection and in greater detail ... the events which took place from the moment you entered Union Station until the moment that you ran away from those men."

I shifted on my seat and frowned. Normally this is an "act" I perform to make listeners think I'm thinking, but in this case I really was thinking.

"I entered the terminal at Union Station around eight o'clock and went up to locker number ninety-six. I pulled the key out of my T-shirt pocket and placed it into the lock. Then I heard a voice say, "Very good. I vill take over from here."

"He said 'vill'?"

"He actually said 'will' but it sounded to me like 'vill'."

"Do you have a hearing problem?"

"No, but I have a vivid imagination. It's just that Heigger sometimes sounded sort of Germanic when he spoke to me."

"You did mention that you know this man Heigger, as well as Weissberger," Boyd said.

"Oh yes. I met them both at … uh … well, there's a lot more to this story than the Union Station episode."

"All right. We'll get to that. But let's stick with Union Station for now. We're still primarily interested in this business about the drawn pistol."

"All right," I said. "After he said 'vill' and so on, I turned around and saw the two men standing behind me. They were blocking my way. Heigger told me to hand him the key. I refused to give it to him. We sort of haggled for a bit, and then Weissberger pulled the gun out of his coat. Heigger told me that people in the terminal might get hurt if I didn't hand over the key. He then told me that he wanted me to go outside with them and finish our business there."

"Where was the key at this point?" Boyd said.

"Oh yeah," I said. "Let me back up. I left out a couple of things. I feel kind of like a rank amateur trying to tell a joke, ya know? Have you ever done that? You start to tell a funny story but then you have to stop and say, 'Oh yeah, I forgot to mention that both of the men were wearing mukluks,' or something like that. And then you go on with the joke but then you have to stop again and tell your audience that both men are named Harvey. Do you know what I mean?"

"Yes we do, Mr. Murphy," Ferguson said. "It can be difficult for a person to remember all the details of a traumatic experience."

"Especially in a comedy club," I said.

"What details did you leave out of your encounter with these men at Union Station?" Ferguson said

"Well first of all, the reason Weissberger pulled out the gun was because I had shoved the key into my jeans pocket."

"Why did you do that?"

"Mainly because I didn't know he had a gun. I wasn't afraid of them up until that point. Especially Mr. Weissberger. He must be about sixty-five, and Heigger is about my age. But I'm an inch or so taller than Heigger. I guess that's why I wasn't afraid of him. Short people don't intimidate me, although I am willing to admit that being short is no proof that a man doesn't, for instance, pump iron."

"That's true," Ferguson said. Ferguson again seemed to be agreeing with every idle remark I uttered. It made me wonder if he was "up to something." I found it hard to believe that he was agreeing with me just because I was right.

"Aside from not knowing that they had a gun, why did you pocket the key?" Boyd said.

"Because it wasn't their damn key!" I said, raising my voice. I regretted it immediately. I frequently do that immediately. But I figured what the hell, these were cops. They were probably used to emotional outbursts, especially during pot busts.

"I mean, I barely even knew these guys and here they were giving me orders like a couple of drill sergeants or something. Of course that was before I found out they were packing heat."

"Say again?" Boyd said.

"Packing heat," I said. "Carrying a gun. Haven't you ever heard that phrase?"

"I have," Ferguson said. "I've heard it in the movies."

Ferguson was starting to annoy me. If he wasn't agreeing with me, he was either confirming or validating everything I said.

"Oh sure," Boyd said. "Now that you bring it up, I've heard that on TV shows."

"That's right," I said. "Movies and TV shows. I guess I haven't really heard it anywhere else."

Ferguson smiled. "You are the first person I have ever met who used the term 'packing heat' in a conversation."

"Oh," I said. "Well." I smiled at him. I felt as if a significant milestone had been passed. "Thank you."

"So when you saw the gun, it changed your attitude toward these men, is that correct?" Boyd said.

"Yes," I said. "My fearlessness was changed into fear."

"Where does the ammonia enter into this?" Ferguson said.

"After I walked outside with them ... oh ... I forgot something. I still had my hand in my pocket, so as we were walking toward the door I let go of the key and took hold of the bottle of ammonia that was in my pocket and started to work the cap off with my thumb and forefinger. We went outside and turned to our right and walked over to a dark spot where luggage was piled on a cart. We stopped, and then Heigger told me to give him the key. So I pulled my hand out of my pocket but instead of the key, I was holding the squeeze-bottle. They didn't know that though. That's what I was counting on ..."

"The element of surprise," Ferguson said. Ferguson was no longer merely confirming my statements, the sonofabitch was finishing them for me. But then I remembered—he was a detective. It was his job to figure things out, although apparently he wasn't interested in figuring out how annoying he could be.

"Yes," I said. "I raised the bottle and squirted Weissberger in the face, then I squirted Heigger in the face. Then I ran across the tracks." Ferguson was writing in his notebook. I wanted like hell to see what he was writing. I wanted to know how much emphasis he was giving my ammonia in his notes. Writers are always interested in the emphasis that might be placed on words, sentences, and witness statements that can be used against them in courts of law—that's what the how-to books say anyway.

"Why didn't you just give them the key?" Boyd said.

"Because I was afraid they would shoot me after I handed it over."

"What made you think that?"

"The gun."

"But I mean," Boyd continued, "did you have any other reason to believe that these men might commit an act of murder?"

"No. The gun pretty much convinced me."

Ferguson and Boyd gazed at me for a few moments without speaking. But I felt I knew what they were up to. They were utilizing a "technique." I decided that they were hoping I would grow uneasy in the silence and start talking until I said something contradictory that would send me up the river. I always feel this way when I talk to cops. But I decided to "play along" with their ruse. I didn't want them to "suspect" that I "suspected" what they were up to.

"The thing is," I continued, "I didn't want to end up like one of those people who say, 'Gee, I should have done this' or 'I should have done that' after something terrible has happened to them. I mean, I didn't want to find myself lying on the platform in a pool of blood and staring up at the falling rain and saying, "Con sarn it, I wish I had squirted them in the face with my ammonia instead of handing over the key.' I mean, it would be like taking an SAT test where they tell you to go with your first answer rather than erasing the answer and changing it to something else because statistics show that your first guess usually turns out to be the right one. So I suppose you could say that pulling out my ammonia was like marking the correct answer on a college-entrance exam."

The detectives continued to gaze at me in silence. They were like an audience in a comedy club waiting for a punch line, so I finished up by saying, "I guess my instinct was right, because I'm not dead."

"Was Mr. Weissberger holding the gun at the time you squirted him?"

"No."

"So he was not armed when you squirted him in the face."

"He didn't have the gun in his hand, but it was somewhere under his coat. I assumed it was in a shoulder holster. To me, that's armed," and dangerous.

"Did Mr. Heigger have a gun?"

"Not that I know of."

"So neither of these men were pointing a gun at you when you squirted them in the face."

"I would have to say no. It was too dark where we were standing to see much of anything, but even if it was daylight I still would have squirted them."

"And you hit both of them in the face?"

"Yes. They were close enough so that I could see their faces. Their faces were a bit lighter, if you know what I mean, than the darkness."

"Did they scream after you squirted them?"

I paused for a moment to think about this, then I said, "I squirted them both in the face and then ran away fast. I hopped onto the ladder of a boxcar. I didn't hear them scream, so I really don't know whether or not they screamed. When I ran across the tracks there was all this noise from the rain and the trains, so if they did scream, I didn't hear it."

"Where is the ammonia bottle now?" Boyd said.

"I don't know. I guess I dropped it."

"You're not carrying a bottle of ammonia on your person at this moment, are you?"

"No."

"But you do carry one when you drive a taxi?"

"Well ... up until yesterday. I might stop doing that."

"You say you drive for the Rocky Mountain Taxicab Company, correct?" Boyd said.

"Yes."

"Is that why you climbed into a Rocky Mountain taxi outside Union Station."

"No, that was just kismet."

"Kismet?"

"Fate," Ferguson said.

I gave him an exasperated glare. "The Rocky Cab was the first taxi in line at the station. I didn't plan it that way. It would be almost impossible to plan a thing like that, although I have done it in the past."

"What do you mean?" Boyd said.

"I mean I have waited … for instance … until a Checker Cab has pulled up first in line at a cabstand before going out to get in. It can be done. I just didn't do it at Union Station. It takes time and patience to wait for a particular taxi to pull up first in line, and I hardly ever do anything that takes time and patience."

"You're not so different from everybody else," Ferguson said.

This really made me bristle. I have always felt that the fact that I am a forty-five-year-old writer with virtually no hope of ever getting published has always set me apart from the rest of humanity.

"Most people take the easy way out," Ferguson continued. This guy was unstoppable.

But I nodded in agreement. He had me pegged. I guess I wasn't so special after all. Keep that under your hat.

"What's this about the boxcar?" Boyd said.

"After I ran away from Heigger and Weissberger, I hopped onto the ladder of a boxcar and rode it out of Union Station."

The two men glanced at each other.

"Okay, this is where it gets a little murky," Boyd said.

It seemed to me that I had heard a cop say that before, but I tried not to remember who, when, or where.

"I wasn't quite clear about that statement," Boyd said. "When we got the preliminary report from the medics we were under the impression that after you ran away from these two men, you reentered the terminal, and then you went out to the cabstand and got into a taxi."

"No," I said. "Well … yes. But that was later. And I didn't just walk out and get into a taxi. A redcap helped me out the door."

"A redcap?"

"Yes, a redcap," I said. "He was a black man about my age who works in the terminal carrying luggage for passengers."

"It doesn't appear that you mentioned the redcap to the medics," Boyd said, looking down at his notebook.

I nodded. Then I shrugged. That pretty much depleted my body language.

"Can you give us a rough estimate of the time that passed between the moment you ran away from these men and the moment you got into the taxicab?" Boyd said.

"Yes," I said. "A hundred years," I wanted to say but I knew what he was getting at and it wasn't hyperbole. "It was less than an hour. I jumped off the boxcar at Sante Fe Drive and Alameda. Then I hopped a bus. I also walked a lot. So I would say it was more than a half-hour, but less than an hour."

Ferguson wrote this down. Every damned word. "What bus did you hop?" Boyd said.

"The zero," I said.

They both nodded. I was surprised. The "0" is the number of the bus that runs from south Denver straight up to midtown. But I guess everybody in Denver knows that. I've always liked riding the zero. It makes me feel like I'm starting my life over again.

"Then I caught the Sixteenth Street shuttle back to Union Station."

"What did you do after you arrived there?"

"I went back inside and … oh wait … I forgot to tell you something else. My car got stolen last night."

"Your car?"

"My sixty-four Chevy. It gets stolen all the time from my apartment building, and it got stolen again last night."

"From your apartment building?"

"No, I mean ... maybe I should have started this story at the beginning. Only ... to tell you the truth ... I'm not sure where this story begins."

"Why don't you start with the stolen car," Ferguson said. He was good. He knew how to cut through the crap. I wondered if he had learned that at the Denver Police Academy.

"I drove my car down to Union Station last night and parked at a curb two blocks north of the terminal. But when I got back to the station after hopping the freight, my car was gone."

They glanced at each other.

Ferguson looked back at me. "I assume this means you want to file a stolen-car report."

I nodded. "I usually report it to Gladys."

They nodded. I felt like I was talking in shorthand.

"You can file the report when you get back downstairs," Boyd said. Ferguson wrote something down, then glanced at me. "Is it possible that Heigger and Weissberger might have stolen your car?"

I stared at Ferguson. I hadn't thought of that. But as soon as he said it, I knew it was possible. Anything is possible in this three-ring circus we call life.

"That's true," Ferguson said.

I realized with horror that once again I had spoken aloud without realizing it. "They could have stolen it," I quickly said. "But mostly my car gets stolen by street punks and junkies. I usually get it back in a couple of hours."

"Why is that?"

"Because it's sort of a lemon. Nobody wants it. Not even people who steal cars and strip them for parts. I don't think my Chevy has any parts."

Ferguson nodded. "Maybe we'll take the stolen car report ourselves and pass it along to the people downstairs."

"That's fine with me," I said. But it wasn't. I was afraid Gladys might get mad. I could not help but feel that Gladys had come to think of my Chevy as "her" car.

I gave Ferguson my license-plate number.

"What did you do after you realized that your car was stolen?" Boyd said.

I gave them a blow-by-blow description of the events that had taken place after I went ballistic. You've been there. The two detectives listened in silence as I described my enraged run to the terminal and my subsequent discovery that the locker was empty. I told them about the redcap escorting me outside and helping me into the Rocky Cab. My story ended when I fainted—although I gave it a kind of epilogue by telling them that the next thing I knew I was staring at two obelisks that transmogrified into them.

"In other words, you came to consciousness in a state of hallucination," Ferguson said.

"Yes," I said.

What I wanted to say was, "Yeah, yeah, that's what happened. Why don't you and I switch chairs and you can tell my goddamn story from start to finish, bright boy."

But I didn't say that. I hoped.

CHAPTER 23

I crossed my arms and gently touched my Adam's apple so I would feel it vibrate if I started talking without realizing it.

"It's odd," I said on purpose. "I mean, you would think that somebody at the terminal would have noticed if two men had been squirted in the face with ammonia. I mean, I would think their screams alone would have drawn a crowd."

"That's what we would think," Boyd said. "But none of the people we interviewed heard any screams last night, and we don't have any reports about two men being … squirted with ammonia."

I immediately wondered what he meant by that ellipsis. I suspected he meant to say "assaulted" but changed it to a word less damaging to my case. He seemed to be on my side—for the moment.

"We've checked the hospitals and nearby clinics, but nobody was admitted with that sort of … affliction."

"So the men made no noise at all?" Ferguson said.

"I was too busy running to notice. But like I said, it was raining hard and there was a lot of train sounds. Maybe their screams were muffled."

Ferguson nodded. "You say these men wanted you to give them the key to locker number ninety-six. Can you tell us what was inside the locker?"

"No."

"Why not?"

"Because I don't know. As I said, it was empty when I opened it."

"How did you come into the possession of the key?" Boyd said.

"Pardon?"

"How did you get hold of the key?"

"Oh. I found it in my taxicab last night."

Both men raised their eyebrows. That was a new one on me in terms of detective reaction. It was almost as if they were displaying emotion. Except for annoyed frowns and the occasional reassuring smile, I rarely saw detectives emote.

"Let me make certain I have this right," Boyd said. "You found a key to a locker at Union Station in your taxicab last night, so you drove down to the terminal in order to open the locker, correct?"

"Yes."

The two men glanced at each other.

"Why didn't you turn the key in to the lost-and-found?" Ferguson said. "Doesn't Rocky Cab have a lost-and-found?"

I started to reply, but then I stopped and stared at him with my jaw hanging open.

"Wouldn't that have been standard operating procedure?" he said.

I closed my jaw and swallowed hard. "The thing is," I said, "I've had a lot of strange things happen to me this week, and finding the key was sort of the last strange thing."

"You do realize don't you, Murph, that finding the key to a locker, and then opening the locker, could be considered a violation of the law?"

"What?"

"Just because you found a key in your taxi did not give you authorization to open the locker."

"No ... I mean, why did you call me 'Murph'?" The men glanced at each other.

"You asked us to call you 'Murph,'" Ferguson said.

"I did?"

"Yes."

"When?"

"A minute ago," Ferguson said. "You did it just before you began caressing your Adam's apple with your right hand."

I quickly lowered my hand and sat up straight.

"Can I ask you something?" I said.

"Certainly."

"Did I say the words 'bright boy' within the past couple of minutes."

"I don't believe so," Ferguson said.

I heaved an internal sigh of relief. At least—I hoped it was internal. Then I nodded. "I do realize now that finding a lost key did not authorize me to open the locker."

"You said earlier that you weren't sure where all this business started," Ferguson said. "Why don't you back up to the first strange thing that happened and start your story from there."

I cleared my throat. "Well, it all started last Wednesday night when a man died in the backseat of my taxicab."

Ferguson and Boyd frowned at each other, then looked at me. "You were the driver of that taxi?" Boyd said.

"Yes I was," I said.

"What was the dead man's name?"

"Zelner. I think his first name was Heinrich."

Boyd crossed the room and opened a filing cabinet. He leafed through some manila folders and pulled out a report. I recognized it. I am familiar with the "look" of police reports. He glanced through it, then tossed the report onto Ferguson's desk. "Two officers in our department looked into that death," Boyd said.

Ferguson picked up the report and looked at it, then set it down. "This was not a homicide," he said. "Mr. Zelner died of natural causes. Our office had no more involvement after the coroner sent the report to us."

"What did Mr. Zelner die of?" I said.

"Coronary."

"Is that what the coroner said?"

"Yes."

I desperately wanted to ask if the words "coronary" and "coroner" were linguistically related, but I kept mum.

Ferguson leaned forward in his chair. It creaked. He looked down at the report for a few moments, then he looked at me. "It says here that you picked up Mr. Zelner at Union Station."

"That's correct," I said.

He looked back down at the report. He looked up at me again. A stony silence entered the room. Boyd was looking at me without expression. So was Ferguson. I returned their gazes with what I hoped was a similar lack of anything.

"Can I ask you a question, Murph?" Ferguson said.

I started to feel uneasy. Whenever I was being investigated for murder or kidnapping or bank robbery, the police sometimes said, "Can I ask you a question, Murph?" even though they had been grilling me for an hour.

"Yes," I said.

"How did you know that this key belonged to a locker at Union Station?"

I shifted on my seat. I coughed. I cleared my throat. I did all the things that experienced criminals never do.

"I deduced it," I said.

"How did you deduce it?" Boyd said.

Rather than give him a thumbnail sketch of my unique methods of inference, I decided to back up and slowly work my way toward the conclusion that I had come to so that he could easily follow the thing that I sometimes loosely referred to as "logic."

I described the death of Mr. Zelner, which was a reiteration of the incident report that I had written at Rocky Cab on Wednesday night. "On Thursday morning Mr. Heigger called my apartment and said he was Mr. Zelner's family lawyer. He wanted me to come to his office and answer a few questions. I ended up going to Diamond Hill with him. I drove my Chevy and he followed me in his Cadillac. He wanted to see the place where Mr. Zelner had died, and wanted to ask around at the office buildings about whether Mr. Zelner had sent any luggage on ahead."

Then I told them about Weissberger's trip to Broomfield on Friday. After that I told them about the law office that disappeared on Saturday. I mentioned the "supe" but I skipped *Plan 9 From Outer Space.*

Ferguson nodded slowly, then said, "So Mr. Zelner died in your taxi on Wednesday, and last night you found a key in your taxi and went to Union Station and tried to open locker ninety-six?"

"Yes."

"And you didn't tell anybody at Rocky Mountain Taxicab that you found this key."

"No."

"Did you find the key on the floor of your taxi?"

"No, I found it in an ashtray."

"What ashtray?"

"It was one of those ashtrays that they build into a door-handle … or I mean a door-rest. You know, where you put your arm."

"Armrest," Boyd said.

I nodded.

"How did you happen to find the key?" Ferguson said.

"I was cleaning my taxi last night after my shift ended. I emptied out the ashtray and the key fell into the trash barrel. So I picked it up and examined it. Mr. Zelner had smoked a cigarette in my cab on Wednesday, so I put two-and-two together."

"And what did you come up with?"

"Zero."

"Because the locker was empty?" Ferguson said.

I was getting used to his quirky perceptiveness by now. "Yes," I said. "The locker was empty."

"What did you expect to find in there?"

I stared at him for a while, then shook my head. "You got me."

"Were you disappointed to find it empty?" Ferguson said.

"I was somewhat disappointed," I said.

"Why is that?"

"Well … it seemed like a lot of people were interested in that locker, and since I had this key, I expected to find a valise or something."

"And what did you expect to find in the valise?" Ferguson said.

I suddenly began rubbing my Adam's apple hard, almost squeezing it, because I began to feel a chortle starting to erupt from my esophagus. I somehow managed to prevent this from happening. "You got me again," I said.

"Did Mr. Zelner say anything significant to you before he died?" Boyd said.

"What do you mean?"

"Did he mention for instance … a large sum of money?" I slowly shook my head no.

"Did he say that there was a valise in a locker at Union Station?" I continued to shake my head no.

"Then why did you expect to find a valise in the locker?"

I let go of my Adam's apple and frowned down at my knees. "Because … because … Mr. Heigger had said something about a valise when I talked to him in his office."

Ferguson and Boyd looked at each other.

"Aside from yourself, do you know of anybody else who has seen this Mr. Heigger?" Boyd said.

"No."

"I see," he said. "All right, Murph, there is one other question I would like to ask you."

"Okay."

"Who is Octavia Brandenburg?"

CHAPTER 24

I swallowed hard.

"Octavia Brandenburg?" I said.

Repeating parts of people's questions is something that I do to buy time when I'm frantically scrambling for an answer. I did not invent the technique of course. I have seen plenty of other people do this. In fact, I'll be honest and admit that I myself sometimes ask people certain questions in order to watch them scramble. It amuses me to see people fidget uncomfortably. Why I find this amusing is open to conjecture, although I'm sure a psychotherapist could answer it in the twinkling of an eye.

"Yes," Ferguson said. "According to the medics, you told them that you were being stalked by a woman named Octavia Brandenburg." He was leafing through his notebook as he said this. When he finished his statement he looked up at me with his eyebrows raised.

"I said that?" I said.

"Yes."

I hesitated before deciding whether or not to make up a lie. As a rule of thumb I never lie to the police. I prefer to just get it done and get it out of the way, whatever "it" happens to be.

"There is no Octavia Brandenburg," I said. The two cops glanced at each other.

Ferguson frowned at his notes. "According to the medic, this woman Octavia Brandenburg told you some sort of lie about taking a post office test. You also said something about this woman removing license plates from a car."

"It was her own car," I said quickly. "She was abandoning it."

"I thought you said she doesn't exist."

"Oh. Yes. That's true. She doesn't."

"This woman who doesn't exist," Ferguson said, "is she connected in any way with the men who drew the pistol on you?"

"I don't know," I said.

"In your statement you seemed to be making a connection between the men at the station and this nonexistent woman named Octavia Brandenburg."

"That's probably true," I said.

"Probably true that you said it, or probably true that she is connected with these men?"

"Both," I said.

The stony silence reentered the room.

I finally gave up. "There no Octavia Brandenburg, but there is a Melanie Donaldson."

The detectives stared at me. I would have given my eye-teeth for them to glance at each other, but their eyes were rooted to mine, if that's a proper metaphor. I wasn't much of an English major.

"We're not quite clear on what you're getting at, Murph," Ferguson said. "I realize that you've been under a good deal of stress, and if you would rather put off answering our questions until things are more clear in your mind, we will understand."

"No," I said. "You could put it off from here to eternity and it still wouldn't make any sense. The thing of it is … I made up the name Octavia Brandenburg."

"While you were in the ambulance?" Boyd said.

"No, sir," I said. "I was perfectly sane … or that is to say, I was my regular self when I made it up."

Ferguson wrote something in his notebook, then he looked at me.

"So this woman is named Melanie Donaldson, but you call her Octavia Brandenburg."

"Yes."

"And Melanie Donaldson does exist?"

"Yes."

"Is she stalking you?"

"I don't have any real reason to believe she is."

"Did she lie to you about taking a post office test?"

I started to say yes. I wanted badly to say no. Melanie had seemingly lied to me about taking the test, but I didn't know why. I didn't know where she fit into all this. Suddenly I felt weary. I let out a soft sigh and closed my eyes. "I guess she did, but I don't know what the post office thing was about. All I can tell you is that I made up the name Octavia Brandenburg yesterday, and I guess I must have said that name in the ambulance rather than the woman's real name."

"Why did you make up such an exotic name like that for this woman?" Ferguson said.

I took a deep breath. Here it came—the thing that I feared most. "Because I'm an unpublished novelist."

There.

I said it.

The words hung in the air between us like a bleached skeleton sprawled on the burning sands of Death Valley for all the world to laugh at. I gritted my teeth and waited for derisive sneers to sprout on their lean cheeks.

"My brother-in-law Pete is an unpublished novelist," Boyd said. "He sometimes calls me 'Boston Blackie.' He's a card."

"Pete once called me 'Flatfoot Ferguson,'" Ferguson said. "Was that at the last New Year's Eve party?" Boyd said.

"Yeah."

"He was plastered to the gills."

"Pete's okay. I didn't hold it against him. My wife laughed when I told her about it."

I listened to this dialogue with an astonishment that turned to chagrin. I wanted them to get back to the subject of me. I hate it when people talk about other unpublished writers.

"Let me see if I have this straight," Ferguson said. "This woman is named Melanie Donaldson, but you refer to her as Octavia Brandenburg because you're a writer of prose fiction who likes to play with words. Is that correct?"

"Yes," I said, although I was frowning when I said it. I had not mentioned the concept of "playing with words."

"Don't ever play Scrabble for money with Pete," Boyd said. "I think he memorized the Oxford English Dictionary."

"I wish you had told me that last New Year's Eve," Ferguson said. "He took me to the cleaners."

Boyd's reference to the Oxford English Dictionary added to my annoyance. I had thought that only English majors knew about the OED. The notion that "ordinary" people were familiar with that massive, multi-volume compendium of words had the peculiar effect of making me feel less special than I ordinarily feel. I'll be honest. After you've spent seven years earning a bachelor's degree in English, you rarely get the chance to feel special.

"Since you have cleared up the reference to Octavia Brandenburg, I have another question to ask," Boyd said.

"Okay."

"Who is Melanie Donaldson?"

As I opened my mouth to reply I began to feel stupid. All of the surmise about Melanie began to fade like a vampire exposed to the light of dawn. Beyond suspecting that she was in league with two men who may have tried to kill me, all I really knew about Melanie was what I ended up saying to Ferguson and Boyd.

"She's a woman I encountered after I dropped off Mr. Weissberger in Broomfield. Her car had broken down, so she removed her license plates and abandoned it. Then I drove her to the Hyatt Hotel. She said she was going to take a post office test, but I later found out there was no test. I guess she was lying, but lying to a cab driver isn't against the law so I figured she was going there to meet a man or something, and had just made up the story about the test. That's all."

"That's everything?"

"No. Three days later she called me for a date. She wanted to buy me dinner to thank me for getting her to the Hyatt on time to take the test."

"Even though there was no test?"

"Yes. She said she was divorced and had a six-year-old daughter and lived near Broomfield ... but I don't know what was really going on."

"Is that everything?"

"No. After dinner she invited me to her hotel room. But I didn't go."

Boyd looked at Ferguson. Both of them raised their eyebrows. I waited for them to pursue their line of questioning and try to find out why I was out of my gourd. But they surprised me by not doing that.

"Murph, last night we were called to Denver General Hospital because a medic reported that someone had drawn a gun at Union Station," Ferguson said. "The report was given to him by a man who was unconscious when we arrived at DGH. That man was you. But so far we have uncovered no evidence that a gun was drawn at Union Station, or that any of these other events took place. We have only your word."

I nodded. I knew what my word meant. It meant nothing. "Can I ask you a personal question, Murph?"

"Yes."

"What I'm going to ask you stays in this room, so I want you to understand that you will not get into any trouble regardless of how you answer it."

"I understand."

"Do you do drugs, Murph?"

"No."

I knew what he meant, and he did not mean alcohol. "Have you ever undergone a drug test?"

"Yes."

"When?"

"Every time we take a physical for the cab company, we drivers have to provide a urine sample."

"Do you always pass the test?"

"Yes."

"When was the last time you took the drug test?"

"A couple months ago."

"Did the death of Mr. Zelner upset you?"

"Pardon?"

"Did the fact of a man dying in the backseat of your taxi upset you in any way? I mean … psychologically?"

"I was … well … I felt rather … you know …"

"Freaked out?" Ferguson said.

"Not exactly that. I just … felt …"

For the first time in my life I was at a loss for words. You should have been there.

"I want to ask you another personal question, Murph," he said, leaning forward with his elbows on his desk.

"Okay."

"Have you ever had any psychological counseling?"

I blinked. "Are you asking me if I've ever had any goddamn therapy?"

"Yes."

"No."

He nodded, then glanced up at Boyd who was standing beside my chair. "All right," Ferguson said. "We're going to turn this case over to the day shift. They'll be going down to Rocky Cab and make some further inquiries about the death of Mr. Zelner. Until then ..."

"The day shift?" I said.

"That's correct."

"Do you mean Duncan and Argyle?" I said with panic in my voice.

"That's correct. Our department wants to follow up on this gun business as quickly as possible, so we're going to turn the information over to Detectives Duncan and Argyle."

"Are they in the building right now?" I said.

"No, they're out on a call."

I heaved an internal sigh of relief.

"Why do you ask?" Ferguson said. "Would you like to speak with them?"

"No!" I said. "I just ..." promised them that they would never see my face again as long as I lived. "I have met with Detectives Duncan and Argyle on previous occasions." I felt like my brain was beginning to float out the window.

"The thing is," I continued, "I met them when they were investigating some other cases connected with ... the Rocky Mountain Taxicab Company." I quietly sighed with resignation. I told them that Detectives Duncan and Argyle could fill them in on anything they needed to know about my background. I did this partly because I wanted to make it clear that I was willing to cooperate with the investigation and had nothing to hide, but mostly because I wanted Ferguson and Boyd—rather than myself—to break the news to Duncan and Argyle that I was back in the loop.

I also felt it would take entirely too long for me to tell them everything that they would inevitably want to know about me. Which is to say, Dunk and Argy probably had a file on me a foot thick.

"When we talk to them later, would you like us to say hello for you?" Boyd said.

"If you wish," I said. "I just thought it might be best to mention the fact that I have already met them."

I felt like a chess master arranging my pawns to protect my king. My king was me. My pawns were the men who had long ago gotten tired of seeing my face.

This is probably as good a time as any to mention the fact that I am lousy at chess.

The "stranger" suddenly stepped in and spoke up.

"Well, gentlemen, if that's all you need me for, I have a number of things to do today."

"We're finished with you for now, Murph. But we may need to talk to you again about this business with the gun."

"I could always come by late at night when you are on duty," I said. "That would be convenient for me."

"All right, we'll see. But after Detectives Duncan and Argyle speak with your supervisor they might want to talk to you about this case." My head started to swivel as if I was looking around for a lost pencil on the desktop.

I stopped doing that and nodded. "That's fine," I said.

"We appreciate your coming in to talk with us," Boyd said. "You're free to leave now, Murph."

I stood up from my chair and looked at the door. I didn't want to go out that door. I was afraid I might run into Duncan and Argyle. But into each life a little rain must fall.

I took a deep breath and didn't let it out until I was on the ground floor walking quickly toward the exit of the building.

CHAPTER 25

After I got outside I exhaled and started walking toward Colfax Avenue. I thought about hopping aboard the #15 bus and heading east, but that idea made me feel worse than I already did. The interview with Ferguson and Boyd, combined with the fear of seeing Duncan and Argyle, had depleted my energy. You need a lot of energy to brace yourself for a ride on the 15. Fortunately the Brown Palace was a couple blocks north of Colfax, so I continued on up to the hotel. I decided to take a taxi home.

When I got to the Brown I saw two Rocky Cabs and a Yellow Cab parked in line. I didn't want to climb into a Rocky. I didn't want to have to explain myself to the driver if he recognized me. I didn't want to climb into a Yellow either because of the bet that I don't want to go into, but I decided that risking my life in the backseat of a Yellow Cab was better than trying to explain myself to anybody.

William was acting as palace guard that morning, so I walked over and used what was left of my depleted energy to smile at him. I told him I wanted to catch a ride in the Yellow Cab. I supplemented this explanation with a five-dollar tip. I told him that I would go into the lobby and wait until the Yellow was first in line. It would take time and patience, but I was desperate.

I went into the hotel, however I didn't go all the way into the main lobby. I looked like hell and I knew it. William hadn't said anything to me about how I looked, but he was used to how cab drivers look. I stood just inside the entryway and pretended that I was a janitor. I didn't know if the rich people walking in and out the door knew what I was pretending, but I pretended that they did. I was draping myself with layers of pretense. It almost felt like I had pulled my bed covers over my face.

After ten minutes William stepped into the entry and smiled at me and said my chariot had arrived. He didn't actually say "chariot" but I pretended he did. When I walked out the door of the Brown I pretended I was a rich businessman headed for DIA. I had four or five layers of pretense draped over me by then, but they didn't fool the Yellow driver. He seemed annoyed after I climbed into the backseat and told him I was going to Capitol Hill. This meant he was either a newbie or an amateur. Professional cab drivers know that short trips come with the territory and they take it in their stride. It takes an ego of monstrous proportions to expect a DIA trip every time I park at the Brown.

The distance from the Brown to my apartment is three dollars and sixty cents, but I handed the driver a ten-dollar bill and told him to keep the change. I did this to teach him a lesson. The lesson can be summed up in one word: "kwicherbitchen." Fishermen often say this although I don't know why. Back when Stapleton International Airport was open for business a ten-dollar trip from the Brown was considered a sweet ride, but DIA had destroyed the perspective of Denver cabbies. This is indirectly related to Parkinson's Law.

I got out of the cab in front of my building and did something that I virtually never did, which was enter by the front door. I glanced at my mailbox before I went inside, and was pleased to note that it was empty. The junk mail people had given up on me.

The mailboxes are nailed to the brick wall right by the door, but since nobody ever writes to me except my Maw, I have found that the law of diminishing returns dictates that I needn't bother checking my box every day. Once a month usually suffices. When Maw gets serious about communicating with me she takes the phone route. As Mr. Weissberger had said, "The art of letter writing has faded from the world," thank God.

But mailboxes themselves fascinate me. They are like atom bombs. They are about the safest things in America. Nobody tampers with them. You never hear about people robbing mailboxes. Oh I know, welfare checks do get stolen from boxes where street punks and junkies run wild, but I'm talking about regular people. I think if you could get them to come clean, most Americans would admit that they are scared to death of mailboxes.

I climbed the interior stairwell and managed not to encounter any of my fellow tenants. Five years earlier I had encountered the woman who used to sunbathe topless on the second floor landing of the fire escape. She was wearing clothes, but I got so rattled that I turned around and hurried back downstairs and went to a bar. I don't remember what happened after that, beyond taking a vow to never again enter my building by the front door. Yet here I was, breaking another vow. I break them with regularity so I don't know why I even bring it up.

I unlocked my apartment door, stepped inside and closed it. I entered the living room and immediately glanced at my AudioMaster DeLuxe. I was pleased to note that I had no messages blinking blinking blinking like a babbling idiot who was fool enough to think I was going to return a call. Even the telemarketers had given up on me—except for the occasional newbie. But I am willing to cut slack for all newbies, having been one myself so many times on so many different jobs before I settled like silt into cab driving. Even when I was in second grade I was tolerant of the first-graders.

I wanted nothing more than to collapse into bed, but I knew I'd better take a shower first and wash all the hospital germs off my body. I was also hungry for a cheese sandwich and a soda. It irritated me to think about all the things I had to do for my body before I could let it topple onto my mattress. But flesh maintenance is the price we pay for the delightful privilege of living on this giant ball of dirt careening through outer space toward oblivion.

I walked into the kitchen, took off my coat, and washed up at the sink in order to kick-start my ablutions. I didn't want to touch anything in my apartment while I still had "hospital hands." I once worked as a janitor in a medical clinic. It gave me a psychological tic.

As I was drying my hands with a paper towel I drifted over to the kitchen window and peeked out the curtain, which I frequently do when I'm in my apartment. You may have experienced this yourself—not in my apartment but in your own living quarters. I am always peeking out curtains just to see what's happening on the street. My mother is the same way. I don't know what sort of gripping scenarios Maw expects to see on the residential streets of Wichita, but I can tell you what I saw from my kitchen window that day: my Chevy was parked in the choice V-spot.

I froze.

I eased away from the window and stood there a moment trying to think. That didn't work, so I tossed the paper towel in the trash and walked through my apartment to the bedroom. I went to the window at the head of my bed and peeked out to see if there were any strange cars parked near my building. The street was filled with strange cars but I recognized all of them. Most of the people who live on my block are in the same income bracket as myself. One of them owns a 1951 Studebaker.

I walked back into the kitchen and peeked out the window. My Chevy was still there. I was sort of hoping it would be gone. I don't mean stolen. I was thinking in terms of "hallucination" as Detective Ferguson had so diplomatically put it.

I peered over at 13th Avenue but didn't see any unfamiliar strange cars except a purple Gremlin. I once had a buddy in college who drove a purple Gremlin. This made me uneasy. I still owed him five bucks. Could that be his car? Could he have driven all the way from Wichita just to get revenge? Was he the puppet-master behind these events? He once glued a chalkboard eraser to a podium in history class. The professor was livid.

I decided not to follow up on that theory. Instead I went down the fire escape. I didn't care anymore. If someone was watching me I would give him what he wanted. I couldn't stay inside my apartment for the rest of my life, unless I was a millionaire. Part of my Big Dream is to have my groceries delivered weekly, and have nothing hanging in my closet except dusty taxi uniforms.

I got down to the ground and approached my Chevy. The keys to the car were in my pocket so I knew it must have been hot-wired at Union Station. The question was whether it was still hot-wired—which is to say, was there a bomb attached to the ignition just waiting for me to go shopping? I cannot tell you how crippling it is to have a vivid imagination. But why would anybody want to blast me to smithereens? There are easier ways to get rid of guys like me. Whenever I was at a party in college, the host would simply tell me that the keg was empty. I was gone in sixty seconds.

I tried to act casual as I approached the driver's side door, although I don't know why. If any assassins were watching me they would probably know I was faking it, and doubtless having a good chuckle at my expense.

The window was rolled halfway down. This annoyed me. Didn't assassins understand that an automobile could get stolen with a window open like that? I leaned toward the window to see if a bundle of dynamite was piled on the driver's seat, even though I knew from movies that the bomb would be attached to the engine. There is a dull predictability to mob hits. I didn't see any dynamite but I did see my Rocky cap. It was lying on the passenger seat. Resting beside it was a bottle of nasal spray. The plastic cap was missing.

I started to reach for the door handle then I stopped. I decided not to open the door. I decided I didn't want to end up lying in a pool of blood while staring at parts of my car raining down from the sky. I decided I would go with my first guess in the SAT of life. This made me feel bad. It meant my test would be graded by the kinds of teachers who carry badges. For the first time in my life I prayed I would fail the test, i.e., I hoped that my answer would be wrong even though the consequences could be more dire than if I guessed right. Which is to say, if I was blown out of existence I wouldn't have to try and explain how the bomb had gotten there—but if the cops didn't find a bomb I would find myself having to explain my imagination to Duncan and Argyle. I had taken that oral exam numerous times and didn't do very well. Detectives don't fool around with letter grades.

With them it's strictly pass/fail.

I turned around and trudged back up the fire escape to my crow's nest. I think I groaned a couple of times on the way up. I usually do. I wanted to shower and go to bed, but I knew that if I didn't call the cops right away and report that my stolen car had been found, and that I was afraid it might be wired to explode, Duncan and Argyle might end up frowning deeper than any two human beings had ever frowned in the entire history of disapproval. Not even twelve years of Catholic schooling had prepared me for a rebuke of that magnitude.

As soon as I entered my apartment the telephone rang.

Normally I would have stopped dead in my tracks, in the same way that I stop dead whenever a small dog charges me when I'm walking toward the front door of a house where a fare has called for a cab. Oddly enough, I have never been charged by a large dog. I know a guy who reads meters for the Public Service Company and he has been charged by large dogs on numerous occasions, but this usually involves backyards. One thing I have learned about small dogs is that they are all bluff. There is something hilarious about a canine the size of a billiard ball baring its teensy teeth. It reminds me of gym coaches.

The phone rang three times before I made my decision. Rather than let the AudioMaster do the dirty work, I grabbed the phone, lifted it to my ear, pinched my nostrils and said, "Yeh?"

"Is this Brendan Murphy?"

"Ooose calling?" I wheezed.

"This is Detective Duncan from the Denver Police Department."

Fer the luvva Christ.

I let go of my nose and cleared my throat.

"Bad connection here," I said. "This is Brendan Murphy."

"Hi Murph," Duncan said. He remembered my nickname. I appreciated that. But I wasn't surprised. I had rebuked him on numerous occasions for calling me "Mr. Murphy."

"Hello Officer Duncan," I said.

"Listen, Murph, my partner Artie and I just finished speaking with your managing supervisor at Rocky Cab and we would like to have a talk with you."

"Artie?" I said.

"Detective Argyle," he said.

"Your partner's name is Artie Argyle?" I said.

"Yes."

I pinched my nose and tried to keep from chortling.

Duncan continued: "This morning Detectives Ferguson and Boyd asked us to look into the report you made that someone had pulled a gun on you at Union Station last night."

"Yes," I said maturely, "they did inform me that they were going to proceed in that manner."

"I was wondering if you could come down to DPD today, Murph."

I closed my eyes and slumped against the wall. I decided I might as well get it done and get it out of the way.

"I was just about to call you, Detective Duncan."

"Oh?"

"Yes, sir. I filed a stolen car report with Detectives Ferguson and Boyd when I was at DPD this morning. But when I got back to my apartment I found my sixty-four Chevy in the parking lot."

"Is that so?"

"Yes."

"Interesting."

"I suppose you could look at it that way."

"I understand that your Chevy was stolen last Monday, too," he said.

"Yes," I said. "It gets stolen a lot."

"I remember you remarking on that a number of times in the past, Murph. Is that why you wanted to get in touch with me?"

"Partly."

"Partly?"

"Yes … partly." I took a deep breath and sighed. "I would have called Gladys and told her that I got my car back but I decided I had better call you."

"Why is that, Murph?" he said, his voice turning level and cold. He had spoken in the same tone of voice the first time I met him. That was during the teenage-girl/kidnap/homicide deal that turned out happily. But I didn't blame him for speaking that way at the time. He hadn't known me from Adam.

I paused a moment because I didn't really want to say what I knew I had to say. Then I said it: "Because I'm afraid of my car."

"Why are you afraid of your car, Murph?"

"I'm worried that there might be a bomb wired to my ignition."

"Where exactly is your car parked right now?" he abruptly said.

"In the choice V … I mean it's parked in the lot behind my apartment building."

"I want you to stay right where you are, Murph. Don't go near the back door. I'll have some people over there right away."

He rang off.

CHAPTER 26

In less than two minutes I heard the wail of sirens in the distance. I wanted to go to a window and look out but Duncan had told me to stay put. Half a minute later I heard another siren, and another. As the sounds of sirens grew louder and closer I started thinking about the Doppler Effect. I had some trouble remembering the significance of the Doppler Effect in relation to sound, just like in high school where I failed earth science. The class was taught by a gym coach. He spent most of his time telling stories about his service in the Korean War. The rowdies at the back of the classroom always got him going on Korea.

By now the sirens were dropping to growling whirs both at the rear of my building as well as the front. I heard a lot of shouting. It sounded like the voices of men who knew their business. I remained by the phone. I had the bizarre urge to call someone and say that I was standing in the midst of chaos. But my friends had gotten tired of that long ago.

Then I heard a pounding on the interior stairwell and more shouts. I realized that the men who knew their business were hammering on tenant doors. Pretty soon they got to my door. I decided to violate Detective Duncan's directive and move from my spot. The last time someone had hammered on my door it was a S.W.A.T. team, but I don't have time to get into that.

"Open up!" a man shouted.

I yanked my front door open and saw firefighters dressed in yellow rubber spacesuits, including scuba tanks.

"We're evacuating the building, you'll have to come with us!"

I went with them. I had been expecting policemen. My reaction was Pavlovian I suppose. The S.W.A.T. team had pointed guns at me, but again no time to explain.

When we exited the front door of the building I saw a fire truck parked at 13th Avenue near a hydrant. There were cop cars all over the place. Emergency lights were flashing. I could see red glows bouncing off the trees even though it was broad daylight. Standing across the street next to a firefighter was Keith. He was wearing normal clothes. His eyes were as big as ping-pong balls. I looked around the neighborhood but didn't see any other tenants, I saw only Keith, and it occurred to me that everyone else was probably at work. I tend to forget that most people have real jobs. I would have hated to have interrupted their daily routines. Thank God for honest labor.

I was about the ask the firefighter if he wanted me to go across the street and stand with Keith, then I saw Detectives Duncan and Argyle coming around the corner from 13th Avenue at a fast walk. I hadn't seen them in quite a while. It felt like old home week. If you have ever spent Christmas with your relatives then you know how I felt—I braced myself, swallowed hard, and wondered if I should apologize for letting them see me again. This is a psychological tic from which I will never be cured unless I leave town forever, presumably under cover of darkness.

Duncan walked right up to me and said, "Are you okay, Murph?"

"I'm okay."

Duncan nodded at a firefighter and said, "O'Malley," in obvious greeting. The firefighter nodded at Duncan and said, "I brought this man down from the top floor."

Duncan nodded. "This is Mr. Murphy," he said. "We need to speak with him."

O'Malley nodded. "All right. The fire investigator might want to talk to him later."

Duncan nodded.

I felt like a "thing" that they were discussing in an official capacity. To a certain extent, I was.

O'Malley walked away. I glanced across the street. Keith was looking right at me. I debated whether to give him a little wave of greeting. I decided against it. There were policemen and firefighters all over the place and I was afraid I would look like one of those cocky homicidal maniacs who hobnob with reporters during a perp walk.

"Come with us, Murph," Duncan said.

We walked up to 13th Avenue, turned right and walked for a quarter of a block until we came to the entrance that led to the parking lot behind my building. I saw another fire truck blocking the avenue beyond the entrance. I saw more police cars. There were also two ambulances. But the best thing I saw was a DPD bomb-squad wagon parked in my lot. It was not far away from my Chevy. Neither was the bomb crew. They were crawling all over my car. The hood was up. So was the trunk lid. This didn't surprise me. My trunk stopped locking years ago. I rely on gravity and a small loop of twine to keep it generally closed. Two men were on the ground peering beneath the frame. The doors were open and the backseat had been removed.

One of the men saw Duncan and began walking toward us. He had the rank of "captain" written all over him although I didn't know if that was an actual rank in a bomb squad, but it might as well have been. He looked like every captain I ever met, and believe me I've met a lot of captains. He was wearing a safety helmet with a Plexiglas visor. He was wearing a protective vest and gloves. I'm sure you've seen bomb-squad gear on TV. If not, you need to watch more TV.

"That automobile is clear," he said, removing his headgear. "No evidence of an explosive device of any sort."

Let me pause here a moment to talk about the adrenaline that had been coursing through my system ever since I had heard the first siren. I was barely aware of it, which is the peculiar nature of adrenaline. You become physically hypersensitive to the extent that you don't notice the adrenaline itself because you are too busy seeing and hearing things that you never perceive in the normal course of existence. Your nerves register every sight and sound within the vicinity, and Time seems to slow down. It's like being in a David Lean movie called I'm Dying Now So Don't Bother Me—it goes on forever, and in CinemaScope. This is all tied in with the anticipation of imminent danger. It's only after the danger has passed that you become aware that the adrenaline is making you vibrate like jelly because jam don't shake like that.

"No bomb?" Argyle said.

"Nosir," the captain said. "No bomb. All we found in the car were these."

He handed the Rocky cap and the nose-spray bottle to Duncan. Duncan examined them, then looked at me. "Are these yours, Murph?"

"Yes," I said, without too much deliberation.

I forgot to add that there was a faint ringing in my ears. Adrenaline does this to me, too. But the ringing was beginning to fade. Time had accelerated back to normal speed, which I guess would be from a negative velocity up to the rate of zero. I don't know if that's possible, but that's what happened.

I looked around at all the policemen and firefighters and bomb crew. I looked at the police cars and fire trucks and ambulances and bomb-squad wagon. Then I looked at Duncan and Argyle. They were looking at me, the last thing on earth I wanted them to look at.

"Hi, Artie," my mouth said.

"Hello, Murph," Detective Argyle said. "Can I ask you a question?"

"Sure."

"What made you think there was a bomb planted in your Chevy?"

I smiled at him with my lips closed. Then I looked at Duncan with my lips still closed. I finally opened them and started to say, "I have a vivid imagination," but something stopped me. The "stranger" I supposed.

"It's a long story," I said.

"Make it short," Argyle said.

I looked at the captain. He was gazing at me with an expression bordering on curiosity. I say "bordering" because I was afraid to look on the other side of that fence.

"Someone threatened to shoot me at Union Station last night, and I was afraid they were still out to get me."

Glance.

Duncan and Argyle did this—meaning they glanced at each other. All cops do this when I talk. It happens so often that I sometimes resort to the word "Glance" just to save time. I don't know why. I guess I like to think I'm efficient.

"Did you see an object attached to your car that you thought was a bomb?" Duncan said.

"No."

"Do you have any reason to believe that there is a bomb planted somewhere in this neighborhood?"

"No."

The captain was now peering at me with an expression on his face that I will describe as somewhat "doleful." Or maybe "doubtful." Or maybe "disgusted." Or maybe all three. He reminded me of Captain Gertler. Especially when he growled, "Is this the man who phoned in the false bomb report?"

"We haven't fully established that the report was false," Duncan said. His words seemed to indicate that he was on my side, although I couldn't say the same thing about his tone of voice.

I heard a vibrating sound. I looked at my fire escape. Two bomb-squad men were coming down from my crow's nest. The door to my kitchen was wide open. Had my Fourth Amendment rights been violated? I hoped not. The last place on earth I wanted to defend my rights was in a courtroom, but this had always been true.

"We will be taking custody of Mr. Murphy," Duncan said. "Why don't you have your men put his car back together. Then you can go." The bomb-squad captain pursed his lips and gave me the 3-D look again, then turned and walked back to my Chevy and started giving orders. I gazed at my car dolefully as the crew began putting it together like a jig-saw puzzle. I wondered if they had found anything lying under the back-seat. I had never looked under there before. I once found one hundred thousand dollars lying under the backseat of my taxi. It almost caused me to take up a life of ease.

"With your permission, Murph, my partner and I would like to es-cort you upstairs to your apartment. We have a few questions we would like to ask you."

I nodded. I put the Fourth Amendment conundrum behind me. I had the feeling that there were a lot of other amendments that I should be more concerned with right then, except for the Second Amendment. I don't own a gun, but the police already knew that from the one hundred thousand dollar debacle.

I led Duncan and Argyle upstairs to my apartment. They entered be-hind me and left the kitchen door open. We walked into the living room. I would have bade them sit down but there was no place for them to sit. I have only one chair, my easy chair, which is located directly across from my TV. After my cable was installed I spent an entire evening lining up my chair so that it was aimed perfectly perpendicular to the TV screen. It has never been moved since.

"Have a seat, Murph," Duncan said.

I sat down on my chair and looked up at them.

Detective Argyle was holding my Rocky cap and the nose-spray bot-tle. It occurred to me that those two items ought to have been sealed in a plastic bag as evidence, but I didn't say anything. Duncan and Argyle knew their business, this I knew.

Duncan blew out a sigh that puffed his cheeks. "We have a problem here, Murph."

I nodded. I didn't know the nature of the problem but I knew it didn't matter. Whenever cops talk to me, it's always in the nature of a problem.

"Last night you reported that one of two men pulled a gun on you at Union Station, correct?"

"Yes."

"Detectives Ferguson and Boyd investigated that claim, and they were unable to come up with any evidence that anything you said to them was true."

I nodded. "They did tell me that they were unable to find any corroborating witnesses." I said "corroborating" because I thought it would sound like I was hip to cop lingo and thus would make me a sympathetic figure.

"They took a look at locker ninety-six," Argyle said. "The key was in the lock."

"I know," I said. "I left it there last night before I went out and got into the taxi."

Glance.

"My partner and I spoke with your supervisor down at Rocky Cab. Mr. Hogan told us that he has no first-hand knowledge of the existence of this lawyer named Mr. Heigger. There is a phone record of a call that came to Rocky Cab last Friday ordering a taxi to go to an address on 10th Avenue. Aside from that he knows nothing about the person who made the call. But he did say one interesting thing."

"What's that?" I said.

"He said you called Rocky Cab on Saturday and asked an employee named Stew for a phone number of a Heigger & Associates. You said that you had gone to that office on Saturday but the place had been cleared out."

"That's right."

"We checked into this, and we could find no Heigger & Associates listed in the phone book or any other directory. In fact, we came to the conclusion that Heigger & Associates does not exist."

"Me too," I said.

"What do you mean, Murph?"

"I couldn't find the office in the phone book either."

"According to the story that you told Detectives Ferguson and Boyd, you went to this office two other times, once on Thursday and once on Friday."

"That's true," I said. "The office existed on those days."

"You told them you spoke with Mr. Heigger."

"Yes, I did. I spoke with his friend Mr. Weissberger, too."

"And you drove him to an address up near Broomfield, correct?"

"Correct."

"Can you tell us anything about Mr. Weissberger?"

"He pulled a gun on me at Union Station."

Glance.

"And you subsequently squirted him with ammonia, correct?"

"Correct," I said. "I carry ammonia in that bottle whenever I drive my taxi. I do it for self-protection, but I have never squirted it while on duty."

Argyle nodded and held the tip of the bottle to his nose. He gave it a quick sniff.

"This doesn't smell like ammonia to me," he said. He handed it to Duncan, who gave it a quick sniff. He shook his head no.

"What do you mean?" I said, sitting forward in my chair.

Duncan held the bottle out to me. I took it. The bottle felt full. I held the tip to my nose and took a bunch of quick tiny sniffs—I was still gun-shy from the high school debacle.

Argyle spoke: "That smells like ordinary nose spray."

I lowered the bottle and sank back into my chair. "Last night it was filled with ammonia," I said.

Duncan held out his hand.

I returned the "evidence" to him.

"You reported last night that someone pulled a gun on you at Union Station," Duncan said. "And this morning you reported that a bomb might be planted in your car."

He stopped talking and stared at me.

I stared back. I didn't know what else to do.

"We have not been able to find any evidence that any of your claims are true," he said. He held up the bottle of nose spray. "How do you account for the fact that this bottle does not contain ammonia?"

I stared at the bottle for a while, then said, "Perhaps it's not the same bottle."

Duncan examined it. He held it toward me. "It looks like a pretty old bottle, Murph. I notice that the text on the plastic is somewhat worn away. Would you take a closer look and give me your opinion?" I looked at the bottle. I had been carrying ammonia for thirteen years. I had bought the bottle at a drugstore called Skaggs, but they went out of business years ago. I reached into my pocket and pulled out the plastic cap. I handed it to Duncan.

"It's the same bottle," I said. "This is the cap. But I can't account for the fact that there's no ammonia in it, except that somebody must have removed the ammonia and replaced it with nose spray."

"Why would anybody do that, Murph?" Duncan said, as he slowly, gently, screwed the cap onto the tip of the bottle.

I shrugged and shook my head. "I don't know."

"Yes … why would anybody go to all the trouble of removing ammonia from a squeeze-bottle and then replace it with nose spray, Murph?" Argyle said.

I looked at Argyle. I had just answered that question, but I knew what was really going on. They were playing a softcore version of bad-cop/bad-cop.

"You got me," I said.

At this point Argyle looked around my apartment. He looked at my TV, then he looked at my RamBlaster, then he wandered over to the bookshelf made of unpublished manuscripts.

"If I remember correctly, you once told us that you were an unpublished writer, Murph. Are you still an unpublished writer?"

"Nothing's changed," I said.

"Do you like making up stories, Murph?"

"Yes," I replied honestly.

"What kind of stories do you like to make up, Murph?"

"Anything that will sell."

"Do you like making up suspense novels?"

"Yes."

"Police procedurals?"

"No."

"No?"

"No. I hope you men won't take this as an insult," I said, "but police procedurals bore me."

"Me too," Duncan said.

"Same here," Argyle said. "We get enough of that on the job."

I nodded. "Astronauts probably don't read science-fiction novels either."

"Likely not," Duncan said.

Argyle turned away from the bookshelf. He walked back to my chair and looked down at me.

"Murph," he said. "We are going to have to ask you to come with us."

I nodded.

"We want to be honest with you, Murph," Argyle said. "You have made some fairly serious charges that do not hold up. We will need you to give us a written statement that covers everything you did from the night that Mr. Zelner died in your taxi until you made the false bomb report this morning. We will also need you to explain in detail this business about the key to locker ninety-six."

"Okay," I said.

"Before we take off, Murph, we want to ask you one last question."

"All right."

"Why did you try to open locker ninety-six instead of turning the key in to the lost-and-found at Rocky Cab?"

I took a deep breath and sighed. I looked at my TV. Then I looked at my bookshelf. Then I slowly stood up.

"I'm not a lawyer," I said. "But if I was one, I would advise myself to say nothing more until I got me."

They nodded. They were thoroughly versed in the strange turns my syntax took when my life was going to hell in a hatbox.

I looked around the living room, then looked at the two men. "By any chance would I have time to take a shower before we leave? I have hospital germs on my body."

"I'm afraid not, Murph," Duncan said. "You'll have time for that later. Maybe you should bring a jacket."

I nodded. I went to the closet and got my "big" coat. As I pulled it on I felt—for lack of a more sophisticated word—icky. I decided I would go to Blanchard's as soon as possible. Blanchard's is the name of the coin-operated laundromat down on Colfax where I take my laundry once a month. They serve draft beer at Blanchard's. Nuff said.

Duncan and Argyle escorted me out to the landing. I pulled my door shut and locked it, then went down the steps. Duncan was in front of me and Argyle was behind me. As we approached the bottom step I noticed that the only emergency vehicle still in the lot was an ambulance. The back doors were wide open. Two men in white were standing beside the doors. They were big men, bigger than Duncan and Argyle, and in a lot better shape than me, which describes everybody in Denver over five feet tall.

Duncan stopped when he got to the ground, which forced me to stop on the bottom rung of the fire escape. Argyle placed a hand on my shoulder. The men in white stepped forward. Duncan turned around and said, "Murph, we would like you to ride in the back of this ambulance."

He stepped away. The men in white gently took me by the upper arms. They led me to the ambulance and helped me climb into the rear. I was too stunned to do anything except comply.

You can carve that on my tombstone.

CHAPTER 27

I t seemed like we drove for an awful long time. I was alone in the rear of the ambulance. There was a partition between myself and the driver's compartment. I had seen similar partitions in movies about taxi drivers set in New York City. Except the partitions in the New York taxis were made of transparent Plexiglas and were designed to prevent cabbies from being robbed, whereas this partition was opaque, although it did have a sliding window that opened and closed on occasion. When it opened I saw one of the nurses look in at me. I thought of the two men in white as "nurses." I don't know why. I had long ago given up trying to get a fix on the random associations that floated like flotsam on my brain. Or perhaps "given up" is not the right phrase. I think the right phrase would be associated with the idea of a disfigured man who refuses to look at his face in a mirror. Not that I have anything against disfigured people—hell, half the fares who climb into my taxi look like they wandered out of a Lon Chaney movie.

"Is that so?" I froze.

I looked around. A man was seated on a chair a few feet away. He was wearing white clothing, but rather than the soulless pajamas that male nurses wear in movies, he was wearing a long white laboratory coat and holding a notebook and pencil. I assumed he was a doctor. I doubted that the nurses were authorized to carry pencils. But he did have the same rubber-soled shoes that nurses wear, the kind of soles that squeak on linoleum. You would think that after thousands of years of wearing the flesh of dead animals on our precious little sensitive feet, someone would invent a shoe that didn't squeak. But then maybe the people who manufacture footgear have more important things on their minds than the things that are often on my mind.

"That may be true," the doctor said.

I looked at him again. Then I looked around. I didn't seem to be in the ambulance any longer. I was lying on a bed. A hospital bed, I assumed. I will stick my neck out here and assert that hospital beds are the ugliest beds ever designed by humankind. They make me sick just to look at them.

"How long did you drive a taxi before you came here?" he said.

I looked at him again. But my eyes kept wandering around the room, which I found ironic since there was nothing worth looking at. It was as rectangular as the inside of a locker. But maybe I was wrong. Maybe it was worth looking at because it was the sort of room that might have been designed by an avant-garde artist who was making a statement about the sterile vacuousness of human existence. If I were an artist, that's the kind of statement I would make. Fortunately I'm not an artist. I'm a commercial novelist. I'm in it strictly for the dough.

"Have you ever made any money writing novels?"

I looked at the man again, but my eyes kept drifting away from him in the way that normal eyes drift toward things that stand out from a background, like a soldier's eyes looking at sudden or subtle movements in a jungle terrain.

"No," I said.

"You have been writing novels for more than twenty years, is that correct?"

"Well ... it depends on your definition of the word 'novel.' I've been writing book-length manuscripts ever since I was in college but so far none of the publishers in New York City have opted to categorize them as 'novels.'"

"You spend a great deal of time parsing the meaning of words, don't you Mr. Murphy?"

"I've never clocked myself."

"I am not so much concerned with the amount of time that you spend doing it as I am concerned with the fact that you do it at all," he said.

"Well I …" I said, then I paused, hoping he would interrupt me the way obnoxious people do in movies during arguments. I wanted him to interrupt me because I didn't really have a coherent explanation as to why I spent so much time parsing words, although I did have what might be termed an "incoherent" explanation.

"And what might that be?" he said.

"I was just pretending to have a response to your observation."

"So you didn't actually have a response?"

"That is correct," I said.

"Why would you pretend to respond to something that another person said?"

"Oh … you know … I never have much interest in anything anybody has to say, so I pretend to respond to their questions in the hopes that they will be satisfied and go away."

"Because you have no interest in hearing what they have to say?"

"That's correct."

"Why do you have no interest in hearing what other people have to say?"

"Oooh … probably because I spent twelve years in school listening to teachers say things that had no relevance to anything on the planet earth. It cured me of listening."

"I beg to disagree with you, Mr. Murphy. I find that your explanation is not at all incoherent. All of your explanations appear to be grounded in a well thought-out system of consistent though unorthodox logic."

"A method to my madness, huh?" I said.

"Nobody said you were mad, Mr. Murphy."

"I didn't mean that," I said. "I was just making a joke."

"Are you sure?"

"Yes."

"You joke a lot, don't you Mr. Murphy?"

"Not about jokes."

"What do you mean?"

"When I told you I was making a joke, I was serious."

"I take it you are referring to your statement about a method to your madness."

"Correct."

"But the madness statement itself was a joke."

"Correct."

"You seem to be awfully concerned about establishing the specific meanings contained in words, statements, and concepts in general, Mr. Murphy. I wonder if you could give me some insight as to why this is."

"I would say that it is most likely due to the fact that I spent my entire childhood listening to adults tell me things that I knew or else believed weren't true."

Case in point: when I was ten years old my Maw told me that astronauts could not possibly leave their orbiting capsules for a spacewalk because they would be swept away by the wind.

"Knowledge and belief are not the same thing," the doctor said.

"You better believe it," I snarled.

"Calm down, Mr. Murphy. I'm your friend."

"Please doctor, I'm not interested in your nickel psychology."

"What do you mean?"

"You are not my friend. I don't have any friends. You're just trying to put me at ease. I can read you like an X-ray."

"You say you don't have any friends. Why is that?"

"Because half the people I used to think of as my friends weren't interested in hearing the truth about anything, so they dumped me."

"What about the other half of your friends?"

"They couldn't handle my sarcasm."

"You seem to feel that you possess some sort of monopoly on the truth, Mr. Murphy."

"You got that wrong, doctor."

"How so?"

"I never have a clue as to what's going on. That's why I'm always trying to ferret out the truth. My friends couldn't have cared less about what was really going on."

"What did they care about?"

"Music and sports."

"Don't you like music and sports?"

"I like the Beatles, and I am suspicious of golf. That's all I have to say on those subjects."

"All right," he said, leafing through the pages of the notebook. "What do you say we get back to the subject of the key."

"What key?"

"The key to locker number ninety-six."

"What about it?"

"When you opened the locker did you find anything inside it?"

"No."

"How do you explain that?"

"You're assuming I have an explanation. But I don't. Unlike twits, jerks, and pompous asses, I never explain things that I don't have answers to."

"What about conjecture?"

"Oh yeah, I do that all the time. But I don't define my conjectures as explanations."

"Are your listeners always aware that you are engaging in conjecture?"

"Perhaps not."

"It seems to us that you were considerably determined to access locker number ninety-six. According to our report, you illegally took possession of the key and went to Union Station and opened the locker."

"I don't know that the illegality of my action has been established."

"What do you base that statement on, given the fact that the key did not belong to you?"

"I base it on the fact that I have not been arrested for theft."

There was a moment of silence. A long, long moment.

"You say that you found the key in an ashtray of your taxicab," he said.

"Correct."

"Is it possible that someone gave you the key?"

"Yes and no."

"What do you mean by that?"

"Anything is possible in this three-ring circus we call life—and no, I was not given the key by anybody."

"Is it possible that Mr. Zelner gave you the key on the night he died?"

"Yes and no," I said.

"Yes it's possible but no he didn't?"

"Correct," I said. I just about had this guy trained.

"Aside from your word, do you have any proof that he did not give you the key? Or any proof that you found the key in your ashtray?"

"No."

"Did Mr. Zelner mention locker ninety-six after you were stopped by the policeman who told you about your defective taillight?"

"No, he didn't say anything. He just sat back and died."

"Do you know for a fact that he died right then?"

"No."

"Then why did you say he sat back and died?"

"Conjecture. But he might as well have died right then. He never spoke another word as long as he lived, which was three minutes tops."

"What made you feel that you were authorized to open the locker at Union Station?"

"Oooh, various things. Mostly the fact that Mr. Weissberger had pulled a gun on me. I guess you could say that after being threatened with a gun, and riding a boxcar in a rainstorm, and having my car stolen, I felt sort of 'special.' I decided I would go to the terminal and open the locker and take a look at the thing that nearly cost me my life."

"And what did you intend to do with this 'thing' as you describe it?"

"I don't know. I never got that far with my plan."

"Would you care to conjecture?"

"Maybe."

"Were you going to keep it?"

"What do you mean?"

"Suppose you had found a valise which contained high-grade cocaine or heroin. Would you have thought about keeping it, or perhaps selling it to a drug dealer?"

"Sure."

"Why is that?"

"I'm only human. I probably would have said to myself, 'I'm rich!' I've had thoughts like that before under different circumstances involving different found things, such as stolen money and plaster of Paris and so forth. But the thoughts didn't last very long."

"Why not?"

"Oooh, various reasons. For one thing, it would take a professional drug dealer to pull off a scheme like you described, and not a professional taxi driver. Taxi drivers aren't very good at most things. But I don't break the law on purpose. I'm pretty honest I guess."

"You illegally opened the locker on purpose."

"That's true, but when I'm filled with umbrage my brain tends to fly out the window."

"What if the valise had contained something far more valuable and deadly than heroin?"

"I would have called the police."

"You didn't call the police after you looked into the locker. You exited the terminal and got into a taxi."

"I know."

"Where did you intend to go?"

"To the police."

"Even though you found nothing inside the locker, and possessed no evidence that anything you said was true."

"That's true."

"Weren't you worried that the police might not believe your story?"

"I'm used to that. But I figured I would tell them anyway, especially since everything I said was true."

"Let's recapitulate," he said.

"Again?"

"Yes. You found the key to locker ninety-six in your ashtray. Nobody gave it to you. You went to Union Station and opened the locker and found it empty. Then you went outside and climbed into a taxicab and fainted."

"Yes, although you left out a number of tangential facts."

"You had no idea what was in locker ninety-six, is this true?"

"Yes."

"Mr. Zelner did not mention anything about a valise being inside the locker, or what might be contained inside the valise."

"No."

"You have absolutely no knowledge whatsoever concerning the contents of locker ninety-six."

"I already told you it was empty. I keep telling you that. Why do you keep asking me what was inside locker ninety-six? There was nothing in the locker except a rectangle of air the same size as the interior of the box. I know that because I stuck my hands into the rectangle and felt all around and there was nothing in it but air!"

"Who is Stew?"

"Pardon?"

"Who is Stew?"

"I know a man named Stew who works in the cage at Rocky Cab."

"The cage?"

"The little room where the cashier sits. We call it 'the cage.' The man in the cage takes my lease money and gives me a trip-sheet and the key to my taxi."

"So you don't get to take the key home with you. The man in the cage keeps the key, is this correct?"

"Yes. Well. No. I mean, if you have a weekly lease you get to take the key home. But I always work a daily lease, so the man in the cage takes the key away from me every night."

"Why doesn't he let you keep it?"

I rolled my eyes with impatience. I hate it when people ask me questions that have obvious answers. I always assume they do it to get attention. I know I do.

"Because the driver who works the night shift needs the key to my taxi," I said.

"So they do not make duplicate keys and let each driver have one?"

I almost rolled my eyes with impatience, but then I realized that the answer to his question was not so obvious. I'm willing to cut people slack when they make ignorant remarks about things they know little about. I'm not like an algebra teacher.

"You seem to take a great deal of umbrage at the existence of algebra," he remarked out of the blue. He frequently said things out of the blue. I assumed he did this to throw me off balance. But what he did not realize was that I had patented the off-balance remark. I decided to play along with his insidious little mind game. Maybe I could "turn the tables" on him. I've always wanted to do that to somebody.

"You bet I take umbrage," I said.

"Why is that?"

"Because I was forced against my will to study algebra for two years in high school, and after graduation I found out that algebra has no relationship to anything on earth."

"Engineers use algebra in their line of work."

"Well I'm sure Julius Caesar used Latin in his line of work but he's been dead for two thousand years!" I barked.

"Calm down, Mr. Murphy. No need to get upset over something as meaningless as Latin."

His words had an instant calming effect. Someone was on my side for once. I felt as if he had injected me with the opposite of an upper.

Some people call it a "downer." Not me, baby. I'll take a downer over an upper any day. When I was in college I once took an upper in order to study for a test during finals week, and I ended up mopping an entire dormitory. I have no idea whose dormitory it was but the dorm adviser gave me an A+. After I got to San Francisco I mentioned my grade when I applied for a job as a janitor in a medical clinic. I think it tipped the scales in my favor. I spent six months mopping floors in Hippie Town before I moved on down the road.

"If you mop floors as well as you drive a taxi, I'm sure you made a very successful supe."

"What?"

He repeated it. I won't run you through that again. But it reminded me of something someone else once said, although I couldn't remember who, when, or where.

"I learned to do it properly in the army," I remarked.

"Do what?"

"Mop floors. Fire grenade launchers. Wrap bandages around sucking chest wounds. But mostly I mopped floors."

He nodded. "You once called this man Stew on the telephone and asked him how you might go about contacting a man named Mr. Heigger. Is this correct?"

I paused before nodding. The pause went on so long that it ceased to be a pause. It became a non-answer.

"We have you on a recording tape talking to Stew about Mr. Heigger's phone number."

My chin started to bob slowly up and down. But I wasn't setting into motion the previously unexpressed nod. I was acknowledging to myself the fact that my phone had been tapped after all. The doctor misinterpreted the nod of course, which was exactly what I wanted. I often want people to think something entirely different. My success rate is occasionally higher than I expect it to be.

"Why did you wish to contact Mr. Heigger?" he said.

I stared at him for a moment, then articulated the most-feeble effective excuse ever invented by humankind—to wit: "I don't remember." I did this because the doctor was a stranger and I had no idea what the consequence of my answer might be. Before he took this grilling any further I wanted to know who he was, where I was, and what was going on. I reached deep down inside myself and hauled out a facial expression that communicated those very questions. I rarely dig down that deep—it can get scary.

He closed his notebook.

"That will be enough for today," he said, as he stood up.

"Doctor?" I said.

"Yes, Mr. Murphy?"

"What day is today?"

"Saturday," he said, just before he opened the door, stepped outside, and closed it.

I nodded, even though he did not see my nod, and even though the day of the week meant nothing to me because I did not know how long I had been inside what I could only conjecture was some sort of mental institution. I was reduced to conjecture because I could not remember being brought there, and because I had seen plenty of movies about insane asylums. My favorite was *The Snake Pit*, which was based on a novel by Mary Jane Ward. I saw the movie version when I was six years old, which is probably never a good idea.

The Snake Pit starred Olivia de Havilland, whom I often confused with Yvonne DeCarlo. Yvonne rose to the summit of immortality by portraying Lily Munster, the wife of Herman on the TV series *The Munsters*, which I always thought of as the poor man's *The Addams Family*. But when you are ten years old and there are only three broadcast channels to choose from you take whatever you can get, like a kid dying of thirst on the burning sands of Death Valley. I prefer Morticia Addams over Lily Munster though. "Tish" was portrayed by Carolyn Jones. She co-starred with Elvis Presley in *King Creole*, where the king of rock 'n' roll sang my favorite Elvis song, which is titled "Trouble." He wears a busboy uniform when he sings it. He looks sort of goofy because the white jacket doesn't fit him very well, but when he belts out "… If you're looking for trouble, you've come to the right place …" I forget all about costume design.

"What are you singing, Murph?"

I looked around.

A woman wearing a long white coat was standing in the open doorway.

It was Octavia Brandenburg.

CHAPTER 28

"Was I singing out loud?" I said.

She nodded and approached my bed. "How do you feel, Murph?"

I wracked my brain for a detailed description of my physical and mental well-being, then gave up. I decided Octavia was merely being polite and didn't give a hoot in hell about my health.

"I'm fine," I said, which was far from the truth. In truth, I felt like I had taken two sleeping pills on the previous night. Did I ever mention the fact that sleeping pills make me feel crappy the next day? That's why I opt for severe depression to put me to sleep.

"Do you feel well enough to travel?" she said.

"I'm not going anywhere with you if I can help it."

Octavia smiled at me. Her smile reminded me of the night she had bought me a pizza, the night I put her in stitches telling a cab story about a time when I accidentally shortchanged a blind man. "You can trust me, Murph."

"I don't know what's going on but I would appreciate it if you would stop calling me 'Murph,'" I said for the first time in my life. "My name is Mr. Murphy."

"I know you're upset, Mr. Murphy. I'll try to reassure you, but under one condition."

"This is non-negotiable," I said.

"Okay. I will explain everything that's been happening to you during the past week under one condition—that you stop calling me Octavia Brandenburg."

I froze.

Her statement did nothing to sprinkle oil on troubled waters. I clamped my lips closed and gritted my teeth. I'll admit it. I was scared. This had been the most unnerving week of my life and that included my first week of basic training. When I stepped off the bus in boot camp and took a good look around the flat red earth of ol' Kentucky, I realized that I had arrived at a place and a time in my life when there was nowhere to run and nowhere to hide. I was forced to improvise. If you are a young man or woman thinking of joining the army, I recommend the mop closet. Sergeants rarely look inside the mop closet after the work details have been assigned.

"You don't have any reason to be scared, Murph," she said. "I served in the army, too."

My lips began to go slack. My gritted teeth began to chatter ever so slightly. I felt like I had been clinging to a boxcar for three days and my strength had drained from my body. I felt like I was about to start crying—this was in conjunction with the idea that I seemed to be losing my mind, which was based on the fact that during the past week I had begun to talk out loud without realizing it.

"The doctor has a theory that you unconsciously talk out loud as a defense mechanism," Octavia said.

See! There! I did it again!

"The doctor also told me that you often chortle uncontrollably when you find yourself in the presence of an untruth."

"Who told him that!" I demanded.

"You did."

"Oh."

"He told me that after the death of Mr. Zelner your inherent fear of mortality manifested itself in abrupt chortles as well as talking out loud without being aware of it on a conscious level. In layman's terms this is referred to as 'babbling incoherently.'"

I nodded. "I wasn't even aware of it on a subconscious level," I said, perhaps a bit disingenuously.

"My name is not Melanie Donaldson," Octavia said.

"I'm glad to hear that," I said. "It confirms a suspicion that I began developing during the past week, assuming I haven't been locked up in here for the past year heavily sedated with excessive doses of downers."

"No. You have been here only three days."

"What about the downers part?"

She shrugged slightly, which I interpreted as a resounding YES.

"That leaves me with two questions," I said. "Where am I, and what is your real name?"

"I can't tell you where you are, and I can't tell you my real name."

"Why not?"

"Because that is classified information."

I froze. I had served in the army long enough to know that I should never be allowed anywhere near classified information.

"Why don't you continue to call me 'Melanie'?" she said.

"Am I going to be assassinated?" I abruptly babbled.

I do remember saying that on a conscious level.

"No, Mr. Murphy. You were brought here for a number of reasons that I have been asked to explain to you."

"Who asked you to do that?"

"My immediate superiors."

I gazed at her for a moment, then blurted out, "Who the hell are you?"

She gazed at me for a much longer moment. It had been a long time since a beautiful woman had gazed at me for an extended period of time. It felt pretty good.

She turned her body one hundred and eighty degrees and sat down on the bed next to my goddamn knees. That felt pretty good, too.

"Do you love your country, Mr. Murphy?" she said.

I sighed. "I gave it two of the best years of my life," I said. "That would be twenty, and twenty-one."

"You were willing to give up your life for your country, weren't you, Mr. Murphy?"

I frowned and peered at the ceiling. "The word 'willing' might not be entirely … well … what I mean to say is … I was drafted, so this might to some extent alter the …"

Before I could finish parsing the Selective Service System, Melanie reached out and placed a vertical finger against my lips.

"You are a loyal patriot, Mr. Murphy, and your government needs your help again."

This did not bode well.

"I can't tell you the specifics of who I am or what my job is," she said, "but I can tell you that your government hopes that you still believe in the oath you took to protect and defend the Constitution when you were twenty."

I shrugged, then nodded. "Once a cab driver, always a cab driver."

"I can tell you only that I work for a government agency," she said.

I mulled this over. "Is your agency in any way connected with Harry Truman?"

"I can't tell you that, Mr. Murphy."

"If I let you call me 'Murph' will you tell me if your agency was ever affiliated with Wild Bill Donovan?"

She smiled. "No I won't, Mr. Murphy. You will have to remain in the dark on that subject. But it sounds to me like you have been doing your homework. Where did you learn all this?"

"Oooh, you know, I educated myself after I graduated from high school. I didn't have time to learn anything in high school. I was too busy studying Latin and algebra."

"I can tell you that I am authorized to explain to you what's been going on," Melanie said. "If I tell you that, may I call you 'Murph'?"

"We'll see," I said. My Maw used to say "We'll see" when I asked her if I could do something that I knew I didn't stand a snowball's chance in hell of being allowed to do. It drove me crazy. I wanted a definite answer NOW. I sometimes wondered if Maw was messing with my mind.

"Before I tell you what has been going on, you will have to get out of bed and get dressed and prepare yourself for a trip. You're leaving this place."

"What is this place?" I said.

"We've had that conversation," she said.

Damn but she was good. I couldn't slip anything past her. I felt like writing a letter of commendation to President Truman.

"A couple of things, Murph," Melanie said, jumping the gun on the familiarity deal.

"What's that?"

"Before you leave this room, you will have to be blindfolded." I froze.

"Here's the other thing, Murph," she continued. "Are you afraid of flying?"

"Of course I am," I said. "Anybody who isn't afraid of flying needs some kind of goddamn ... well, I guess that doesn't apply to airline pilots."

"I'm sorry you feel that way, Murph, because you and I are going to take a flight out of here. It won't be in an airplane though. It will be in a helicopter."

Fer the luvva Christ.

"I'll explain everything on the second leg of our journey," she said. She got up from the bed and walked to the door. She opened it and nodded. Someone reached in and handed her what I immediately recognized as a taxi uniform: T-shirt, blue jeans, socks, tennis shoes—thank goodness the underwear was discreetly hidden inside the jeans. Have I ever mentioned the fact that I was raised Catholic?

Melanie left the room while I got dressed. Up until then I had been wearing one of those hospital gowns that fasten in the back. Next to hospital beds they are the ugliest things ever designed by the AMA. On top of that, the gown was blinding white. I finally understood why George Lazenby had been so panic-stricken when he held his intervention when I shopped at the mall.

Five minutes later Melanie returned. She was wearing a long overcoat and carrying my "big" coat as well as a rather complicated blindfold that looked like it might have been designed by a private firm under government contract. I don't know why I say this except that the blindfold actually worked. It resembled the sort of cap that WWI flying-aces wore, except the brim effectively cut off my eyesight. After it was securely fitted in place on my head, I waited for the cuffs to come out. Habit. Instead, Melanie took me by the hand and led me out of the rectangle and into what I had to conjecture was a hallway. I just prayed that we didn't start running. I'll admit it. The moment she told me we were leaving this place, the word "escape" welled up in my mind. This was not unusual. I would have to say that of all the places I have ever left in my life, 23 percent could arguably be defined as "escapes."

Pretty soon we were outside. As we walked along I could feel the wind buffeting my body. I could hear the sound of a helicopter idling on what I conjectured was a "pad." Everything was conjecture now. I felt right at home. Due to the nature of the Doppler Effect I could tell that we were walking toward the eggbeater. The engine gave off a whining sound that I recognized. I conjectured that we were moving toward a HUEY. I remembered the sound of HUEYs from the army. When I was stationed briefly at an army base that shall remain nameless, a HUEY showed up every day at noon and landed in front of the headquarters building to pick up the battalion commander and ferry him down to the main base for lunch. I conjectured that it was a three-martini lunch, although I have no proof—yet.

I myself never drank alcohol at lunchtime in the army, not even beer, since alcohol diminished my ability to effectively hide out from work details. One of the undeniable facts about military service is that a gold-brick has to keep his mind sharp at all times if he expects to fulfill his self-imposed mission. I can't begin to tell you the number of times I secretly watched captured GIs trying to mop floors with booze on their breaths while buck sergeants holding clipboards stood around shooting the breeze with off-duty cooks. After I received my discharge I tried to put those terrible images out of my mind, which is why I rarely talk about my military service, unless I'm at Sweeney's, or there's nothing good on TV.

Melanie helped me climb aboard the chopper. She guided me to a seat, then handed me the two straps of a seatbelt so I could buckle myself in. Okay. I'll admit it. I pretended to fumble with the seatbelt in the hopes that she would get exasperated and buckle it tight for me. But it was no-go. She was probably onto me. I figured she had learned her business at Langley.

I heard Melanie holler something, presumably to the pilot, because the rotors picked up speed, the most disheartening sound I ever heard in my life next to an accelerating airplane. I do hate flying, but then I hate almost everything that involves traveling faster than the posted speed limit. If Charles Darwin had meant for Mankind to fly, he needed some kind of goddamn therapy. As the helicopter arose from the pad it suddenly occurred to me that I myself had just undergone some kind of goddamn therapy. I suspected I needed a bit more because I had let a woman blindfold me and stuff me into a flying machine, and I knew exactly why I had let her do it: she was pretty.

I don't know if you have ever ridden in a helicopter blindfolded—my guess would be no. The only comparison I can make is riding on a Ferris wheel blindfolded, and if you're anything like me you probably did that a couple of times when you were a teenager. I'm pretty sure I did. That was during the summer of my first beer, but let's move on.

Since I was blindfolded I had to rely on my body to ascertain what was going on, which was surprisingly effective. Thanks to the magic of centrifugal force I conjectured that the chopper was circling above the place we had just departed, but then the nose dipped and we shot forward. This caused my arms to flail. My left arm struck what I conjectured was Melanie because she took my hand and lowered it to my side and held onto it. Suddenly I blurted out, "I know how to land a helicopter!"

I said it to reassure the pilot.

"Where did you learn that!" Melanie hollered above the whine of the rotors.

"The motor pool!" I hollered back.

That was where the army officer had explained the concept of 0+0 to me. I still don't remember how I ended up having a conversation about helicopters with an army officer. He was probably bored.

As we sailed through the sky I was grateful that I was wearing a blindfold because the last thing I wanted to see right at that moment was the earth. On the plus side, the blindfold eradicated the effort it would have taken to hold my eyes shut. This got me to thinking about evolution. Given the importance of eyesight to the survival of the species, eyelids are about as indestructible as soap bubbles. If I were Charles Darwin I would have created eyelids as hard as silver dollars. I mean, look at eardrums. You can't even see the damned things.

They're hidden deep inside your head, yet eyeballs are sticking out where an orangutan could rip them to shreds. Frankly I would rather be deaf than blind. I don't read books with my ears, and Europeans long ago had learned to put subtitles on their movies, so to hell with eardrums. Give me optics any day.

These are the kinds of thoughts you have when you're trapped inside a carnival ride run amok. I don't know how long we were in the air—maybe thirty minutes—but suddenly I felt my stomach crawling up my esophagus and I knew we were descending. I had the sudden urge to lean forward and explain landing procedures to the pilot. But people were always leaning forward to tell me things about driving that I didn't want to hear, such as informing me that my taxi meter was defective because it ticked even when we weren't moving, as in a traffic jam. But this is due to the fact that when a taxi slows to below eleven miles an hour the meter automatically switches over to a clock so that the monetary rate is measured by time rather than velocity. I don't tell this to my customers though. I just thank them for pointing it out and promise to have the mechanics look at it when I get back to the shop. It saves me from having to make the kind of long-winded explanation that you just endured.

Ergo, I decided not to explain anything to the pilot. I sat back, crossed my fingers, and waited for 0+0 to take effect. When the chopper finally did set down, it was anticlimactic, thank God.

To my surprise, Melanie unbuckled my belt. It felt pretty good. At least, I think it was Melanie. I was guided out of the chopper by what I assumed were her hands. I expected her to remove the blindfold, but instead she guided me away from the breeze generated by the rotors. The chopper took off a few moments later. I listened to the rising whine as it dwindled into the sky, and I suddenly wondered whether it was daytime or nighttime.

I decided not to ask. If it was nighttime I might have gotten retro-actively nervous because I knew that night flights were more danger-ous than daylight flights, although I didn't know the ratio factor of the risk. The army officer never explained that to me. But I did know that it was more dangerous to drive a taxi at night, and I'm not talking about drunks and weirdos. I had to assume that chopper pilots rarely encoun-tered drunks and weirdos, but there were such things as power lines that could be struck by rotor blades. Taxis rarely hit power lines but there were plenty of other fixed obstacles. I suddenly wondered who the genius was who invented headlights. But then I recalled that horse-drawn carriages had sported lanterns in the olden days. This made me wonder who the genius was that invented the carriage lantern, not to mention the klaxon. Leave it to the human race to invent things that go fast in the dark.

"Where are we?" I said, as the last sounds of the eggbeater faded away. The air smelled strange. No smog.

"You'll know in a minute," the voice of Melanie said. "We have one last thing to do."

I waited for the cuffs to come out. Instead she led me approximately fifty paces toward a rise in what I took to be the earth. "We're getting on a train," she said. She helped me up what I took to be the steps of a Pullman car. We walked a few more paces, then I heard a door close.

"You can take off the blindfold now," Melanie said.

I reached up and removed my WWI cap. I found myself standing in a sleeping-car compartment. Melanie was standing next to me. I glanced at her hands instinctively to see if she was holding a gun. She wasn't. Then I looked out a window. It was dark outside.

I was right.

I grew retroactively nervous.

"Have a seat, Murph," Melanie said.

There was a small couch in the compartment. The couch was the same size as the type of furniture that is commonly referred to by upholsterers as a "loveseat." But I didn't kid myself. After I sat down next to her I couldn't help but feel that I was just sitting on a regular couch.

This turned out to be true.

CHAPTER 29

M elanie looked me right in the eye and said, "Would I be correct in assuming that you have heard of deoxyribonucleic acid?"

"Sure," I said. "That's LSD."

"No," she said. "That's lysergic acid diethylamide. I'm talking about deoxyribonucleic acid."

"Oh yeah," I said. "I always get those two confused."

"Are you serious?" she said.

"I'm afraid so," I said. "One is DNA and the other is LSD. I learned that in college—in a classroom I mean, not at a beer blast or anything."

This was true. To my knowledge I had never taken LSD. On the other hand, I knew that you didn't take DNA, you were born with it inside you. Imagine what the world would be like if we were born with LSD inside us. Our lives would probably be nasty, brutish, and short, but interesting.

"You are familiar with the concept of recombinant DNA, correct?" she said.

I swallowed hard. I suddenly felt like I was talking to a nun. "We did cover that material in class, but I've forgotten the details," I said, summing up my entire education.

"Murph, the man who died in the backseat of your taxi was a scientist who had been experimenting with a malevolent form of recombinant DNA. Our agency has been tracking him for the past three years. Mr. Zelner was not an American. He was from a country where scientific research is not bound by the restrictions that American scientists have to cope with."

"You're not going to tell me the name of the country, are you," I said. It was more of a statement than a question, although the question was implied. But it didn't matter because she continued to talk as though I had not implied anything.

"What do you suppose the world would be like, Murph, if a scientist developed a virus that could be transmitted from one person to another like the common cold, except the effects of inhaling the virus would be similar to that of being bitten by a rattlesnake?"

I thought about this, then said, "You mean if I sneezed in your face, your whole body might end up looking like it got bitten by a rattler?" She neither nodded nor shook her head no, the kind of answer I hate.

"My agency became aware of the nature of his research in recombinant DNA three years ago," Melanie said. "Mr. Zelner entered the United States illegally ten days ago. We picked up his trail when he passed through Vancouver."

She stopped talking and gazed at me.

During the gaze I thought about the class I had taken at UCD. It was a three-hour credit divided into three subjects that covered the study of waves-and-beaches, cosmology—which is about the universe and not hairdressing—and biochemistry, which included the history of the double-helix discovered by two men named Watson and Crick. If you don't know who they are, look them up in the encyclopedia, laddie.

"Waves-and-beaches" was my favorite subject, though, because it explained why England hadn't been washed away by the tides years ago. The biochemistry class covered experiments with e.coli, a bacteria that exists naturally in the human intestine. Scientists had performed experiments where they injected genes from animals into e.coli cells, which theoretically could create a mutation that could become a genetic part of the human body and be passed along through reproduction. You're probably way ahead of me by now—I'm talking lizard people!

I subsequently wrote two hundred pages of a novel about lizard people before I abandoned it. The manuscript lurks near the bottom of my steamer trunk next to Draculina.

"I know," Melanie said. "While you were in our custody we went over your apartment with a fine-tooth comb."

"What?" I said.

"We came across a manuscript you had written which indicated to us that you are familiar with the concept of recombinant DNA."

"What?"

"After Mr. Zelner died, our agency descended on the morgue and took possession of his body ..."

"You examined my unpublished manuscripts?" I said, diverting her from further extrapolation.

"Our people looked them over," Melanie said. "We needed to know exactly who you were and what your relationship might have been with Mr. Zelner."

"They read my books?"

"That included the bookshelf that you built out of manuscripts," she said. She didn't seem apologetic. She seemed like an agent of the government who had more important things to worry about than a stalled writing career.

"Can I ask you a question?" I said.

"Yes."

"Did any of your agents like my books?"

"That information did not make it into the report," she said. "After we took possession of the body we searched Mr. Zelner's clothing for papers that we believed he was going to pass along to two men whom we had tracked from Paraguay. The men were known to you as Mr. Heigger and Mr. Weissberger. Mr. Zelner was known to be carrying a valise, and we were concerned that he might be carrying a sample of the malevolent DNA that he had been experimenting with. But we found no papers, no bottles that might have held a virus, and no valise in his possession."

Suddenly I forgot all about my ego and found myself thinking about the night Mr. Zelner had died. The rain. The windshield wipers.

The fare who came out of nowhere and climbed into Rocky Mountain Taxicab #123. I also thought about hospital germs.

"Mr. Zelner traveled to Sea-Tac airport, then flew to Denver International," she said. "He must have suspected he was being followed. He took a shuttle to downtown Denver, and at some point he eluded our people. After our agency learned that the valise he was carrying was not in his possession, we began to trace his moves from the moment he arrived in Denver. We were afraid that he had already made contact with the persons to whom he intended to transfer his research information."

By this time I had a half-dozen questions, but Melanie made me forget all of them when she said, "Our investigation led us to a taxi driver named Brendan Murphy."

My mouth was starting to open when she said this. It remained open as she said, "We wanted to know if you might be one of Mr. Zelner's contacts in the United States."

You wouldn't believe the chortle that erupted from my throat. Melanie ignored it. She probably had a file on my chortles a foot thick. "You have to understand, Murph, that many of the people whom our agency encounters around the world are not all that different from you. There are taxi drivers from Singapore to Beirut who have been the focus of investigations that have threatened the security of the west."

I didn't know whether to swell with pride, or vomit.

"It's an ugly game we are forced to play, Murph. That's why you were finally taken into custody. We had to find out what you knew. We put a wiretap on your telephone because we needed to know if you had taken possession of the valise that Mr. Zelner was carrying. We wanted to know if you had anything to do with the death of Mr. Zelner. We had to know the extent of your knowledge of the unsanctioned research that had been performed by Mr. Zelner before he died. We had to know if you were a danger to the security of the west."

"What about spider venom?" I said.

She nodded.

Fer the luvva Christ—she knew exactly what I was getting at, i.e., would it be possible to create a virus that would turn a human being into a giant spider bite?

"Who are Heigger and Weissberger?" I said.

"They work for a foreign government."

"Enemy agents?" I said.

She nodded. "They arranged to meet with Mr. Zelner in an obscure location in the United States."

I nodded slowly. "That makes sense," I said. "Denver is the most obscure city in America, and I once lived in ..." but I never got to the punch line. I closed my eyes. I suddenly felt as small and helpless as a ping-pong ball batted around by opponents in a game of geopolitical subterfuge beyond my ken.

I opened my eyes and looked at Melanie.

"Was Mr. Zelner going to meet Heigger and Weissberger on Diamond Hill that night?"

She nodded. "We learned that Mr. Zelner had originally arranged to meet them there and give them the valise. We surmised that Mr. Zelner had put the valise into the locker at the train station after he realized he was being followed. Apparently he was going to give Heigger the key to the locker in exchange for a large sum of money. When you failed to leave Diamond Hill on Wednesday night, Heigger and Weissberger became wary and didn't approach your cab. After the police and ambulance showed up, they were scared off."

"Did your people get around to opening locker ninety-six?"

She nodded. "The authorities at Union Station cooperated with us."

"Did you find the valise?"

She nodded.

I started to ask related questions, but then I paused. My pause had to do with a recollection of certain previous "experiences" with classified information that had nothing to do with mops. It had to do with a two-star general whose army career had ended on a somewhat sour note.

So instead I said, "What about the supe?"

"Who?"

"The janitor who cleans the building where Heigger & Associates was located."

"He's only a janitor. He works weekends. He had nothing to do with this investigation. We discovered that Mr. Heigger had leased the office last week, then cleared out after it had served its purpose."

"Was I its purpose?" I said. She nodded.

Damn. I had been certain that the supe was in on this. I decided not to ask any more questions about him. I didn't want Melanie to know that I would make a terrible secret agent.

"Your government needs your help, Murph."

I almost raised my palms to indicate that I wanted no part of anything conceived of by another human being as long as I lived. But instead I just sat there staring at Melanie and experiencing the same gut-wrenching sensation that I felt on the day I got drafted.

"What does the government want me to do?" I said.

"They want you to remember the oath you took when you became a soldier, and forget that any of these events ever took place. They want you to do nothing."

I almost fell out of my loveseat.

The agency could read me like an X-ray. Suddenly I sat up straight.

"Wait a minute," I said. I pointed a finger at my face, an instinctive gesture that served as a kind of visual aid for the statement I was about to make. "What happened to Heigger and Weissberger on the night I squirted them in the face with ammonia?"

For the first time during the train ride Melanie cracked a grin. "They suffered," she said.

"But I didn't hear them scream."

"Such men are trained not to scream. You and the two men who called themselves Heigger and Weissberger were not alone at Union Station that night. We had agents at the terminal."

"How did you know I was coming to the terminal?"

"We didn't," she said. "Our people followed you there, just as Heigger and Weissberger followed you there. We were trying to find out where Mr. Zelner had secreted his valise."

"Did the valise ..." I paused, then continued, "... contain any bottles?"

She nodded.

I looked down at my hands, then looked at Melanie. "I don't quite know how to say this ... but ... I put my hands into the locker that night. What I'm getting at is ... do I have to worry about laboratory germs?"

She gazed at me for a moment, then shook her head no. "You were given a complete physical as soon as you were taken out of the loop. You have a clean bill of health. You have nothing to worry about."

Obviously she did not know me as well as I unfortunately did. I pictured myself in the very near future climbing naked into a washing machine down at Blanchard's, which was not beyond the realm of possibility, especially during Happy Hour. I once had a similar experience at Kansas Agricultural University during a spring break festival, minus the international implications. Ironically the machine I climbed into was a taxicab, but I don't want to talk about it. Neither did the cab driver, especially when he found out I didn't have any money on me, or anything else on me.

"After you squirted the two men with ammonia and ran away, our people swarmed," Melanie said. "They gave your victims immediate first-aid and spirited them away."

"Why didn't your people grab me?"

"You were too fast," Melanie said. "Your move was unexpected. We didn't realize that you had jumped a boxcar. By the time we understood what had happened, you were gone."

"You mean I escaped from your agents?"

"It's not something we're proud of," Melanie said.

"Did any Singapore cab driver ever do that?" I said.

"No."

"Wow."

The compartment grew silent but for the clickety-clack of wheels on the rails outside the window. I looked at the darkness. I could see the reflection of my own face in the window. I once did that in a dream. I was riding in a Pullman car at the bottom of the ocean—you know how dreams are. In the dream I looked out the window and saw my own reflection looking in at me. I looked the same way I've always looked. This disappointed me. I was hoping that I would see a graphic depiction of the true nature of my very soul.

Perhaps I did.

"Was my car stolen by your agents at Union Station that night and returned to my apartment?" I said.

She nodded. "We also stole it on Monday morning to keep you at home so I could call and offer to buy you dinner. I wanted you to come to the hotel in the hopes of finding out what you knew."

"So I threw a monkey-wrench into your plans."

"Yes. To be honest, we didn't believe you would have the willpower to turn down an offer to come to my room."

"Yeah. My willpower is pretty unpredictable I guess." I gazed at Melanie for a moment, then said, "The night we went to Bombalini's

I noticed that you were driving a rental car. I thought you told me you had gotten a new car."

Her eyes squinted at me ever so slightly. I didn't know if she was impressed or annoyed. I never can tell that about women. She didn't respond verbally, so I decided not to pursue the subject. I think we both understood that my unpredictability had tweaked the Fed again.

"What about the bottle of ammonia that got switched?" I said.

"We retrieved your hat and the bottle of ammonia where you dropped them on the tracks. We placed them on the front seat of your car where you would find them."

"Why did you replace the ammonia with nose spray?"

"We were concerned that you might go to the local police with your story, and we wanted to eliminate the evidence. We wanted them to think your story wasn't true if you told them about the ammonia. This business is out of their jurisdiction and we wanted to keep it that way. But we didn't anticipate that you would report a bomb in your car."

"You mean ... I tossed another monkey-wrench?"

"Yes," Melanie said. "You couldn't have thwarted our plans more effectively if you had been on the payroll of an enemy power. Up until that moment we did not know how paranoid you were. After you called the bomb squad we realized the time had come to take you out of the loop and learn what you really knew."

"You mean ... you decided to find out the things that you hoped to learn at the hotel?"

She nodded.

"Why did you make up a lie about a postal test, of all things?"

"How do you know I lied?" she said.

I flushed with embarrassment, almost as if I myself was the one who had been caught in a lie. I realized I had made a mistake. I hate letting people know I'm on to them, since it usually leads to further conversation, the last thing in the world I ever want from anybody. I was losing my touch.

"I went to the Hyatt on Tuesday and asked the clerk if there had been a postal test," I said.

"That was a setup," she acknowledged. "I followed your taxi to Broomfield, then pretended my car had broken down. I needed to meet you. I needed you to do me a favor so I could ask you out to dinner."

"What if I hadn't stopped for you that day?"

"We would have crossed paths eventually."

I nodded. I didn't know why I bothered to ask. Every bizarre thing that occurred that week had an explanation. Melanie's agency was the exact opposite of life.

As the Pullman car rolled across the dark plains toward Denver, Melanie explained that after I had arrived at DGH I was taken to the psychiatric ward for observation, which was not unusual. Whenever a citizen makes a false bomb report, psychiatrists are often brought in to examine the perpetrator. Two hours after I arrived at DGH I "disappeared." The agency transferred me to the place where I had found myself coming down out of the clouds talking to a doctor about Lon Chaney movies.

"It's odd that I don't remember anything that happened to me after I climbed into the ambulance," I said. "It's as if I was given some kind of 'forgetfulness' drug."

Melanie stared at me impassively. She didn't make an attempt to extrapolate. I suddenly thought of her silent resounding YES.

"Where is this train taking us?" I finally said. That was one of the half-dozen questions that I had forgotten earlier.

"Denver," she replied. "We'll be arriving in half an hour."

"Are we traveling north or south?" I said.

"South."

I wondered if she had inadvertently given away top-secret information.

"No. You would have figured it out by yourself anyway," she said. "It will be dawn by the time we arrive."

This woman—I don't know. Did Langley teach mind reading?

I hoped not because I was trying to figure out where that helicopter had picked me up. The train we were on obviously had come from the direction of Cheyenne, Wyoming. I once took the same route on the Zephyr after a disastrous trip to Reno. This meant the chopper had picked me up at a place somewhere out on the plains. The phrase "Leavenworth, Kansas" came to mind but that was not unusual. For someone who has never committed a felony, I spend a great deal of time thinking about Leavenworth, Kansas.

"Your part in this investigation is almost over," Melanie said. "There is only one thing left for you to do."

"What's that?"

"Forget everything that happened to you this week."

At that moment I felt the train begin to decelerate. It was a gentle deceleration. Railroad engineers know their stuff. But it caused my body to lean slightly toward Melanie. The irony is that the deceleration also caused her body to lean slightly away from me. I may not have been much of an English major, but I could spot a metaphor a mile off.

I forced my body erect, then leaned back against the seat and smiled at her. "I have no idea what you're talking about," I said.

She gave me a smile of approval.

I'll admit it. I was hoping she would give me a kiss of approval. But it looked like I would be forced to accept the standard rule of non-fraternization. There has always been somewhat of a disconnect between me and hope.

CHAPTER 30

I turned and looked out the window at my back. The horizon was paling. I realized we were sitting on the eastern side of the Pullman car. I hadn't thought about that earlier. The jarring movement of the train, and the fact that I had been told we were headed south, ought to have given it away. To what purpose I don't know—but it seemed like the kind of tactical information that a Singapore cabbie would have deduced rather quickly. This made me feel inept. I made a personal vow right then that I would never again think about Singapore.

The sun was cresting the horizon when we pulled into Union Station. I got a glimpse of the rising red ball just before we entered the industrial flats of the Platte Valley where the sun was hidden behind abandoned factory buildings. The sun is always red at dawn in Denver due to the smog, but it's a pretty sight if you have the ability to deny reality. Picasso obviously possessed that ability, and the world is a better place for it I am told, although I don't understand anything about painting. I'm not sure Jackson Pollock did either, but let's move on.

Melanie opened the door and we sidled along a narrow corridor toward the exit of the railcar. We stepped down onto a platform where people were crowded around preparing to board the train. It was not as noisy as it had been on the night I had escaped on the boxcar, but this was due to the fact that it was not raining and the crowd was comprised of morning people, who were never as noisy as night people. This was also true of taxi passengers.

I turned and looked at Melanie. I don't remember if I described her earlier but she was about four inches shorter than me and her hair was dishwater blonde and she had a pert nose and her lips were as red as ... Aaah, I don't want to talk about it.

"Can I ask you one last question?" I said.

"Yes."

"Do you really have a six-year-old daughter named Beverly?"

"No," she said. "That was part of my cover story."

For some reason this made me feel bad. When Melanie and I went on our fake date, I began looking forward to meeting Beverly. The thing I like best about little kids is that none of them have heard the hundreds of knock-knock jokes I've accumulated during my lifetime. Telling a stale joke to a six-year-old kid is like starting your life over again.

I smiled at Melanie. "I guess this is goodbye."

Melanie nodded, then she smiled. I hoped she was going to hug me as she had on the day I drove her to the fake post office test. Instead she did what she had done on the night of our fake date. When I realized she wasn't going to hug me I tried to use body language to indicate that I wanted a hug. One problem though. I had never used body language to indicate that I wanted to do anything, so I didn't know how to go about it. I normally used it to avoid manual labor, big favors, and invitations to gatherings of strangers. I suddenly felt like a physical functional-illiterate.

"I hope I never see you again," Melanie said, as she stuck out her hand for a shake.

I was startled by this seemingly insensitive remark. But then I realized it was rife with multi-layered meanings that existed on a literal as well as a metaphorical level that indicated an affectionate regard for my personal safety. I wondered if she had majored in English at Langley.

"That makes two of us," I replied, as I squeezed her hand a little harder and longer than I normally squeeze hands. When I shake hands I usually try to get it over with as quickly as possible, like the snappy salute. Frankly I think society would be better off if people would salute each other rather than shake hands. It would certainly be more hygienic, and it would stop giving individuals the impression that I want to be their friend. Army officers know what I'm talking about.

"I hope you will always think of me as your friend," Melanie said.

Fer luvva Christ. Was I talking out loud again?

"Yes," Melanie said. "But the doctor told me your psychological tic should fade with the passage of time."

I noticed she didn't say how much time.

Instead she reached inside her coat and pulled out an envelope and handed it to me. "The government would like to offer you this small remuneration for your services to your country," she said.

I frowned at the envelope. "Remuneration?" I said.

"Look it up in the dictionary, laddie" she replied, then she turned and climbed the steps. She paused and glanced back at me, discreetly waved, and disappeared into the sleeping car.

"Wait!" I hollered. "I know what 'remuneration' means!"

I hopped onto the first step. "Melanie!" I cried plaintively. "I know what …" but a conductor suddenly appeared in the doorway. I hopped off the step, backed away from the train, and looked at the windows of the sleeping car.

"I wasn't asking for the definition of 'remuneration,'" I said. I wanted to yell it but the conductor was staring at me. I began trotting alongside the car peering at the windows. "I know what the word means! I was just expressing my surprise!" I looked through one of the windows but couldn't see anyone. "Melanie! I know what 'remuneration' means! I have a degree in English!"

I looked back down the line and saw the conductor standing on the platform frowning at me. It was your standard dog-track frown. I decided

I had been in enough trouble this week, so I turned and trudged toward the terminal wishing I could somehow clarify Melanie's misunderstanding before the train pulled out of the station. But it was no-go.

I felt a psychological tic coming on.

I entered the station, which was as crowded as it had been on the night I hopped the freight. I paused and looked over at the wall of lockers. People were placing valises and suitcases into them. I looked at locker number ninety-six. The key was in the cylinder. I stared at it. I felt like going over to the locker and pretending to put something inside it, then removing the key and slipping it into my pocket and taking it home and keeping it as a souvenir of the worst week of my life. I would hide it in my steamer trunk next to my lizard book.

But I decided not to do it. I felt that somehow, in some way, Amtrak would track me down. Instead I decided to go into the terminal bar and do something I had not done in a long time, which was drink a shot of hard liquor before noon. I have been known to drink beer before noon, usually after weeks similar to this, but I always steer clear of hard liquor when I'm feeling morose. If I have to explain that to you, I recommend that you avoid hard liquor altogether.

I slid onto a stool, laid a five-dollar bill on the bar, and ordered a shot of Johnny Walker Red. The bartender didn't bat an eyelash. They teach that in bartending school. That's what Harold told me anyway. He graduated from bartending school prior to going to work at Sweeney's Tavern. He also uses the indoor track at the YMCA. He likes to run. I should introduce him to Heigger.

I opened the envelope and took a quick glance at the "remuneration." The long green was in a tight stack, so I was forced to discreetly make a fan out of the bills inside the envelope.

I froze.

I'm not going to tell you how much money the federal government thinks my time is worth—I don't want to get busted for fraud. But I can tell you that I finally learned where all of your goddamn tax dollars are going. I was never very good at mathematics but a quick calculation indicated that whatever the IRS had taken away from me over the years, Langley was giving it back.

I quickly closed the envelope.

By then a shot glass had appeared in front of me. I picked it up, swallowed the contents, slid off the stool, and walked out of the bar. I always wanted to do that. I figured it would make me look like I had somewhere "important" to go. I fought the urge to glance back and see if the bartender was impressed. It was one of the biggest battles of my lifetime but I made it to the front door with my willpower intact.

I stepped outside.

The sky was glowing beyond the glass skyscrapers of 17th Street. A line of taxis was waiting at the cabstand. Two Yellow Cabs, a Rocky, a Checker, a Metro, and a taxi from a company that has since gone belly-up and therefore doesn't rate mentioning.

I thought about waiting for the Rocky Cab to pull up first in line, but external evidence indicated that the mad rush to grab taxis had already passed and the cabbies were playing a little-known taxicab game that I refer to as "I hope the other cabs leave so I'll have Union Station to myself."

Been there.

I decided to hop a Yellow home. After all of the things I had been through this week I no longer felt any fear of Yellow Cab drivers, in spite of the money I had cost them when they made the mistake of betting against me that time I went to Hollywood to bring the murdered girl home alive. Sore losers are a tedious bunch. I still remember the week I became addicted to gambling. I won eight hundred dollars in the twin-quin at the dog track, and for some reason I expected to win eight hundred dollars every night for the rest of my life. Big Al explained the flaw in my reasoning: "Anybody who does the same thing over and over again expecting the same result needs some kind of god-damn therapy."

I gave the Yellow driver my address on Capitol Hill, then sat back and gazed at the sunlight glinting off the skyscrapers of downtown Denver. I didn't go into my "passenger" act and ask the driver inane questions. Suddenly role playing didn't seem so important to me anymore. It seemed like all my life I had been pretending to be someone I wasn't, usually while driving a taxi. I did it to increase the size of my tips. If a businessman climbed into my backseat I became a hardcore aficionado of Ayn Rand. If a Marxist climbed into my backseat I was ready to burn down the Establishment and scream "Power to the people!" But I thought about the fact that almost all of the strangers I had encountered during the past week had been role playing and every one of them had fooled me—except the "supe" who had not been role playing at all. He really was a supe, an ordinary blue-collar Joe like me. I knew he was just like me because he obviously suspected me of being someone I wasn't—a burglar—and he was wrong. I was only me and nobody else. That's what bothered me most as the Yellow wheeled onto Colfax and drove up past the state capitol building with its golden dome sparkling in the morning sunlight.

I had told the doctor back in "the room" that I was a fairly honest guy, but I could see that there was a certain amount of dishonesty in role playing, in tricking people into thinking I was something I was not in order to get more money out of them. Back in the Old West people like that were called "snake-oil salesmen." Back in the Old West people like that got hung a lot. As long as I'm on the subject, I don't know why it's called the "Old" West. The West is older now than it was a hundred years ago, but let's not get into that.

A few days earlier I had pondered whether there was a difference between lying and not telling the truth, but I now realized it went deeper than that. It's true that there is a difference between lying to get big tips, and lying to save the western hemisphere, but where is the line drawn? If you lie to a cop you can get into serious trouble, which is why I never lie to cops, but it seems like there are no lines drawn when you ascend to the geopolitical level where the air is thin and nobody knows who is real and who is lying and who is telling the truth.

Maybe I was in the wrong line of work. Maybe my inherent duplicity could be put to better use. Maybe the Atlas who held the weight of the free world on his shoulders could use a helping hand.

That was what I thought about as I rode along east Colfax. I couldn't help but feel that my ability to skirt reality at a moment's notice and in all kinds of weather could be transformed from a vice into a virtue—with a little bit of training. A couple of months at Langley and I just might be qualified to go undercover and start lying.

But the word "training" pulled me up short.

Who was I kidding? Maybe Atlas was a thimble-rigging fraud with a shish kebab of exotic nom de plumes, but he was still built like Hulk Hogan. I had barely made it through basic training at the age of twenty, so I was hardly in shape to repeat that nightmare at the age of forty-five. No, it looked like the nasty, brutish, and short life of a deep-cover agent wasn't in the cards for me. I was stuck with the nasty, easy, and endless life of a taxi driver. I had been questioned, studied, psychoanalyzed, and sized up by men who knew their business—I'm talking shrinks—and they had come to the conclusion that the greatest contribution I could make to the survival of western civilization was to do nothing.

When we arrived at my apartment I handed the Yellow driver a ten-dollar bill and told him to keep the change. The tip came to almost six dollars. I could tell that the driver was an old pro because he went into a briefly effusive whirlwind of somewhat fawning gratitude that I knew would last only as long as it took for me to climb out of the cab and shut the door. I felt like Lawrence Olivier watching John Gielgud strut his stuff. His performance was impeccable.

As the cab rolled away I stood on the sidewalk and looked at my building. I decided not to enter by the front door, but not because I was afraid of running into a tenant, and not because I was afraid of my mailbox, but because I wanted to walk around to the rear and see if my car had been stolen while I was "away"—literally, mentally, and metaphorically, which was a new record for me.

I took the same route that I had taken during my perp walk, around the corner and along the block until I came to the entrance of the parking lot. And there she stood, my portable dump. Suddenly it occurred to me that I had never given my Chevy a nickname, like "Ol' Betsy," which was Davy Crockett's nickname for his rifle according to Walt Disney. I wasn't sure if "portable dump" qualified as an official nickname, but it was as good a nickname as any, and more accurate than most.

I thought about climbing into the driver's seat and starting the engine just to see if it would explode, but this only made me think of my date with What's-her-name. I decided to leave it alone. There would be plenty of time for that after I ran low on beer. I suddenly had the funny feeling that it would be a long time before I rented *Plan 9 From Outer Space* again. But that was probably for the best. It usually is.

I trudged up the fire escape and unlocked the door to my crow's nest. When I entered the kitchen I glanced up at the empty light socket. I started to get annoyed because it meant my psychological tic was still with me. But I put the brakes on my annoyance because it felt kind of good to know that things were back to the way they had been before the federal government had whisked me away to an unknown location. It was as if all the things that had taken place during the past week had never happened, which is how I always like things.

I went to the cupboard and opened the door, grabbed the lightbulb and carried it to the middle of the kitchen where I screwed the bulb back into the socket. The tungsten filament exploded with a blinding white flash—accompanied by an audible "tink."

In disgust I unscrewed the bulb and tossed it into the wastebasket, then decided to get on the mission that had been draped over my shoulders by an unnamed agency of the federal government. I headed toward the bedroom feeling a swell of patriotic fervor stir inside my chest. I had been given my marching orders and I was prepared to obey them without question: kick off my shoes, collapse into bed, and pull the covers over my head.

Uncle Sam was counting on me.

CPSIA information can be obtained at www.ICGtesting.com
Printed in the USA
LVOW08s1929131215

466484LV00007B/1377/P